Wolfe
in
Shepherd's
clothing

Wolfe
in Shepherd's *clothing*

a SHEPHERD & WOLFE
mystery

COUNIOS & GANE

ynwp
YOUR NICKEL'S WORTH PUBLISHING
www.ynwp.ca

prologue

"*Bueno*, Jack?"

The young server behind the counter nods at the glass of rum she's set before him, waiting for an answer. Her face shines from the heat of the tropical night, but she's used to it.

Anabel looks like a typical local, her skin olive dark and her lips full and rich. Everything about her is tight: her tank top, her jeans, the way she pulls her black hair into a ponytail to reveal big hoop earrings. She's young and attractive, but offers very little challenge for pursuit.

Definitely not his type.

"The three-year rum. You like it?" she persists.

"Yes. Very good," he lies.

The truth is he's tasted better, but he doesn't care to waste words arguing with her. After a few glasses, it's all the same— weakening you, making you less capable of being your true self.

He pulls out a polished silver money clip, inlaid with a pearl dolphin, and slides a few bills across the counter.

Anabel half grins and takes the money, satisfied enough to move onto the next customer.

Jack came to the island several weeks ago to deep dive the nearby four-hundred-foot deep submarine sinkhole and its dangerous caves. The locals told tales of people unable to handle the depths, who fell prey to euphoria and disorientation. Rapture of the deep, they called it. Nitrogen narcosis. They'd run out of oxygen too far below the surface and disappear into the dark blue depths.

But as he watches the ice cubes slip around the bottom of his glass, his disappointment is strong. He pushed himself—hard—during his dives but never once experienced any of the thrills promised by the brochure. There had been no fear factor, no risk. Not once had this so-called adventure taken him to his limit.

Of course, not everyone in his group had been so capable. One stupid tourist swam too far out and got lost. Jack's guide had had to rescue the woman, supplementing her oxygen with his own before both of them were endangered in the swift-flowing currents. When they finally made it back safely, the excursion was cut short to take the woman back for medical treatment.

Now, at the end of the day, Jack just wants to relax. He likes this bar and its distance from the glitzy hotels and safe resorts. The odd "snowbird"—whose only excuse for leaving home is to escape the winter freeze—stumbles in off the beach now and then, but for the most part it looks like the place was made for adventurers like him, those who long to seek out the real *edge* of a place, to uncover its true nature.

He studies the couple at the table across from him. They're speaking German and laughing, flirting, intoxicated by more than just cheap liquor. A dahlia, probably purchased from a beggar kid on the beach, sits between them, tied with a long purple ribbon. Watching the two of them together in their own little world provokes a hot sting of envy.

On the other side of the room, two weathered young men loudly debate the best shores to surf. Although he dislikes their brash conduct, he appreciates their passion, their outspoken wanderlust. Jack enjoys travelling and diving and work but has yet to experience that ferocity of desire for any of it. If only he could inflame such passion—

A woman sits alone under a light at the other end of the bar.

It's surprising: most women avoid travelling alone in this part of the world. Perhaps she has someone back at her hotel. She's not too young, somewhere around his age. Long wavy hair, strong features, dark eyes—maybe European. The heat doesn't seem to bother her at all. She takes a drink and meets Jack's eye with a confidence that seems to say "I dare you."

She's definitely his type.

Well, that's something, he thinks.

2

Unfortunately, the feeling doesn't last.

Jack glances over his shoulder. There's a tourist in the corner staring at him.

The man is alone, out of place, awkward. Sweat blooms dark and soggy on his powder blue linen shirt. He pulls off a woven fedora, setting it on the table in front of him, to reveal damp, matted hair. He yanks out a handkerchief and wipes his brow, dumping it in a wrinkled heap on the table.

Jack doesn't like the look of him. No, that's not it. He doesn't like the *feel* of him. It's not that the man's a tourist or that he's distinctly uncomfortable in the climate. There's just something *off*, a stickiness like an oil slick spreading out from the corner where he sits to foul things up.

Getting too close to that guy would only drag himself into the muck, Jack's certain.

Anabel steps between them to set a fresh bottle of beer down at the tourist's table and pick up his empty.

"Where's the tourist from?" Jack asks, nodding at the corner when she passes him again.

"Canada, maybe?" She stacks a few glasses. "He came two days ago."

"He with anyone?"

"No. I only see him alone so far." She seems to have taken note of the way the man's been watching Jack, though, because she adds teasingly, "Maybe he likes you."

Jack shakes his head. He only wishes it were that uncomplicated.

Get lost, man.

The tourist waves Anabel over and she tends to him.

In the mirror, Jack catches a glimpse of Anabel taking the man's money. When she comes back, she grabs a cold beer and sets it in front of the woman, gesturing to the tourist.

The woman turns and smiles politely at the man but shakes her head—she's not interested.

Wise woman, Jack thinks.

Anabel shrugs, walks back to Jack and pours him another shot of rum.

Jack reaches for his money clip.

"No. *Es un regalo del turista.*"

Jack doesn't even look over his shoulder, refusing to acknowledge the man for his "gift."

He knows Anabel's judging him, probably thinks he's an asshole for not being gracious, which only pisses him off more. Not at Anabel—no, just at the man for spreading his oiliness over the whole bar.

Jack pulls a few bills from his clip and sets them on the counter. He's had enough.

Anabel has no reservations about snatching it up, though her "Good night, Jack" is a bit curt.

He ignores it. He nods to the pretty lady at the end of the bar—his fellow kindred spirit—and she smiles back.

He feels an unfamiliar rush and embraces it, enjoying the feeling.

3

The light breeze is welcome relief from the stuffy bar as Jack steps onto the sand. The moon is full and sits low on the horizon, shimmering on the ocean's surface as waves break in long lines up the beach.

This tranquility is marred by exhaust fumes and head-lights on the highway behind the bar; everyone's headed home from the beach.

Jack decides to take the long seaside walk back to his room.

He strolls along the water's winding edge and around the piers, past a couple of fishermen casting their lines, toward the soft orange glow of the village's fringe. As he moves far-ther away from the bar on the beach, the din and vehicle exhaust surrenders to the rhythmic pulse of waves on sand and the wind in the palms.

Yet Jack feels unsettled. He glances back, searching the shore.

Nothing.

He exhales, trying to release his stress, but he can't shake the restlessness. He stops again, peering into the darkness of the night more carefully. But again, nothing.

He presses on, no longer settled, no longer calm like he wishes he could be. He looks over his shoulder once more, and there, in the inky black distance between him and the colourful gleam of the bar's lights, a figure approaches.

It's a weeknight and late. Most of the residents should be in their homes. The tourists ignore the village for the most part—it's working class, with no attractions.

Could be a fisherman, late to join his buddies, or a drunk out for a stroll.

Or...

It's the fedora Jack notices first, then the powder blue shirt as the man passes under the naked bulb of the pier's entrance lamp.

Jack's instincts kick in. Adrenaline hits his bloodstream. He lengthens his stride, focusing on his destination, not wanting the man too close.

He's still a mile from the village. He can see the small fires of more night fishermen far ahead, but between him and them, the shoreline slips into darkness. There's no trace of people—no streetlights or buildings—nothing except for the outline of rowboats anchored by thick lines, like hulking beasts resting in zigzags along the shore.

Jack turns.

The man is close now, a silhouette moving toward him in the moonlight.

"Hey," Jack offers, heart pounding.

The man doesn't respond, maybe hasn't heard him in the crash of the waves—

"Hey!" Jack repeats, this time louder, as the man rushes toward him.

There's a small reflection, a flash of moonlight, down by the man's hip.

Knife! Jack thinks, twisting and running toward the moored boats.

"Wait!" the man yells. "I have something for you." He's only metres behind and Jack feels the hot, oily blackness that soaks the man's every word.

Fear grips him and Jack shoves a hand deep into his pocket, grabbing his diving knife. He keeps it for utility, not protection, but now he pulls it out and opens it with a quick, sharp flick, pivoting to meet the tourist.

The man stumbles toward him and Jack doesn't pause, plunging the blade into the man's belly. It sinks in easily and a sticky warmth flows over his skin.

The tourist seems shocked by the way things have suddenly turned out. He stares down at Jack's fist pressed tight against his gut.

Jack pulls out the knife and the man yells, "Why'd you *do* that?"

Jack doesn't have an answer, but for some reason he's certain it was the right thing to do.

A deep, low moan escapes the man and he starts to shake. His strength is draining—quickly, all over the beach—his eyes rolling back in their sockets, his legs buckling. As he drops, he releases the silver money clip Jack accidentally left at the bar.

Jack's embarrassed by the display. The man's down in the sand now, unconscious but wheezing. A fish out of water.

Looks like he pissed himself too, Jack thinks. Disgusting.

Yet he leans down, trying to hold the tourist's gaze in the dark. He has a sudden, incomprehensible, urge to witness this man's last moments: the blood draining out, the heart slowing down, the mind slipping away...

All this, Jack realizes, because of him.

4

Jack's focus returns. He rises from between the boats, worried someone may have seen what's happened.

But no one's around. The closest people are the fishermen he passed, but they're too far away to have noticed.

He listens to the rhythm of the waves and the rush of the wind. Even they don't seem to have heard the man's cries. He stares up at the moon and calls out at the top of his lungs, "I killed a man!"

Nothing.

No one comes running. No sirens blare. The earth doesn't open up to swallow him whole. No one seems to care at all.

He feels a surge in his heart. He's discovered something, a secret that's lain dormant at his core for a very long time. The capacity to do things that very few are willing to do. The opportunity to push himself to his furthest edge.

He kneels again by the body. Despite the blood on his hands and a little on his knees, he's clean. He searches the man's pockets, taking the money he finds and folding all the cash into a tight bundle, then picks up the money clip.

He peers over the boat hulls, checking all directions to be certain he's still alone before sloshing out into the ocean. He tosses the clip out as far as he can but pockets the money—no sense wasting it. He washes the knife and his hands in the warm water and glances up at the moon—that glorious transformative moon—as it reflects off the crests rolling toward the shore.

Once the tide comes in, there'll be no trace of Jack left on the beach, and the water will wash away any evidence remaining on the man. In the next day or so, the local news might report the story of a foolish tourist who wandered too far from the safety of the resorts and got knifed by a mugger.

An old fisherman once told Jack, "The ocean eats everything." The ocean will eat this too.

5

Jack has one last thing to do.

He swaggers back to the bar. The place is empty now, and Anabel is behind the bar, chatting with the woman.

He walks up to them.

"You're back," the woman says, her tone acidic.

It sends a chill down his spine, but he can give as good as he gets. "You noticed."

"Only for a second."

She's cool to him but her actions betray her. The dahlia from the German couple's table lies on the counter before her and she's fiddling with the purple ribbon tied around it.

He flashes a smile, showing his teeth, and turns to Anabel. "I don't suppose I left my money clip behind? Silver, with a little pearl dolphin?"

Anabel shakes her head, but Jack's sure she would've denied it even if she'd had it.

"That tourist took it," the woman says, indicating the now empty corner.

Jack likes that she'd noticed.

"Ran out of here almost ten minutes ago. Figured he was on his way to chase you down."

Jack glances halfheartedly at the door, then back to the woman. "Well, hopefully he'll come back."

She takes a thoughtful sip of her beer. "Or maybe he's on his way to spend it."

"You're not very trusting."

She raises an eyebrow. "Pays to be cautious."

She's loosened the ribbon from the flower entirely now, and runs it in long strokes between her fingers.

Jack grins, sliding up on the barstool beside her, turning up the charm. "You never know the sort of person you're dealing with, right?"

"Nope, you never do." She finishes off her bottle.

Jack doesn't allow a pause. "Thank you for your help. I'd buy you another—"

"Well, now *that's* quite the invitation—"

"What do you mean?" Jack plays dumb, but he's certain she's onto him.

"Offering to buy me a drink when you've just made it clear you don't have any money so I'll feel obligated to buy *you* one."

She is whip-smart.

And he's appreciative.

"Did it work?"

"You're still sitting here, aren't you?" She winks at him and gestures for Anabel to bring another round.

She sets the ribbon aside to turn to him and he makes a mental note to pocket it later—a memento of the evening.

He puts out his hand.

She takes it. "Nice to meet you."

Seems like his day might end well after all.

part 1

chapter 1

"Tony! You coming to help us soon?"

I'm almost asleep in my room, relaxing to the smooth beats of Zion I, when muffled thumps disturb my zen. I pull out my earbuds.

Heather's at my door. "Are you ever coming out of there, you hermit?"

At least she's respectful enough not to barge in.

"Be down shortly," I yell through the door.

"You better not be doing anything weird in there."

I cringe. "Geez, Heather, just stop." I can't believe she even went there.

"Okay, little brother, but people are showing up soon. Mom wants you to give us a hand."

I can't help it. I throw the joke back at her. "Just a few more seconds. I'm almost finished!"

"Ew! You are *so* gross! I'm sending Jodi up!"

A real enough threat, but I'm enjoying my break from the bustle, so I'll chance it. I know I'm pushing my luck, but being the baby of the family has its advantages.

I slip the earbuds back in and lean back, closing my eyes, and lose myself to the music once more.

chapter 2

It's my parents' twenty-fifth anniversary. The big two-five. They celebrate every year, but this year is a bigger deal than usual. Since they've managed to stay married as long as they have, they've decided to celebrate, Shepherd-style. And it's true, lots of my friends' parents have split, so this big anniversary blow-out, with all the friends, family, neighbours, and co-workers invited, is maybe understandable. Dad gets to shine on the barbecue, and Mom can relax and laugh with people who care about them.

We're expecting a full house. Spring thaw came early this year, and the weather is supposed to be warm, so people will be mingling inside and out. I'm going to help—I promised I would—but my plan is to hole up in the peace and quiet of my room until I'm absolutely needed.

I don't mind these events, but I need to gear up for them. There'll be lots of questions, as there often are, but with the past year and a half I've had, they're getting a little more awkward. Oh, people try to be kind in their curiosity and side-step the big discussion points like my dead girlfriend and my new talent for finding trouble, but they usually end up tripping all over themselves in their efforts, and then I have to come up with a new topic.

But the new year has been good so far. After the frightening events of last summer's woodland adventure, we've finally fallen back into a groove, and life feels almost normal again. Mom's practice is thriving, and Dad's busy at whatever it is he does—hopefully someday I'll figure that out. They try to keep the drama to a minimum, despite my worst efforts, so for them an uneventful house is a happy house.

My sister, Heather, travelled from Calgary, where she is studying law and loving it. She rarely complains. From what she's shared, she's having the stereotypical college experience of too much work coupled with just enough fun. She's driving back early Monday morning so she can finish up some big final project. She already has plans for a summer internship at a fancy law firm—no doubt she's earned it—and I'm proud of her.

My other sister, Jodi, and her husband, Bryan, have been home from Winnipeg for the week, visiting Mom and Dad and helping prepare for tonight. Jodi is now full-time as a veterinary technician at the zoo, while Bryan's been working at his architecture firm. They're also buying properties—putting in a ton of renos, then flipping them—so their lives are more than a little hectic at the moment, but I've overheard Mom and Jodi talking about them slowing down in a few years to start a family.

And I'm as busy as the rest of my family. Grade 12—last year of high school. My marks are great, so Mom and Dad aren't complaining. They've been discussing post-secondary options, but I've been stalling on making a decision. Two years ago, I was certain I wanted to go into medicine like Mom, but then my life turned upside down and it's left me reevaluating most things, including what I want to do with the rest of my life. Fortunately, my parents keep the talk to a minimum, trusting that I'll make a choice soon enough. I only wish I could have the same faith in myself.

This indecision hasn't, however, slowed down my efforts to get back on course. I've been putting in the time with my studies, trying to get my grades as high as I can so that when I do decide on a career path, I've got something to show for it. I've also made training as important as my marks. I've learned that being in top form athletically is as important as having a brain that fires quickly, especially after all I've put my body through over the last year.

Unfortunately, I've earned a bit of a reputation at my school the past few years. The whispering in the halls has nearly stopped, but I know people still think of me different-ly. Some criticize me and believe I'm some sort of vigilante, trying to right the wrongs of the world. Yet, I'll also get the occasional teen asking for my help, whether it's finding out if their boyfriend is cheating or if their friend stole their money. Of course, I politely say no, because almost losing a friend last summer and having my family's lives threatened was enough to make me stop chasing mysteries.

This has made things a little better. Every time I turn some-one down, the heavy feeling deep in my gut melts away a bit more. My social life has become steadier. I hang out with my teammates—and my buddy, Mike Raynor, and I keep out of just enough trouble not to get bored.

Actually, I think the only one in our family still struggling from the effects of last summer is our golden retriever, Ollie. He got knocked around pretty hard during the home invasion and lost the hearing in one of his ears, making him skittish and not his usual self. He's more protective of us, and when strangers visit or he hears an unexpected noise, it sets him off. It makes me sad but I suppose things could have been a lot worse for him.

And as for Charlie Wolfe, he's an ongoing fixture of the household. The first Sunday of every month, he arrives for supper, dessert in hand. He even sticks around afterward to help with the dishes before disappearing into the night. Or he'll sporadically show up with a coffee and doughnut for me, or drop a book off for Dad or tea for Mom. He's even agreed to come to tonight's party. Yet he still keeps his distance, for the most part. He seems to like it that way and we try not to pry. Maybe one day he'll bridge the gap, but for now, what we have works.

chapter 3

A heavy knock interrupts my daydreaming. The door blows open and the hallway light spills into my sanctuary. Heather has sent the hellfire of our older sister, Jodi, at me!

"Little brother!" she yells.

"Sorry, what?" I ask, pretending like I can't hear what she's yelling at me through the music in my ears.

Jodi raises an eyebrow.

I pull the headphones out and give her a "will-this-get-me-out-of-trouble?" smile and jump off the bed.

"Whatever, Mr. Charm. Get your butt downstairs and help out."

"Copy that," I say, carefully edging past her through the doorway.

Yup, things are definitely back to normal.

chapter 4

My family's got me running in circles for half an hour before the guests start showing up. Mom has me do a quick spot-check vacuum and sweep, as well as set the table for a buffet-style feast before sending me outside to see how Dad's doing with the barbecue.

It's sunny and hot out, but there's still a small pile of snow in the shadows of the yard where the sun can't reach. Patches of green and puddles are everywhere.

Dad's nowhere around, so I wander over to the makeshift bar and grab a pale ale from the ice bucket, crack it open, and sneak a sip. I don't get to enjoy it for too long before Dad steps out behind me.

"Hey, Pops. Need anything?"

He grabs my beer, taking a big swig. "Nope, just this, thanks." He gives me a wink.

"Not yet, huh?"

"Nope. Not quite yet."

I surrender. "No harm in trying."

He tells me to go help in the kitchen, but when the doorbell rings, I rush to answer it, hoping it'll get me out of chopping veggies.

Of course, it's Aunt Sally and Uncle Sheldon who arrive first—they always do—because they never, ever leave anything to chance.

I love my Aunt Sally, but I have to say she's the perfect fit for him. Uncle Sheldon's a tax accountant for some big firm out in Toronto, and he has always believed in being precise. She retired several years ago from teaching and now spends most of her time running their lives like a finely tuned machine. They have a son, Malcolm, who's the same age as Jodi, but he stayed home this weekend, studying for his last exam in dentistry.

Aunt Sally shoves a big gift into my hands, immaculately wrapped in blue foil and tied with a silver ribbon. "Anthony, set this somewhere safe. I don't want it being battered around."

Sheldon is right behind her, already worrying. "Is my rental going to be okay on the street? The street signs say only two hours."

"Only on weekdays, Uncle Sheldon. It'll be fine."

He double-clicks the key fob twice more to make sure the door is locked. "They should mark the area better," he grumbles, heading past me into the house.

I place Aunt Sally's present on the growing pile in the living room. A couple of flower arrangements showed up earlier in the day from distant family members and acquaintances who were unable to make the trip, and gifts and cards had arrived throughout the week in the mail.

"Hello?"

I hear a familiar voice in the front hall. Mom beats me to the door this time and greets Irene—her longtime friend and receptionist—and Irene's partner, Barb.

"Happy anniversary, Keya!" She wraps Mom in a huge embrace. "Where's Ben? I want to get his secrets to a happy and successful quarter-century of marriage."

Mom laughs. "I don't think you two need any help for that!"

"Agreed," Barb admits as she gives Mom a less exuberant but no less friendly hug.

Irene's been working with Mom since forever and has a magical ability to keep the most irate patient calm. Barb is a clerk for the city, but the two of them also run a thriving business on the side, doing residential yard maintenance in the summer and house-watching for "snowbirds." In fact, business has been so good for them this year that they've brought me on part-time to help with the load. Although Irene assures Mom that she's not going to quit working for her for a very long time, I think the fact that they've hired me has eased Mom's worries. Besides, they're great bosses and the job puts a little extra cash in my pocket, so I'm not complaining.

A couple of our neighbours arrive shortly afterward, bringing presents and food, and I'm back and forth throughout the house delivering it all to the appropriate places.

As I pass through the kitchen, Heather calls me over. I worry she's going to get me chopping, but she's on her toes, stretching for a top shelf. "Can you reach the big salad bowl up there?"

I reach for it easily. "No problem, shorty."

Jodi looks up at me. "When did you get so tall?"

I consider the question but shrug. Like most things, I wished for it for a long time and then it just happened without me noticing.

I watch the impressive food assembly production line they've got going. Bryan's chopping, she's mixing, and Ollie's at their feet, waiting for extra scraps to come his way.

"Can you take him downstairs before more people arrive?"

I nod and call our pup to the stairs. He's hesitant to leave the kitchen but comes along without much of a fight. I guide him over to a little bed I've set up and pat it so he'll lie down.

I hate putting him in the basement, but the bigger the crowd gets, the more uneasy he's likely to be. He hasn't acted aggressively to anyone—yet—but we'd rather not put him in a situation where he might. I give him a good rubdown and a deep scratch through his fur, and he gives me several licks of thanks.

I go back upstairs, avoiding the kitchen, and hover by the door, waiting for more arrivals.

The front room is filled with even more guests. I see Dad's former research assistant and friend, Cory, and his wife, Cynthia, talking with Irene and Barb, and then I notice Uncle Ed talking with Dad outside.

Uncle Ed's not really my uncle, but rather a grade school friend of Mom's; he's been in our lives forever. He's sporty and athletic, and always made camping trips fun. He also helped grow my love of basketball when I was a little kid, teaching me how to run the ball down the court and shoot. He used to work with Mom ages ago, but then started doing something in computers and making big money. His job keeps him on the road all the time now and he's rarely in town, so it's a real surprise that he's able to make it today.

Aunt Ayana, Mom's younger sister, arrives next. Although she's from Vancouver, she's working in the art department on some film production in London right now, but flew in late last night to surprise my parents. Mom says Ayana has always been a free spirit, even as a child.

She bustles into the house now, travel bag slung over her shoulder and several bottles of wine in her hands. "My goodness, nephew, you're handsome for being so pale!"

She likes to tease because she and Mom emigrated with their family from Jamaica in the 1970s, while Dad is third-generation Canadian, making my sisters and me what I affectionately call "mocha."

However, she doesn't even give me a chance to respond before asking, "You think this'll be enough Chardonnay for your mom?"

"I think so, Aunt Ayana." I try to grab something from her to help but she pulls away.

"Mind yourself, kiddo. I can do this myself. Just point me to my room."

"All right," I say, laughing. "You're up the stairs and to the right."

She barely makes it halfway. "Oh Lord, is that Ed out there? All the trouble has certainly come out of the woodwork for this big day!" She forgets about her room and aims for the backyard but immediately veers off again to give Irene, Barb, Cory, and Cynthia hugs.

I shake my head. It's amazing that she's even made it this far into the house.

I tuck myself into a corner by the buffet table, watching the busy flow of friends, neighbours, and co-workers streaming from room to room. The place is bursting at the seams. Everyone seems to be here, except…

The doorbell chimes again.

chapter 5

"Anthony," Mom calls out, "come say hello to Maggie."

I have no clue who Maggie is, but I guess she's dining with us.

In the front hall with Mom stands Detective Gekas, in a party dress—and with a man.

I don't know if I'm more surprised that she's in my house or that she's got a date and is being normal and stuff.

The truth is, like Charlie, she cares about our well-being and checks in on us a fair bit. I guess you could say she's developing a close relationship with the whole family.

I get over my knee-jerk reaction and put out my hand. "Detective-" Strange how I can't bring myself to use her first name. It doesn't feel right.

"It's okay. Will you just call me 'Gekas' tonight—not 'Detective?'"

I nod. "It's good to see you," I smile sincerely.

I admit there's some relief in seeing her outside of work: it means no one's hurt or gone missing...or worse.

I'm absolutely done with that.

"You too, Anthony." She turns to her date. "This is Spencer."

I don't hesitate to offer my hand again.

Spencer takes it, shaking with a solid grip. "Nice to meet you, Tony. I've heard a lot about you."

I glance at Gekas, unsure how to take his comment. Every interaction between us has been me lying to her, evading her questions, telling her about dead people, or dealing with the killers that Charlie and I find.

No telling what Spencer's heard.

I look for a way to shift the focus, but Dad's former colleague, Cory, does it for me.

"Detective Gekas?" he asks, strolling over. "Haven't I been seeing your name in the paper?"

Barb perks up, realizing what he's talking about. "Oh my, you aren't the detective looking into those ghastly murders, are you?"

Gekas glances at me before answering. "Unfortunately, yes."

She's uncomfortable and for good reason.

Last fall, two bodies were found. One was discovered floating in the lake in September, while the other showed up in October on a small island along the creek near the RCMP barracks on the west side of the city. Although the victims seemed to have no connection, both had been shot in the head, dismembered and dumped into canvas bags tied with purple ribbons. The gruesomeness of the crimes had set the public and the police on edge, and everyone expected another body to appear in November, but nothing happened, with some attributing it to the early bitter cold.

Mom and Dad's guests flock around Gekas, asking in an innocent but intrusive way whether there've been any recent developments. She is polite in her refusal to answer questions, but I can see the strain in her eyes and hear the exhaustion in her voice.

Spencer interrupts, "Honey, perhaps you'd like something to drink before you start talking shop? Anthony, maybe you can help Maggie out?"

I take my cue. "Can I get you wine or— You know what? There are so many— Why don't you come and see your choices?"

The edge of Gekas's mouth creeps upward and her eyes brighten a bit. "That sounds great." She excuses herself to follow me outside. Once we're clear of the crowd, she leans in close, grinning. "Thank you, Anthony."

"No worries."

She studies me. "You and Charlie haven't been snooping around—?" She wants to say something more but pauses.

Although Charlie and I are certainly aware of the murders, the events of last summer have kept us from tossing ourselves back into danger. In fact, since our last adventure, we haven't even *talked* about acting on any of these stupid notions.

"Don't worry—" I try to muster "Maggie" but can't do it. "The truth is, Detective, we're trying to leave that business to the professionals."

She gives a weak smile and sighs, but if I'm not mistaken, it doesn't seem like relief.

"Detective?"

She covers the look quickly with a nod. "Never mind. Good. That's good to hear."

She's holding something back, but she's already moved on. "I think I'll take an IPA," she says, cracking it open and taking a couple of big gulps.

I stand there for a moment, wanting to ask what's going on, but that's when Dad appears, and she turns away from me to give him a warm hug.

And I guess that's the end of the conversation.

For now.

chapter 6

I stand awkwardly beside Gekas and Dad, racking my brain, trying to figure out what Gekas was really asking, but I can't get anywhere with it.

Dad, working the barbecue, interrupts my wandering thoughts and hands me a huge tray of cooked meat. "Take this in to your sisters."

I carry it inside and set it on the table.

Heather arrives with the last of the salads. "We're all here?" she asks.

"Everyone but Charlie," I answer.

"Can you text him, please? I'll wrap the meat—it's better if it sweats a little—but we should start eating soon."

I rush upstairs and check my phone. There's a text from my buddy, Mike, about tomorrow morning, and a couple from a few other classmates I'm doing a project with for law class. But nothing from Charlie.

I send him:

Meal's ready
Where are u?

I'm about to leave but stop to add:

Come even if ur late

chapter 7

The party begins without Charlie.

The table looks great, filled with heaping platters of barbecue, huge bowls of salad, and delicious side dishes. Since it's a buffet, people progress in waves, filling their plates before finding a seat anywhere they can. They're everywhere, milling back and forth between the dining room and the patio.

I build myself a huge serving of veggies and meat, knowing I can eat it all and likely go back for more. I try to be conscious of what I put into my body, but since I'm working my ass off in training, I can't stop eating. I take a seat beside Irene and Barb.

Dad's at the doorway by the dining room, giving me a look: *Where's Charlie?*

I shake my head and lift a shoulder.

If he's coming, he'll simply drop in whenever it's convenient for him rather than respond to my text. I've learned to accept this. We all have.

Dad turns to the room. "Thank you, everyone, for coming to celebrate with us today." He gestures to the food. "It looks like we've got some work ahead of us!"

Irene raises a glass, "To the happy couple!"

The guests cheer and toast.

I raise my soda can, slightly disappointed that it's not something a bit stronger.

"And no one's allowed to leave until it's all gone," Mom says. She's smiling but I don't think she's kidding; I know how much she'd hate trying to find containers for all this food if it's left over.

Ed pipes up, "No problem!"

Everyone laughs.

Dad gets everyone's attention again. "I'd just like to say that twenty-five years of being together hasn't always been easy. Sometimes it's challenging and sometimes a little tougher than you want, and I could say it's felt like a lot of work." He looks over at Mom. She beams back at him. "But it hasn't, Keya. You make everything easy and wonderful. And now, as I look around at this room full of our wonderful family and friends, and our amazing children, I see the beauty that love can bring."

"I love you, Ben." Mom takes his hand.

"I love you too, and I can't wait to celebrate with you again after another twenty-five." He pulls her close and gives her a big kiss.

Everyone whistles, whoops, and applauds, caught up in the moment.

"All right," Dad announces, "let's eat!"

chapter 8

We dig in, stuffing our faces with delicious food.

It doesn't take long for the stories about Mom and Dad to start. There is a lot of razzing them, and a lot of anecdotes they try to interrupt or protest with much laughter. There's also a lot I've never heard, hints about how wild my parents actually were in their youth. They've always seemed so ordinary to me—maybe they've already lived their exciting years.

Once everyone's finished eating, the stories slow down and people rise to stretch their legs and refill their glasses. Neighbours chat with neighbours, friends and family reconnect, and eventually people start peppering me with questions:

"What kind of career are you thinking of getting into?"

"What's your major?"

"Are you going to school?"

"What school are you going to?"

"Are you moving away like your sisters?

I try and answer all of them as best as I can, but I can barely keep up.

Uncle Sheldon asks, "Do any of your post-secondary choices have sports scholarships?"

"I've applied for a couple."

"Of course, you've still got to make the teams," Uncle Sheldon points out.

Thanks, Uncle Sheldon, but you're not really helping—

Irene changes the subject. "But which way are you leaning? Medicine like your mom or public policy like your dad?"

"Or something else?" Barb asks. "Maybe a lawyer."

"Never encourage anyone to be a lawyer," Gekas's date, Spencer, chimes in.

"So says the lawyer," Gekas says.

My sister's nearby, gathering plates, and I divert their attention. "Heather's studying law in Calgary."

The group turns and Heather's ready for them. "Only undergrad in political science."

"But you plan to go into law?" Uncle Sheldon asks.

"If all goes well."

"Litigation? Criminal? Family?" Spencer wants to know.

"Isn't that badgering the witness?" she asks.

"Ah, only if I were trying to antagonize—"

"For an emotional response—"

"Ack, I've stepped into my own cross-examination."

I notice Gekas squeeze his hand. It's kinda weird to see her as something other than a detective.

"What law do *you* practice?" Heather turns the tables.

"Corporate."

She nods, considering. "I have a couple of acquisitive friends who may come knocking on your door."

I'm curious to know what type of people she hangs out with.

Spencer laughs. "The money is indeed good. And there never seems to be a lack of clients."

Heather holds up her hands. "No, thanks. I'm not merciless enough."

The crowd chuckles at the burn but it doesn't seem to faze Spencer. He grins in reply. "Good, we need crusaders fighting against us cold-hearted scoundrels."

Heather steps away and I'm again alone with the group.

"I read that your school had a successful season on the court," Ed praises.

Thank you, Uncle Ed. My own relatives don't even care that much.

"Yeah, we've had a really good run. Can't complain."

"You're being modest. Look at your stats: 26.1 points per game, 4.8 on steals, 8.3 on assists—"

Although most of this crowd has no clue what any of it means, they seem impressed.

"Yeah, but I had a lot of help from my buddy, Mike—"

"You two run the court pretty well together," Gekas puts in.

I'm surprised she's even been to one of my games.

Uncle Ed continues, "Tony, you've got serious potential. You can do great things. But you're holding back. You need to quit selling yourself short and letting the other guys look good."

Although I hear what he's saying, that attitude is bad for the team. I yield, hoping he'll move on. "Okay, Uncle Ed."

Uncle Sheldon and Aunt Sally grimace at my use of the title, but the way he's rattled off my stats, Ed's earned it.

"Being such a good athlete must make it hard to keep the ladies away," Cynthia calls out.

Damn, why'd she have to go and ruin it? I don't blame her, though—I'm pretty sure she has no clue what the past few years have been like. My old girlfriend, Sheri, still holds a place in my heart, and it's only recently that time has begun to ease the pain of her loss.

Aunt Ayana strolls over. "Ah, leave him be. The boy doesn't need to be rushed into a relationship. He needs to stretch his legs, travel the world, encounter other cultures, have a few adventures."

Mom's right there with the follow up. "Are you trying to fill my son with wild ideas, sister?"

"Of course I am. He's young! He needs the chance to discover who he is."

Mom's face says it all. She doesn't hate the idea of me travelling or finding myself, but she *may* think I've already had enough adventures.

Uncle Sheldon insists that "A good, solid, education can lead to a promising career," and the debate over my future kicks into high gear.

It's times like this I wish Charlie were around to create a diversion—like maybe starting a fight or burning down a shed.

chapter 9

It only takes a few minutes of questions for my head to spin and my brain to feel full. I grab some dishes and carry them into the kitchen, where I find Jodi and Heather chilling over glasses of wine.

"They finally broke you too, huh?" Heather asks.

Jodi takes a swig from her glass. "I was asked, 'When will we hear the pitter-patter of little feet?' *so* many times."

The phone rings. "I'll get it," Jodi says.

"And you, little brother," Heather turns on me, "*you* threw me under the bus."

"Desperate times, sis." I crack open a soda since my sisters will never let me get away with a beer.

"No worries. I'll get you back. And my revenge will be slow and sweet."

I know she'll make good on that promise, but I'm actually kind of relieved that I'm not the only one feeling this way.

"Tony?" Jodi says pensively, handing me the phone. "It's Charlie."

chapter 10

I grab the cordless and run downstairs where it's quieter. Ollie sees me and growls.

"It's okay, buddy."

When he realizes it's me, he wags his tail. I feel sorry for this good dog who is now damaged and not himself. I'll find him some leftover scraps from the barbecue later.

I put the phone to my ear. "Charlie? What happened to you?"

"How's supper?" He ignores my question.

"Um, good."

"How was the barbecue sauce? I gave Ben the recipe."

"It was fine. Did you get my text?"

Again, he ignores the question. "Yeah, it's a pretty sweet sauce on ribs and steak."

"Charlie, what's up?"

"I'm in a bit of a predicament."

This ought to be good. "Okay. So what's up?"

"I need help moving some things."

"Moving things?"

"Yeah, you know, boxes."

"You need help moving boxes? Right now?"

"That'd be great if you could."

"What's in them?" Please don't tell me it's drugs or a body.

"Stuff."

"That's pretty cryptic, Major Tom."

There is a long pause.

"You know what, just forget—"

Before he hangs up, I bark, "I'll be right there. Wait. Where am I going?"

"Meet me at the convenience store on the corner of Twentieth."

"Wait, you're by my house? Why didn't you come over?"

"Dude, can you please stop with the questions and just come get me!"

Sometimes it's better to just let things go. "Okay. Fine. Be there in five."

"Cool. Thanks, man." He hangs up.

Rarely a dull moment with this guy.

chapter 11

I walk back upstairs into the buzz of chatter and laughter.

Heather and Jodi are waiting for me in the kitchen.

"What's up?" Jodi asks.

"He needs a ride."

"Where?"

I sigh and both of my sisters are alert.

"What's going on?"

"He has some boxes he needs moved."

"Please don't tell me there's drugs or a body in them," Heather says.

Clearly we're related.

"Nope. Just stuff." I really hope he doesn't make me a liar. "Do you think I can borrow Dad's car?"

They both put up their hands, neither wanting to make the call.

I head into the living room. The party's in full swing and I'm happy for my parents; this is how their anniversary should be spent. I hate bringing Charlie's crap into the middle of it.

I scan the room for Dad. Shit—he's telling a story to Gekas and Spencer.

"So the whole tent's asleep when I let out this loud squawk! Keya thinks I'm having a heart attack—" he sees me approach and drags me into his tale "—and Tony's about six at the time and jumps up screaming, thinking I'm a pterodactyl!"

Everyone laughs and I force a smile, leaning in to catch Dad's ear only. "Uh, could I borrow the car for twenty minutes?"

Even though no one hears, Dad's look of concern quiets the group. "What for?"

"Charlie needs a ride."

Somewhere over my shoulder, I'm sure Mom's worrying what I'm up to, but Gekas is doing a good job filling in. "Is he in trouble?"

"It's okay, Detective. Nothing like that."

But she and I both know that, with Charlie, it usually *is* like that.

"Twenty minutes?" Dad asks.

I nod.

"And no more?"

I nod again.

"Okay. But you two get back here immediately."

"Will do, Pops. Thanks."

chapter 12

It's Sunday evening and the drive is quick. There's barely any snow left on the ground and the shopping traffic is done. In five minutes, I'm at the convenience store.

Charlie's leaning against the wall, hands in pockets, scruffy blond hair hanging down, waiting patiently. He's wearing a light jacket, well-worn jeans and his scuffed All Stars. His well-used backpack that holds most of his earthly possessions is hoisted on his shoulders. Except for the fact that his shaggy hair looks wilder than normal, it's pretty much the same look he's got all year long, more or less.

I pull up and he jumps in.

"Hey, you missed supper."

"Yeah, sorry about that."

"I'm pretty sure Dad has a plate waiting for you."

"Ah, Ben. Always thinking. Your dad's a good guy." He doesn't do his ritual rummage through the car—searching through musical choices, opening the console, poking at things—like he usually does. Tonight he sits quietly. "Head east, please."

He's using manners? What the hell's going on with him tonight?

"What's up, Charlie? Where are we going?"

"To my mom's."

chapter 13

The words hits me. This is it. Tonight, I finally get to see where Charlie Wolfe lives.

He's been to our place a lot. In fact, he knows a lot about my life, my house, my summer cabin, my family. He knows what's on my fridge, and he definitely knows what's in it as well. He sits at my supper table, shoots hoops with me in the driveway, visits with Dad, hangs out with Mom. But I've never been to his house. Ever. In the almost two years I've known him, he's never invited me and I've never asked. We've fallen into a delicate friendship, and I've chosen never to push it, in case he pulls away. It seemed to be the best—and perhaps the only—way to grow this friendship.

He points right. "Turn here."

When I turn onto Arcola Avenue, the direction we're travelling clicks in my head. This is the road I would've taken to Sheri's.

It's been nearly two years since I've driven out this way. After she went missing, I came out here twice. The first time was to search the locker at her school for clues about her disappearance. That was when I met Charlie for the first time. The second was when I returned to ask Charlie for help finding her. I never went back after that, partly because she was gone and I had no reason to, but mostly because it hurt too much. But, as I should've expected, it's because of Charlie that I'm returning.

We drive over the expressway and the walled-in neighbourhoods stretch out before us.

"At the four-way, take a right."

Sheri's school appears and I expect a pang of misery but nothing comes. I wonder if something deep inside me has started to let go.

"Take another right."

I hit the turn signal, happy to turn off the road. We go down a street I've never been on. The wall that acts as a noise barrier to the expressway appears ahead. The road seems to end in a cul-de-sac.

"After the apartments, angle it right."

The road bends past the buildings, and I drive down what appears to be a back alley. But I'm wrong. It's a straight-up trailer park—exactly like he once told me. And if he was honest about this, I wonder what else he was telling the truth about.

There are no streetlights and we creep through the dark. My headlights reveal mobile homes in great condition, with beautiful gardens and goofy gnomes. But the further we go, the more we see pretty damn unfortunate ones, with dead lawns, broken toys, ripped bags of garbage, and empty liquor bottles strewn across their yards.

"Here."

Charlie points to an abandoned-looking trailer and I pull to a stop. It's more desolate than I could have imagined.

"Um, Charlie, is this your home?" I try to keep my tone light.

"Nah, man. Home is where you hang your hat."

Here we go with the Charlie-isms.

"Do you live here?" I try again.

"I did."

The place is dark, not a light to be seen. "Where's your mom?"

"You know," he waves a hand in the air, "wherever she is."

He never seems to complain about anything—even a missing parent.

He stares at the trailer. "All right, let's go."

chapter 14

I take a deep breath and follow him to the trailer. An official-looking eviction notice, dated two days ago, has been posted on the door, with a padlock to enforce it.

"Son of a bitch," Charlie says, but he seems calm, laughing as he shakes his head. He takes a breath and runs his fingers through his thick hair.

"Charlie, what's going on?"

"Oh, you know. The usual. Your mom can't pay rent, you get evicted, you have a hearing, you lose, you have another hearing, you lose again, then the court and the sheriff's department kick you out and take all your shit."

I stare at him. Sometimes I think that the way I've grown up has left me too insulated from the world.

He's grinning, and I can tell he wants to make fun of me, but he holds back.

"Up for one more B&E?" he asks as he scoots around the back.

"Charlie?" He's already disappeared. "Charlie!"

I don't want to break into someone's house—not today, not any day, really—even if it is his own.

When I get around the corner, Charlie's standing on a wooden pallet he's leaned against the siding, stretching for a window. He can't quite make it.

"Hey, All Star, give me a hand." He tosses me a flat metal bar. "Push the window up, just a bit, and slide this in the gap."

I climb up and feel for the gap between the window frame and the screen before sliding the bar in. It takes only one small pry for the entire screen to pop out. I push open the sliding window.

"Thanks, Shepherd."

He jumps up and effortlessly pulls himself in. I'm impressed with how well he's healed from last summer's attack.

His head pops back out. "You coming?"

That's a great question.

I hope I don't regret this.

chapter 15

I pull myself through the window, landing softly.

Charlie's already gone.

I'm in a bedroom—I think. It's so dark and desolate I can't really tell. I try the light switch by the door, but there doesn't seem to be any power. I pull out my phone, turn on its light, and look around.

There's a mattress on the floor with some crumpled sheets and an old blanket. An abused dresser is against one wall and above it, a matching mirror, though the glass is broken. There's an ugly straw ornament thing on the wall, random in its placement. The closet door is pushed in, hanging off its hinges. It's a sad and neglected space, with almost nothing else in it except the smell of stale cigarette smoke soaked into the brown carpet.

I step out of the room, searching for Charlie, making my way down the narrow, wood-panelled hallway and into the main living area. Another blanket, this one knitted, lies on a velour couch beside a frayed pillow. Empty glasses and bottles litter the coffee table next to an ashtray overflowing with ashes and cigarette butts. The whole place has a pungent, lived-in smell of sweat mixed with the stink of old nicotine. Linoleum peels in the kitchen corners. An empty box of doughnuts sits on the counter. There are dishes in the sink; clumps of mould have formed on the food-crusted edges.

I study the fridge. A couple of magnets hold overdue bills. A sticky note with a phone number and the name James is stuck beside them. No light turns on when I open it. It's empty but smells sour and rotten.

I wince. This can't be Charlie's home. He's weird but clean; he cares about the details. This grim space doesn't suit him. I close the fridge door quietly, head spinning.

"Can you grab a box?" Charlie yells from another room.

I see one under the kitchen table and grab it. It smells like cat pee but I haven't seen any animals. I carry it down the hallway until I find him in a cramped room, sitting on a mattress, working by flashlight. The foot of the bed is flush against a small closet whose doors have been removed. Inside is another beat-up dresser with an old television hooked up to an original Nintendo console on top. At the head of the bed, a bedsheet's been pinned over the window as a makeshift curtain. On the wall beside it are two posters: one for Deep Purple and one for *Apocalypse Now*.

Man, talk about irony.

"This is your room?" I ask, handing him the box.

Charlie ignores me, busying himself opening drawers and dumping things into the box. "Can you unhook the game and toss it in here?"

"Sure." I get that he doesn't want to talk about it.

He pulls a few shirts off hangers and yanks some jeans off a top shelf.

I look at the things he's put into the box. A coffee mug with a local radio station logo on it, a few books, some cassette tapes. Two picture frames lie face down. I reach in to take a look but before I can turn them over, he slaps my hand away.

"What the hell, man!" he growls.

I raise my hands in surrender. *He* never seems to have a problem going through other people's property. "Sorry. Just curious."

"Are you only here to snoop through my shit and judge?"

Ouch. He's like an exposed nerve.

It isn't until his voice drops and he whispers, "Just help, okay?" that I realize how much courage Charlie needed to even let me be here and see how he lives.

"Okay. What do you want from me?"

He points to the top of his closet. "Above the inside trim is an envelope taped to the wall. Grab it."

He's so very odd sometimes, but I should be used to this by now. I reach up and feel along the edge, finding an eight-by-ten manila envelope. I pull it down.

"What's in it?"

"Well, Mr. Curious, open it and find out."

I rip the seal. Inside is about two hundred dollars in cash, photocopies of his IDs, a credit card—I'm sure it's not his—a gift card from a grocery store, and a SIM card for a phone.

"You never know when you need to scramble," he says.

I study him before realizing. "Wait, you have more of these?"

"All across the city."

I think back to the day I first met him, digging in the dirt. "That day outside your school?"

"Burying some cash, as well as some juicy evidence on a couple of people, in case I ever needed to get out of a jam. Always be prepared, is my motto." He picks up the box on the floor and hands it to me. "Okay, we're out of here."

I look at the meagre collection of stuff. "That's it?"

"Life isn't about possessions, Shepherd."

"Fine. We done?"

"Yup."

"Where now?"

"Far from here."

chapter 16

We sit in Dad's car, all of Charlie's worldly belongings in a box in the back seat. I've known Charlie for almost two years, and rarely see him worry. But in the glow of the dashboard, I can see he's having trouble.

He drops his head, struggling to get the words out. "Shepherd, I need a favour…"

I know exactly what's on his mind. He needs a place to stay tonight. I don't make him suffer. "I've texted Mom and Dad already. They're waiting for us." I nod to the trailer. "You want to torch it before we go?"

He laughs, letting out a deep sigh. "Thank you."

"No worries, man." Then, almost without thinking, "Let's get you back home."

chapter 17

The party is in full swing by the time we pull up in the driveway.

We decide to leave his stuff in the car and go through the back door, avoiding a big *tah-dah* entrance through the front.

The kitchen is a mess. Dinner plates are piled up on the counter along with dessert dishes. Glasses are lined up beside the sink, and dozens of empty bottles of wine sit beside unopened ones. Containers of leftovers are stacked high.

"Looks like quite the party." He honestly could've talked about the excess, especially after what we'd just walked away from.

He opens the container of barbecue. "Wow, that smells fantastic."

"Maybe we should let Mom and Dad know we're back first."

"You don't think me going in gnawing on a T-bone is a good first impression?"

"When do you ever make a good first impression?"

"Oof, Shepherd, you're getting some sass on you."

"Being around you helps."

"Fine," he says, putting the lid back on the plastic container. "Let's meet the herd."

chapter 18

Everyone is in the living room when we come around the corner. Gekas sees us first, then Mom, then Dad, then everyone else. Silence slams down on the room like a cartoon mallet.

"We're ba-aack," I joke.

Mom, clearly thoroughly enjoying Aunt Ayana's wine, glides over to Charlie. "Charles, you made it. Excellent." She gives Charlie a tight squeeze, surprising both Charlie and me.

Dad jumps up and pats him on the back. "It's good to see you, Charlie."

There is a lot of affection flowing in this room and I'm certain it's not just the party. He's made an impact on our family—he's part of us now. And the fact that he nearly died trying to protect us has never been forgotten.

"Happy anniversary, Mr. and Mrs. S.," Charlie stammers.

I've never see him at a loss for words, and now it's happened twice in one night.

"Let me get you some food," Dad says, heading for the kitchen.

A few guests exchange looks, and Mom notices. Some of them have heard about this kid, and many are perhaps taken aback that he's received such a warm welcome.

"Everybody, this is Charles Wolfe."

Heather's shaking her head. "Hey, Trouble."

He nods at her, smirking. "Heather." Without missing a beat, he looks over at Jodi and Bryan. "And you must be the wise, sensible sister and brother-in-law?"

Jodi ignores Heather's protests but doesn't leave her chair. "Oh, you do not disappoint, do you?" By the look in her eye, she's still deciding what she thinks of him. Out of all the people he'll meet tonight, she'll likely be his worst critic since she knows exactly what all Charlie's gotten into.

Charlie and Detective Gekas size each other up. He's never been her biggest fan—I don't think any cop holds much of his enthusiasm—but she saved his life, so he tries not to be an asshole.

"Detective."

She grins. "Charles, how are you?"

"Oh, you know. Trying to keep my nose clean."

His eyes drift to the man perched beside her and she introduces them. "Charles, Spencer."

Spencer stands to shake his hand.

Dad returns with a heaping plate of food. "Hopefully, I hit all your necessary food groups."

"As long as it's your cooking, I don't think you can go wrong, Mr. S."

Dad sets up a TV tray with cutlery and a napkin for him as Mom continues to guide him around the room, introducing him to everyone else.

I stand at the doorway watching Charlie and my family do their thing. What gets me is that less than an hour ago, I was helping Charlie move out of his place, but here he is, acting like he doesn't have a care in the world.

Dad comes over to lean beside me. "Everything okay?"

"His mom took off and he's been evicted."

"Do we know where she is?"

"He might, but he's not saying."

Dad sighs slowly.

"He's homeless, Dad."

"No, son," Dad says, smiling, patting me on the shoulder. "No, he's not."

chapter 19

The party lasts a few more hours but once it ends and the guests leave, it doesn't take long for Mom to sober up and call out, "Tony, could you put on the kettle. It's teatime."

Teatime is Mom's signal that it's time for a family meeting. She's a big believer in holding family conversations over the soothing effects of infused fruit, leaves, and flowers, and since Charlie's come into our lives, we've had some pretty big discussions.

Charlie goes to the kitchen immediately, taking a seat across from Mom at the kitchen island. Dad pulls a seat up beside her, and Heather, Jodi, and Bryan stroll in from the living room, not wanting to miss out. Even Ollie has made his way upstairs from the basement and plops down at the foot of Charlie's chair for some much-missed love.

Mom rummages through the basket and finds a flavour that pleases her. The house rule has always been that whoever calls the meeting gets to pick the tea.

I pull out cups for everyone and grab the tea she's selected, laying everything on the island, along with spoons, sugar, and the honey pot. It feels a bit like an over-the-top ceremony, but if I'm right about what's going to go down, this family needs all the help it can get.

Once the kettle finally whistles, I fill the pot, Mom *clinks* the top on, and the discussion begins.

She asks the first question. "Can you tell us what's happened?"

There is a thick silence.

Charlie's fingers dance around the edges of the cup, studying the pattern along its handle. "Do you know why Japanese teacups don't have handles?"

"Charles—" Mom cautions.

"If it's too hot for the hand, then it's too hot for the mouth."

"Charles…?"

All at once he gives in. Maybe it's a relief? "I have no idea where my mom is. There's usually two ways it goes with her. Either she's at home, passed out, leaving the door unlocked so people can steal our stuff—that is, if we had stuff to steal— or she disappears for weeks at a time. Nothing new with any of it. I've been on own for a very long time."

No one at the table seems shocked by this.

"But when I went to the trailer park today—that shithole—"

"Charles."

"Sorry, Mrs. S., when I went to that stink hole of a trailer, I found a lock on the door and an eviction notice. Seems like Mom forgot about our rent. Again."

"Is there no way you can contact her?" Dad asks.

"Usually she has a phone, but when I tried calling, it was disconnected. Seems she forgot to pay that bill too. Surprise, surprise." He holds his teacup in his hands for a moment before taking a sip. "Ah, perfect. Darjeeling?"

"What's your plan then, Charles?" Mom asks.

"Well, thanks to your kindness, I've got a belly full of delicious food—props to you, Mr. S.—and a place to stay tonight."

"And then? What happens tomorrow?"

"I'm not sure. I know people I can stay with, or I can go downtown and apply for a Section 10."

I've heard about this. Social services gives a place to stay and a very small amount of money to kids whose parents don't want them, who have nowhere else to live, or who don't want to be in a group home or can't be. Unfortunately, those kids are rarely successful in the end. Maybe it's the program or maybe it's the person, but most of those kids don't make it to high school graduation.

"Nonsense. We have room for you here, Charles. You don't need an invitation. You're always welcome. You can stay as long as you like."

Dad leans in. "However, we do have rules."

Charlie is quiet.

I don't know if it's because of my parents' kindness and hospitality or his resistance to being told what to do.

Maybe both.

"You'll need to stay in school and contribute to the household."

"I think that's fair."

Mom takes a turn. "But that will mean you'll need to switch schools. Anthony's is closer and we've got a good relationship with the administration."

"That's fine. It's time for a change anyhow."

"We'll work on that first thing tomorrow," she adds.

Dad's not done. "We'll also want you to join some kind of activity at school, even if it's just until the end of the year. It's to keep you active and busy, and it may also help you feel connected."

"Any activity?"

"Extracurricular," Dad says.

"And legal," I chime in.

Charlie scowls at me.

"And we'd like you to get a job. Something that requires responsibility and time management," Mom adds.

"Also puts a little money in your pocket," Dad finishes.

"I already have a job."

We're all surprised.

I can't help it. "Again, legal?"

"Of course!" Charlie fakes being offended. "What sort of hoodlum do you think I am?"

I choose not to answer that question.

"Where?" Heather wants to know.

"At the Sugar Dough Stop."

She laughs. "Of course."

I've never been to the place, but I know it's north of downtown in the warehouse district. Whenever I've driven by, it looks like it's about ten years past needing to be torn down.

Mom and Dad glance at each other. There's something on their minds, but Charlie beats them to the punch.

"One thing you haven't mentioned—the big thing. Tony and me, and our knack for getting into trouble."

By the looks on their faces, he's hit the nail on the head. Dad takes Mom's hand before urging him on. "And?"

"Well, after last summer," he unconsciously rubs his belly where he was stabbed, "my desire to solve mysteries and catch bad guys has declined considerably."

"Has it?"

He smirks. "Yeah. It's proven to be not so hot for my health."

Mom seems to approve of what she's heard. "Then those are our terms. You can say no thanks, Charles, but considering your other options, and that we care and would like to help you out if we can, I think the choice is simple."

He nods. "I understand."

Mom gets up and puts a hand on his back. "Make what you believe is the best decision for you."

"Okay." He slurps down the last of his drink and sets the cup on the table. "And thank you for the warm beverage."

"No problem, Charles. We always enjoy sharing our tea with you."

chapter 20

Charlie and I walk out to the car to grab his stuff.

"Soooo…," Charlie draws it out. I can't imagine what's going through his head after the family discussion. "Gekas has a boyfriend?"

Should've known it wouldn't be what I was expecting.

"And he's a lawyer," I add.

"And here I was, thinking she was an android."

"Programmed to fight crime?"

"And keep us in line."

I laugh. "Takes quite an ego to think a robot was designed just to deal with you."

"Well, when they make you *this* special…," he gestures to himself. "Hey? What about the Research King? How long has he been married to the young Diane Keaton?"

It takes me a second to figure out who he's talking about. "You mean Cory and Cynthia?"

"Sure."

"Almost as long as Mom and Dad."

"And Mrs. and Mrs. Good-Looking?"

"Charlie!"

"What? They're together, aren't they?"

"Yes."

"Then what's the offense?" He leans in and grabs his box. "This is an open-minded household, isn't it?"

"Irene and Barb have been together longer than Mom and Dad. But married only six."

"Stupid laws."

Charlie probably hates any rule that limits people's ability to be who they are.

He looks at the front window of the house, the soft light coming through the curtain. He sets his box of stuff down. "Uncle Ed's a good-looking dude. I'm surprised he's not hooked up with someone."

"He had someone in his life a while back—Jackie—but she disappeared a couple of years ago."

"Like—?" He slides a thumb across his throat.

"No! He said her job took her to another continent."

"Sure, it did," he says, unconvinced.

"Not everything ends in murder."

"You sure about that?"

I'd hope not, but after the last few years with Charlie, I'm a little more suspicious.

He carries on. "How long are your aunt and uncle staying?"

"Sally and Sheldon? They head back tomorrow."

"Same with Jodi and Bryan?"

I nod.

He breathes a sigh of relief. "Your big sis doesn't like me much."

"I wouldn't say that. It's more like you need to re-earn her trust."

He considers this. "Fair enough. I haven't been the easiest on your family."

My gut tightens at his words, an uneasiness that he'll be now living in our house. It must show on my face.

"Relax, Shepherd. Those days are done."

Are they?

"Your Aunt Ayana is hot."

"Charlie!"

"What! She is. Definitely as hot as your mom."

"Charlie!!"

He's got that shit-eating grin I've come to know well. He baited me and I fell for it.

"You've got some nice people around you, Shepherd."

"Yeah, I'm lucky."

"Do you really think luck has anything to do with it?"

"Fair point." My parents taught me that being kind and good is an action, one that requires hard work each and every day.

He looks to the house. "Time to go back in? I think we've given them enough time to mull over why letting me stay may or may not be a horrible idea."

I'd argue, but I know he's right.

He picks up his box and backpack and I follow him inside.

chapter 21

Mom and Dad are alone at the kitchen island, finishing their tea.

Charlie props his box on the counter and pulls out the radio station mug.

"Where can I put this?"

"Clean or dirty?" Dad asks.

He sniffs inside. "Normally, I'd call this clean, but new place, new rules."

"Into the sink. I'll clean it with the rest."

He places the cup carefully among the rest of ours. Its radio logo stands out amid the matching set Mom and Dad hauled out for the party, but then sometimes so does Charlie.

I lead Charlie upstairs to his room.

Originally, it was Jodi's, but she's been gone long enough that it's just a spare bedroom now. Mom and Dad used it briefly for a treadmill and storage space, but it's been repainted since then and left as a makeshift guest bedroom. The walls are bare, except for the mirrored closet doors.

An old twin-sized bed with a wooden headboard is pushed against the wall. Beside it is a nightstand holding a reading light and a stack of tattered paperbacks, and there's a chest of drawers beside that. A small desk and chair fit neatly opposite the bed.

Charlie goes in and sets his box down on the desk and his backpack on the floor. He steps back and sits on the bed, testing the springs with a bounce.

He pulls out his phone. "Wifi password?"

I give him a look—as if he doesn't know.

He grins and taps on his phone.

I smile. "That's what I thought. You'll find towels in the closet and an extra blanket if you get cold." I look around, trying to think of anything else he might need. "Do you want a nightlight? In case you get scared?"

"Don't be a dick."

"Just saying. New places can be creepy."

"Get out of here, Shepherd."

I laugh as I leave and head to my own room for bed.

chapter 22

My alarm yanks me out of sleep. I squint at the time. Feels too early, but it's not. Crap.

And it's a Monday. Double crap.

Bleary-eyed, I grab my phone to see what I've missed. Mike's asked again about picking me up this morning, and it seems that Randy from my law class didn't get his work done on our project and went nuclear, wiping everything off the online drive.

The day's barely started and it's already crashing and burning.

I drag my ass out of bed, not ready to deal with any of this quite yet, and make my way to the bathroom. The door is locked and the shower is running and, for a moment, I think someone is trying to drown a cat, but then I realize it's Charlie. Singing opera.

I've heard him sing in the car and he's not the worst. But now, unrestrained by an audience, he's belting it out, and it's not great. As he tries to hit the high notes, his vocal register cracks, and it sounds like metal screeching slowly together in a car crash.

I don't listen for long—I really have to go to the bathroom. I do, however, feel reassured: despite his many talents and skills, singing is not one of them.

I go downstairs, popping into the main floor bathroom before wandering into the kitchen to find Dad.

The smell of coffee and cooking fills the air. On the counter is a small stack of bacon and eggs.

"Morning," he says, biting into a breakfast sandwich.

"You're in the kitchen early."

Dad shakes his head. "Not me. This is all Pavarotti."

I pour myself a cup of coffee. "He brought his own beans, didn't he?"

"Actually, no. I guess he feels he's fixed our ill-begotten ways."

However, as I take a sip, I can't help but detect a smoother, more flavourful taste. "Better be careful or you'll be out of a job."

"Oh, he's taking full advantage of the place, but soon he'll become just another lazy teenager in my house," Dad says, giving me a parental look.

"Oof," I say, laughing. Then, "Do you really believe that, Pops?"

"I have to cling to my small hopes."

I stuff a piece of bacon in my mouth and wander back upstairs, coffee in hand. As I walk past the bathroom, Charlie's putting everything into "Black Dog" by Led Zeppelin and this time, it's awesome. His enthusiasm is infectious and I'm caught up in the moment, pausing to sing along.

The door suddenly whips open and Charlie Wolfe stands there, dripping wet and buck-naked except for the towel he's drying his crotch with.

"What the hell, Shepherd!"

"*Me?* Why the hell are you naked? Wrap a towel around that!"

"You don't believe in the natural process of the air-dry? I only want to be kind to my gentle skin."

"Dude, that's not the point. You just bounced from shower to hall and barely covered yourself. My family—my sisters!— are in the house!"

"What? You don't want them to feast upon my teenage magnificence?"

For a fleeting moment, I worry he's going to drop the towel and strut around. He's still in as good a shape as last summer, except he's now got that rough-looking scar across his torso below the compass tattoo on his chest.

I try not to stare.

He catches me looking. "Like it? It's going to help me get *all* the girls."

"It's pretty intense, actually. But, please, cover yourself up."

I know he's enjoying my discomfort, which is only making things worse, but I really don't need Aunt Ayana to come out and witness this. "Charlie, I'm *begging* you."

"Fine." Unashamed, he pulls the towel away to spread it out and wrap it around his waist. "You have a fantastic facility. You should try it. Go in, let it all out. The acoustics are great."

It finally sinks in. We've allowed this kid to stay in our house.

What have we done?

chapter 23

After my shower—I don't dare test the acoustics—I dress and head downstairs. The whole family is up now, gathered around the table. Jodi and Bryan and Heather plan to get on the road soon, and Aunt Ayana leaves this afternoon. I'm pretty sure Aunt Sally and Uncle Sheldon won't bother to stop in between the hotel and the airport.

Everyone's feasting on Charlie's cooking. Even Ollie has found a place, lying in the centre of the kitchen, hoping he'll get tossed a piece of bacon.

I grab a seat beside Heather and help myself to a glass of juice. "Smells good."

Mom hands me the plate of eggs. "Tastes even better."

Charlie, spatula in hand, calls from the stove, "Better be. Organic, grass-fed. Sometimes you guys are too much—" he pauses, glancing at Mom and Dad, adjusting his tone, "but in a good way!"

"Why don't you come eat with us, Charles?" Mom says.

I can tell she's a little embarrassed to have invited this boy into her house only to have him act like a servant.

"Let me just finish the last of these pancakes."

I mouth, "Pancakes?" and Dad nods, handing over the plate.

"You'll make a good wife someday," remarks Heather.

He doesn't even pause. "If only someone were so lucky."

I want to be a smartass, but I decide not to push my luck—after all, Charlie has made my breakfast. I see him flipping through the newspaper as he waits by the grill.

"You going old-school over there?" I ask.

"I think I scared your paperboy this morning when I came back from my walk," he says.

Jodi looks up. "Why were you up so early?" She hasn't been as hard on him as I expected—she must still be forming an opinion.

"New place. Couldn't sleep. Took Ollie for a walk." Before the family comments further, he carries on, distracted, "I didn't even think paperboys existed anymore."

Dad asks, "What's caught your attention that you're not minding my pancakes?"

Charlie hesitates and glances at me before answering. "Uh, another body was found."

I peek quickly around the table and see all the nervous looks. "Like the ones from the fall?"

He nods, not looking up. "The cops say they're still investigating, but if the press is already asking questions, there's got to be a connection."

"Maggie has her work cut out for her," Mom says offhandedly, but I know it's anything but that. It's her warning to Charlie and me both to stay out of it.

Charlie doesn't seem to register this. "The whole business is getting creepy. They've started asking the public for information."

Dad tries to catch Charlie's attention and divert him from trouble. "Of course, Detective Gekas is smart. They'll find new evidence. She'll figure it out."

"Yup, but she better get her ducks in a row. The city's going to freak out soon."

Sometimes with Charlie, you just need to hit him right in the head with a mallet.

"This is Gekas's case," I say. "She'll deal with it."

Charlie looks up, seeing everyone's expressions. "Oh yeah, totally. Let her do her job. She's got it covered." He closes the paper, pushing it away, hoping it will punctuate his point.

Mom and Dad study him, deciding whether or not to believe him.

Charlie knows it. "Listen, I'm not interested in figuring out what happened to these poor dudes. Gekas doesn't need us messing around. Less is more."

He carries over the last three pancakes on his spatula and plunks them straight onto his plate. He fills the edges with bacon and eggs, and drowns the whole thing in syrup.

My family is stunned by this pile of food, but he's still thinking about Gekas. "Besides, did we ever *really* help, or did we just add to the problem?"

Good question. The events of last summer were nearly too much for us to handle.

Yet, as the talk at the table moves on to other topics, my brain floats back to the conversation I had with Gekas last night, and how she asked about Charlie and me. It wasn't what she said but *how* she said it...

Was she actually hoping we'd been digging around?

chapter 24

We say goodbye to Heather, Jodi, and Bryan, and wish them a safe journey. For once, neither of my sisters pulls me to the side to warn me to behave. After they drive away, Mom and Dad send Charlie and me upstairs to finish getting ready while they clean the kitchen.

I'm still wondering about Gekas's comment last night and the body that was found, so I crank up the tunes to drown the thoughts out of my head.

I grab my phone to text Mike.

No need for a ride today

Mike must be hanging by his phone this morning because the reply bubbles up immediately:

What's up?

Dad's driving

Why?

I really don't feel like telling the whole story, but Mike will keep asking if I don't.

**Charlie's staying
with us for a while**

Although the two of them have never met, Mike's a good friend and he's heard the stories.

CHARLIE Charlie?

Yup

Silence on his end. Then:

K

That's it. I know Mike's got more questions, but he'll wait to ask them when he sees me at school.

I catch a look at myself in the mirror and I'm immediately dissatisfied. I change my shirt—a couple of times—before settling on a casual button-up.

Although we're not supposed to care about our looks, guys still get wrapped up in all that teenage image bullshit. I used to care a lot more—then Sheri happened and my priorities changed and I quit caring about a lot of things. However, some of my old ways have been seeping back and I study myself one last time.

Charlie comes barging into my room. "Hey, pretty princess. You done preening?"

"Can't you learn to knock?" I yell, embarrassed.

"Gear down, Shepherd."

Charlie's got on jeans and a T-shirt, with the phrase "Feelin' Groovy!" written in bold, colourful letters on the front.

"You're wearing that to school?" I ask.

Charlie looks down. "Why?" He frowns. "You the fashion police now?"

"Sorry, man. I—" I stammer. No one can cut me down to size like Charlie.

"Aw, quit apologizing. Let's get movin'!"

chapter 25

We're at school early. Dad's phoned ahead to make arrangements to meet my vice-principal, Mr. Barry, before school starts and sort things out with Charlie. When we walk into the main office, Mrs. Opal, the school secretary, is behind her desk in the main office.

"Good morning, Mr. Shepherd, Tony—" She looks over at Charlie briefly, trying to get a read on him, before asking, "What can I help you with?"

Dad leans against the counter that divides the room. "We're here to see Wayne."

She checks. "He's just on the phone. Likely won't be too long. Take a seat."

She gestures to the moulded plastic chairs against the wall.

We all sit but don't talk much. Dad's on his phone, answering emails, and Charlie's studying every nook and cranny of the office—probably trying to figure out the best way to break in when he needs to—so I just sit there, listening to Mrs. Opal's radio playing Top 40 quietly at her desk. The hallways are empty and it's eerie without the noisy buzz of students.

A feeling of déjà vu washes over me. I try to avoid this place as much as possible, but I find myself thinking about when I sat in this exact spot after Sheri went missing.

My heart beats a little harder and I'm grateful when Mrs. Opal says, "Mr. Barry can see you now."

He opens the door as we approach, and of course he's smiling.

Mr. Barry has been at the school for a couple of years, and at the start, we called him Mr. Smiley—but we never meant it as an insult. Most of us like him. He's a young and good-natured guy who loves sports: he's a back-up coach for badminton, volleyball, curling, golf, and cross-country. More importantly, though, he seems to have this way with students; even if a kid is in trouble and gets suspended, they somehow leave his office without a lot of freaking out.

I think it's all him.

He welcomes us into his office. A dark red folder sits on his desk. "Morning, Ben." He looks over at me. "Tony, shouldn't you still be in bed?"

"That'd be nice."

Mr. Barry turns to Charlie. "And you're Charlie Wolfe?" He offers Charlie a hand.

Charlie shakes it.

"Looking to register at our school?"

Charlie nods, not giving much of anything.

"Your transcripts—" Mr. Barry flips open the red folder, looking through it, his eyebrows rising "—are certainly excellent. When you show up, that is."

I can't help but want to get a peek at what's in there.

Mr. Barry continues, "But it's April. There's only three months of school left."

Dad speaks up. "Wayne, I understand that it's unusual to register this late in the semester. However, like I said on the phone, Charlie's got some special circumstances."

Mr. Barry nods, thinking it through, before asking Charlie, "And you think this is the right choice for you?"

I know Charlie could bullshit his answer here—in the time I've known him, he's rarely handled authority well—but I don't think he's doing that when he says, "Honestly, sir, I think this is for the best."

I catch Dad's smile. He seems to understand exactly the importance of Charlie's words.

chapter 26

Dad and I step out of the office while Charlie fills out paper-work with Mr. Barry. After a quick goodbye, Dad's on his way to work, and I'm on my way to my period one class.

I head over to the Psych 30 classroom and find it empty. Not even the teacher, Ms. Statten, is here. I take my seat at the back and pull out my phone while I wait for people to show up. I send Charlie a text:

What classes did you get?

And then I send one to Mike:

Where are you?

I don't hear from Charlie, but Mike responds.

Getting breakfast. Want anything?

After Charlie's cooking, I'm stuffed.

Nope

I hang out, checking sports scores, what music and movies are being released this week, and it's not until I'm looking at a new pair of basketball shoes that Mike lumbers into class. He's juggling a breakfast sandwich (with extra bacon) and a coffee in one hand, and his phone in the other.

He's a tall guy—like me—but he's also built bulkier. He has to fold himself up to slide into his desk. He's barely in his seat before he starts grilling me. "Charlie?"

"He got kicked out of his house and needed a place to stay."

"What if he robs you in the middle of the night?"

Obviously, Mike's interpreted my stories about Charlie the wrong way. "He's not like that—"

"What if he pisses off some crazy person and then they attack you—"

Well, *that's* more likely to happen.

"He's not—" I'm fumbling for words, knowing I'm as much to blame for what's happened as he is. "We're not chasing weird mysteries anymore."

"Sure, you're not," he says dismissively. His phone *bings* and he's immediately distracted. "Hey, check this girl out."

He's Snapchatting some intense-looking girl I don't recognize. She's got a dye job that is literally pink on one side and black on the other. She's a hundred percent not my type.

"No, Mike. Just no."

"What? Why not? She's cool."

I shake my head. "It'd be like dating two girls at once."

"Is that so bad?" He studies her picture some more, shrugging his shoulders. "Says she's got a piercing on her—"

Ms. Statten walks in—thankfully—and Mike is distracted again.

Statten is all legs and long strawberry blond hair, but she's also one of the most demanding and thorough teachers I've ever had. She expects a lot from her students but only because she really thinks we're capable of giving our best.

Unfortunately, Mike can't seem to get past her looks. As she takes a seat at her desk, I hear him sigh. "It's those glasses, man. Whenever she does attendance…it just gets me every time."

I point at his breakfast. "She *will* get you if she catches you with that in her class."

Statten takes a hard line about food in the classroom.

He realizes his mistake and mumbles, "Shit." He ducks behind the guy who's just taken the seat in front of him and shoves the rest of the sandwich into his mouth.

"Gross, dude!" I say as I watch him chew; his cheeks pop like a chipmunk's.

The bell rings and Statten shuts the door.

"Good morning, everyone." She goes straight to business, turning down the lights and turning on the slides. "Today's lesson: Development Theories of Gender Identity."

Then I hear it.

Bzzz.

Mike forgot to silence his phone.

Bzzz.

Statten stops mid-sentence, eyeing the room like a hawk.

He panics, looking at me.

I shrug. He's on his own.

Statten follows the sound to his desk. "Mike? Would that be your phone?"

"Maybe?"

"So, let's pretend that you know how important it is to me for you not to have your phone on in class." She notices his food wrapper and coffee cup. "And let's also pretend you know how important it is to me for you not to bring food into my class."

Mike is like a deer in the headlights.

"Now, let's pretend that you simply forgot to silence your phone and dispose of your garbage before my class only because you were too busy studying for the exam on Friday that you most certainly need to pass."

"Ms. Statten?"

"Yes, Mike?"

"Can you pretend to not care while I toss my garbage away?"

"As long as you put your phone on my desk on the way over, so I don't make you take it all the way to the office."

"Deal," he says, peeling himself out of his desk and clomping to the front of the room.

Now that he's not in her line of fire, he reminds me of someone's big goofy pet: not a care in the world, only wanting to chase cars and hump your leg.

I have to stifle a laugh at the thought.

Before I know it, the bell goes and Mike grabs up his phone before we file out into the noisy hallway.

"How could you forget to shut your phone off?" I ask, shaking my head.

"Hey, what can I say? I got to keep an open line to the ladies."

I shake my head, checking my own phone. Nothing yet from Charlie. I look over at Mike. "You're lucky she went easy on you."

"Don't I know it."

He looks down at the Snap he was sent. "Wasn't even worth it."

He shows me a shot of a guy from our team sleeping in class, a big pool of drool covering his textbook.

We head for our lockers, flowing through the river of teenagers, but there's a pile-up ahead. A group has formed outside Mrs. Shelley's classroom, and the way they're circling around, their phones out, taking video—

"Fight!" shouts Mike.

Shit. Please don't let it be Charlie.

I remind myself he's too strategic to get into a brawl on day one and too low profile to want that kind of attention, but then again—

"Maybe we should break it up," I say.

"Lead the way, Mr. Do-Gooder."

I push my way through the wall of students.

In the centre of the crowd, two girls are rolling on the ground, wailing on each other like animals. One has a fistful of hair—she's definitely been in a fight or two—while the other flails her arms, scratching the air, screaming, "He's mine, bitch!"

"Pfft, they're in Grade 9," Mike says. "Dumb."

I'm relieved that's all it is.

"Still want to break it up?" he asks.

Before I can answer, Mr. Quint from physics and Mr. Barry ram their way through the crowd, along with Mr. Martin, the head of maintenance, to break up the fight, mostly to the jeers of the crowd.

"Shit, man. Your school is ghetto," I hear behind me.

Charlie's standing there, backpack on his shoulder, holding a binder, wearing a school hoodie with the logo on it. He takes a bite out of a puffed wheat square.

"Where'd you get that?" I say, nodding at the treat.

"From Karen, a girl in my Math 30 class."

"Karen Witzki? She just *gave* you food?" Mike asks.

He shrugs, swallowing his mouthful. "She thinks of me as a lost stray."

Mike shakes his head. "Damn, I've been trying to get with her for a year."

I do proper introductions. "Mike, Charlie. Charlie, Mike."

They give each other a short nod. Having these two aspects of my life stand side by side feels weird. Mike seems tense, but Charlie doesn't let the moment linger and points to the two girls. "I can't believe Penny tried to go toe-to-toe with Carol over Bruce."

"Wait. Didn't you just get here this morning?" Mike asks.

Charlie shrugs, taking another bite of gooey square.

"You just have to get used to it," I smile, patting Mike on the shoulder. I point to the hoodie. "Where'd you get that?"

"Mrs. Opal's lost and found." He shows me his binder. "I also got this, full of loose-leaf."

"You know Mom and Dad could have given you stuff."

"Aw, they've done enough. Besides, why pass up gently used, but perfectly good school supplies that have been left by kids whose parents have too much money and too little time to care when it's lost?"

"Ask and the universe provides?" I say.

"Precisely. And Mrs. Opal loved that I cared about the environment so much that she gave me school swag too." He pulls out a pen from behind his ear, emblazoned with the school logo.

Mike shakes his head. "You are too much, man." His phone *bings* again and he glances at it. "Sweet. Got some arranging to do with the ladies. Boys—"

Mike might just be using this as an excuse to get out of this conversation, but I can't really blame him. Charlie is a lot to take in.

Charlie puts out his hand to shake as Mike attempts a fist bump. They totally miss each other's signals.

"Awkward," I say, shaking my head.

Mike shrugs, giving me a proper goodbye before saunter-ing off with his head down, face in his phone.

"Who fist bumps?" Charlie says, chewing the last of the puffed wheat square.

"Who shakes hands? What are you? A forty-six-year-old realtor?" I laugh.

"I prefer travelling salesman. Maybe vacuums or encyclo-pedias."

This kid is from another time. Maybe another planet.

Charlie's already moved on, pulling out the printout of his schedule to study it.

"What's next?"

"Chem 30. Down the hall and to the left?"

"Well done, Mr. Wolfe. Meet back here after next class?"

He throws up a peace sign and walks away.

chapter 28

After English, I head to my homeroom. I'm not surprised to find Charlie there, this time eating a cookie.

I take the seat beside him. "Looks good. Where'd you get it this time?"

"Brynn's mom made it."

"Who's Brynn?"

"Grade 11. Moved here at the start of the year from Ontario. Dad and Mom divorced after he couldn't quit being a genuine asshole. She hangs out with Zack and Paula on the weekends playing D&D. She's also a lightweight grey hat."

"Grey hat?"

He rolls his eyes at me. "A hacker. A little good, or white hat, as they like to say—and a little bad, or black hat."

"Ah! Put them together and you get—"

"Grey. Does it mostly for the entertainment."

I nod, admiring him. "I've been around you for almost two years and I still don't understand how you pull off finding out about people's shit so quickly."

"I ask questions, Shepherd, and then listen to what they have to say. Most people say way more than they need to."

He makes it sound easy, but he and I both know there's a lot more to it than that. He seems to have an innate ability to ask the *right* questions.

"But I also use familiar patterns. There are always certain types of groups, like jocks and nerds. There's always relationships: students with students, teachers with teachers, and depending on age, likely one teacher or student attempting to cross that line."

Considering Charlie and I saw this happen once, it doesn't shock me.

"The sooner you figure out the power dynamics of a situation, the sooner you can manoeuvre through the different players and take advantage of it."

"But aren't you relying on stereotypes?" I ask.

He shrugs. "Of course. I mean, there will always be outliers—people who move on the fringes or navigate between the spaces—but there are always those who define the groups."

As if on cue, Charity Pelton, class princess, sits herself in front of Charlie. She's wearing short shorts even though it's not that hot out yet, and her cardigan is slouching off one shoulder. Her hair is up in what seems like a messy bun, but I know every piece of it has been precisely styled.

"Hey, Tony," she turns sideways in her desk, knees in the aisle, crowding into our space.

"Hi, Charity."

"You didn't come out to party this weekend." She leans farther toward me. "What's with that?"

"My parents had their anniversary."

She shrugs her bare shoulder. "That's too bad. We had a good time."

"Well, maybe next time." I find her presence claustrophobic, but I'm trying hard not to be a dick.

She cocks her head, turning to Charlie, giving a big fake smile. "And who is this?"

He stares at her, expressionless, saying nothing.

I intervene. "Charity, this is Charlie."

"Hello. New here, huh?" She reaches across his desk to give his arm a little squeeze. "And so late in the year?"

Charlie suddenly forces a smile. "Well, you know. Life does that. Moved from Ontario after Mom and Dad divorced. Dad was an alcoholic and an asshole, and Mom came out here to start fresh."

He's going to have to thank Brynn for the backstory.

Not that it matters much to Charity. She continues smiling, but her eyes have glazed over and dart to the door where two of her friends have entered.

"Well, nice to meet you. You two should definitely come out with us next weekend."

Before either of us can answer, she winks at me and is on her way to the other side of the classroom.

"And *that* would be an example of bad listening," I say.

"Charity Pelton. French Immersion student. Good grades, not great. Likes the attention but is noncommittal. Your buddy, Mike, is unfortunately one of those who falls for it nearly every time." He takes a breath before rattling off more. "Rumour has it she's hooked up with a guy from university, but nothing's been confirmed. And despite her attempt to cover it with some nice perfume, she likes to have a smoke in the parking lot before school."

I stare at him, dumbfounded.

He leans forward and copies Charity's wink. "And that would be an example of *good* listening."

chapter 29

After homeroom, Charlie leaves for Native studies with Statten, and I meet Mike for our spare. I have a few scenes of *King Lear* to read and my group project in Law 30 is a mess, but I'm mostly caught up in the rest of my classes. I need to get outside and grab some fresh air, though, so I convince him to play some one-on-one on the outside court.

Even though the sun is out, the weather's still cool, so we have to keep our hoodies on to begin with. Snow and slush still lie along one end of the fenceline, so it's a restrained game of streetball. I use this to my advantage; Mike uses his size and muscle to control the game while I use ball-handling and speed, and I keep pushing him against the muck to make him back off. This only annoys him and he starts throwing a lot of smack talk my way. After he nearly takes a spill into a puddle, I ease up, and he catches up to my five.

I go for a crossover for my six and pull off a wraparound fake for the last point.

"Good game, man," he says, giving me a fist bump before leaning forward to put his hands on his knees.

"Thought you had me," I lie.

"Figured I'd let you have the win."

"Thanks."

He lets out a big sigh, still breathing hard. "So, Charlie?"

After this morning's meeting, Mike must still be trying to decide what to think of him.

"Yeah...?" I say, hoping he'll guide the conversation.

"How long is he staying with you?"

"Not sure. I guess until things get sorted out for him."

Mike nods, considering what I've said. "He's weird."

"Yup, I know." I'm not going to argue with the truth.

"He's not going to pull any shit, is he?"

"I honestly don't know, but he's trying to not mess things up, so I hope not."

He picks up the ball and dribbles it back and forth between his hands. "You trust him?"

"I do."

He bounces the ball toward me, nodding. "Then I guess I better get used to him."

"Thanks. I appreciate it." I keep it low key but I have tons of respect for Mike's willingness to accept Charlie so easily. Mike can be a lot of things, but in this moment, he's being a really great friend.

He smiles. "Besides, if he screws up, somebody's got to have your back."

Fair enough, Mike. Fair enough.

chapter 30

At the end of our spare, we meet up with Charlie for lunch.

We find a table in the cafeteria, and I'm digging into my lunch bag, pulling out leftovers from last night, when I catch Charlie's look. He hasn't touched his bag.

"You okay, man?" I ask.

"I just realized, no one's ever packed a lunch for me."

I'm staring at him and he knows it, and I don't know what to say, but Mike does it for me.

"Good thing Tony's dad is a good cook then."

We both consider him. I doubt Charlie realizes how much of a leap Mike just made, especially after our little talk outside.

Mike continues, "I'm just saying, it'd suck if your first packed lunch tasted like crap, right?"

Charlie smiles before offering a fist bump. "True."

Mike reaches across the table and delivers it back.

I quietly admire the gesture and move the conversation along. "How was Native studies?"

"Fantastic. I wish I'd taken the whole class." Charlie takes a bite of roasted barbecue pork bun before adding, "But what's the deal with Statten?"

Mike nods. "I know. Hot, right?"

Charlie shrugs. "Yeah, I can see that. But she's going through something."

He's piqued my interest. "What do you mean?"

"I don't know. Something's off about her."

"You only met her today. How can you know that?"

He sets his sandwich down and digs out a juice box. "Well, she seems really put together. She's smart and confident. Like Mike pointed out, she's attractive, but more importantly, she knows it but doesn't overthink it. Her clothing is sharp, business casual—"

I interrupt, "But not always. Sometimes she's in jeans, but it's often matched with a dress jacket or high heels." I wouldn't have given these things much thought a couple of years ago, but since hanging around Charlie, I've started noticing these details. I'm also aware that Mike is looking at me, but I ignore it.

Charlie continues, "There's barely a hair out of place, her makeup is on point, and even the frames of her glasses are high-end and expensive. She also has quality tech gear: smart watch, computer, phone. I'm betting the newest and best?"

I confirm Charlie's suspicions. "Always. And styled to match the rest of her outfit. So what makes you think something's going on?"

"I feel some of that confidence has slipped. Sharp noises, like a door slammed too hard or the bang of a desk, seem to affect her. Also, if students get too close, she takes a step back."

Mike's curious now. "How do you know she hasn't always been like that?"

Charlie turns to me for confirmation and I know he's right. Although I've never paid attention to it, somewhere along the way I *have* noticed something's off with her.

But where's he going with this? "Even if something *is* off—"

"We're not doing a damn thing." Charlie glances at Mike as if he's saying it solely for Mike's benefit. "School, work, home, sleep. That's our focus. Mysteries are no longer our business."

I almost want to believe him.

After lunch, we all go to our classes. Mike has gym, Charlie has Graphic Arts 20, and I head to my law class. Most of it is spent cleaning up Randy's mess and putting together all the pieces of our project. Fortunately, Shannon, our other project partner, had almost three-quarters of the work saved on a USB drive from when she transferred all our individual sections onto the computer. Then we tracked down any backups we had on our computers and added them to the file. By the end of the hour, we'd Frankensteined together a nearly usable version and Shannon volunteered to clean up the rest of it tonight. Thank you, Shannon.

At the break, I get a text from Charlie:

Working a shift at the
The Sugar Dough Stop

What about class?

Spare
Texted your folks to let them know

K. You home for supper?

Are we an old married couple now?

Now that he's said it, I can't help but feel like somewhere along the line, that's exactly what we've become.

And I hate it.

I try to think of a comeback—even punched in *you're not my type* before deleting it—totally aware that Charlie can tell I'm struggling.

Shepherd, quit it. You're a manly man
Come by and I'll give you a doughnut

Then, just when I think he's done:

And if we WERE a couple,
I'd be the one wearing the pants

My last class of the day is Biology 30, which has been far more enjoyable since our usual teacher, Mr. Harriet, went on leave a while back and was replaced with a substitute, Mr. Hall.

None of us are sure what happened to Harriet, and the staff isn't talking. Of course, there are plenty of rumours: cancer, death in the family, inappropriate conduct, outpatient psych ward, and last but not least, mid-life crisis. But like most gossip, the truth probably lies somewhere in the middle of all that—though it's likely more boring.

Harriet's never been exciting. In all the time I had him for a teacher, he talked in the same monotone voice, wore the exact same kind of dress shirt and tie, and always expected our notes to be completed in a very specific, detailed way— and if we didn't follow his system, we were penalized.

Hall, on the other hand, is young and casual, with a trendy beard and a badass sleeve tattoo. On his first day, he pulled up on a Triumph Bonneville motorcycle, which definitely caught people's attention. Over the past few weeks, he's told us stories of how he spent the first year after high school touring across Canada, the US, and some tropical places in South America before coming back to get his education degree. A lot of the guys in my class find him relatable, but I also know a couple of girls who wouldn't mind corrupting his teaching career.

The interesting thing, though, is that he's strict too. When the final bell for class goes, he shuts the door. Normally, this is annoying because most teachers do it just to be dicks, making a false claim to power. Yet, Mr. Hall has fun with it. If you're the dumbass who's late, he makes you draw your punishment out of a bucket, which is usually doing some sort of exercise reps, answering biology questions, or singing something of his choice. Although push-ups would be pretty easy, I have no interest in performing "I'm a Little Teapot" in front of the whole class, so I make sure I'm always on time.

As Hall turns on the data projector and gets into the processes that enable movement in unicellular organisms, we scramble for our notebooks. Mr. Hall doesn't wait and we start diagramming an amoeba and a paramecium and don't stop until the bell rings.

chapter 33

After school, Mike spots me a ride over to Charlie's work before he takes off to pursue his two-toned-hair girl.

The Sugar Dough Stop is in the corner of a strip mall at the intersection of two busy streets in the warehouse district. The place is filled with blue collar and emergency service workers—at least one ambulance and a fire chief's car are outside—and it's a noisy racket of conversations.

Charlie's behind the counter, sliding trays of doughnuts into the display racks. He's wearing a Sugar Dough Stop shirt that he's tucked into his pants and a visor that fights to contain his trademark shaggy hair, which has been scooped into a net.

He waves me to an empty table and comes over with a large coffee and a Boston Creme doughnut.

"On the house," he says.

I'm staring at his clothing and I want to say something smartass, but he stops me. "Just don't."

I'm still tempted, but he's gone before I can open my mouth.

I look around the restaurant. There's nothing fancy about the place. No art on the walls or televisions in the corners. Absolutely no attempt to brighten it up. The clientele seems to be here to meet over coffee and doughnuts and not much else.

Then I taste the coffee. It's rich and flavourful—something I would never have expected, or noticed, until Charlie started making it for me—and I wonder how much he's a part of it. I take a bite of the doughnut and marvel at its freshness.

Yup, I definitely understand why Charlie works here.

Since he's busy working, I grab my backpack and pull out my copy of *King Lear*. I'm supposed to be on Act 4 and I still need to get through Act 3, so I start reading.

I'm deep into Lear's storm rant when I hear, "Anthony?"

I look up to see Detective Gekas standing beside me.

"May I?" she asks, indicating the chair across from me.

"Of course."

She sets down her cup of coffee and a piece of apple pie, served with a dollop of whipped cream on the side, and slides into the seat. When she looks at me, her eyes are fresh and focused, but her brows are furrowed, the corners of her lips drawn down with unease. She seems tense, nothing like the Gekas I saw at yesterday's party.

I glance over at Charlie. He's not paying attention, but if she's been to the till, I'm sure he's aware of her presence.

"I wouldn't expect this to be quite your type of hangout," she says.

"I guess it's all about the company we keep."

"I suppose it is." She smiles, intentionally ignoring Charlie. "You two hanging out lots?"

"Yeah, you could say that. He's moved in."

At first Gekas seems surprised, but then she relaxes. "After last night, I wondered. But I think a house like yours may do him good."

I don't know Charlie's history, but I do know Gekas has a thick file on him back at her office. She knows his secrets—some of them, anyway.

"How's he doing after last summer?" she asks, genuinely curious.

"Good. At least, I think so. You know him. Never shares much with anyone even on a good day."

Gekas smirks.

"How about you, Detective?"

"Healing. A little slower than my liking, but I'm coming along."

I nod. I can't help but feel a little guilty since Charlie and I are very much responsible for her current condition.

"It's been a steady stream of OT." Then, based on my look, she explains, "Occupational therapy, physio, and desk work."

"That doesn't sound like fun." I add, "I once tore ligaments in my ankle. Physio sucks."

Shut up, idiot! Torn ligaments do not equal being stabbed in the back!

The comment doesn't seem to bother her, though. "I'd take it over desk work any day."

"Really?"

"Yeah. I hate being in an office." She laughs a little. "I guess I should just be glad to be on a case again."

She's talking about the bodies that have turned up. With the new one that was found today, I'm guessing she's feeling the pressure.

She's got something on her mind. Maybe she's waiting for me to ask questions about the investigation, but I stay quiet.

She goes on, "You two keeping out of trouble?"

Again, the same question as the night before. I wonder if she's worried about us messing things up again.

"Yes, Detective, we're behaving."

And again, that brief hint of disappointment.

Am I missing something here? I'm about to ask when Charlie's appears at our table.

"How's the coffee, Detective?"

She looks up at him with a smile. "Very good, thank you."

"And the pie?"

"Just like something my father would have made."

"Since he ran a bakery, I'll take that as a compliment," he says, all nonchalant.

She looks at him, surprised, and shakes her head.

"Hey, you've got your file on me, so I figured I better have one on you too," he counters.

She studies him, and I expect her to yell, but instead she asks, "So what else have you found out?"

"Besides your parents, grades, and service record? Not much. You keep a pretty low online profile."

"It pays to keep your private life private when you're in my line of work."

"Too much dealing with the riff-raff?" he asks, grinning.

"Yeah, something like that."

I laugh, knowing we're probably included on that list.

Without pause, Charlie switches gears. "You're pretty busy with those murders, huh?"

Gekas's smile fades and the tension returns to her face. Sometimes he's so blunt, I really want to facepalm myself.

"Got any leads on who's killing those people?"

And then sometimes I just want to facepalm *him*—so hard that it knocks him on his ass.

He continues, "What can you tell us about the victims?"

"You know I can't—"

"Any connections between them?"

"This is a police matter—"

"How about leads on the killer's M.O.?"

"Charles—"

"C'mon, Detective. You must know *something*?"

"Charles, enough." She raises her voice and people turn to look. It's very un-Gekas-like. "Sorry, it's just— Please..."

I gesture at Charlie. "Go. Do something. Maybe frost some doughnuts."

"Geez. Fine, Shepherd. I was only curious." He leaves, looking a little sheepish, to take his place behind the counter.

I turn back to her. "Sorry. He's just being...Charlie."

"It's all right. It's not him. It's—" she breaks off. "He's not a bad kid. Pretty smart, actually. Just sometimes, he pushes a little too hard." She sighs, gripping her coffee mug. "The truth is, this case has been a series of dead ends so far."

I'm a little surprised that she's telling me this.

"Two bodies—" she realizes her mistake, "*three* bodies now... And sometimes, it just feels so personal. Like the killer's mocking me."

I've never heard her speak this way, and it actually sends a chill down my spine.

She sighs again, staring into the murky depths of her mug before glancing up at me. "You boys really haven't been snooping around at all?"

I shake my head.

"This guy's been so methodical and confident…"

I notice her slip—they assume the killer is a male. For her to casually mention it, giving me details of the case… What is she up to?

Charlie reappears. "Two fresh chocolate-glazed doughnuts. Still warm." He pushes the plate under Gekas's nose. "I promise you won't be disappointed."

I'm still searching her face, trying to understand why she's revealed this clue, but she breaks my gaze and looks up at Charlie.

"You don't have to do this, Charles. I was out of line—"

"No, Detective. I insist."

She studies the plate, takes one, and tastes it.

Although she's not in the mood, I can tell she's impressed. "Very good. Thank you," she says through a mouthful.

Charlie slides in beside me. "I don't know if you know this, Detective, but I can be a little socially inept around cops."

She laughs. "It's all right. It's what makes you good at what you do…" She trails off, suddenly distracted by her phone, checking it as if it buzzed, though I didn't hear anything. "I should be going. Thanks again for the doughnut, Charles." She glances at me briefly. "You boys behave yourselves. Stay out of trouble."

She rises, desperation plain on her face, and strides out of the restaurant, not looking back.

But all I can wonder is: What the hell just happened?

chapter 34

While Charlie works, I attempt to do homework, but my head is swirling, trying to understand what Gekas was up to. I want to ask Charlie what he thinks, but he's busy at the till.

His shift ends, and I think I'm finally going to get my chance, but he says, "Your dad's on his way to pick us up." And as if on cue, Dad honks his horn as the car pulls up. Before I can say anything else, Charlie calls, "Shotgun!" and rushes outside.

We pile into the car and I stare out the window while Dad and Charlie talk about his first day of school.

I'm only half listening when Dad asks, "And how was your day, son?'

I mumble something —"Good," I think—before the conversation moves on without me.

When we step through the front door, Ollie rushes down the hall, barking, until he realizes it's us and immediately goes into chill mode, wanting love.

Mom calls from the family room, "Food's in the fridge. Help yourselves."

Dad wanders off to be with Mom, and I follow Charlie into the kitchen.

He pulls out plastic containers full of roast beef, scalloped potatoes, and salad, and sets them on the counter. "Working around food makes a guy hungry!" he says, piling it all onto his plate. "It's like Christmas dinner here every day."

Supper looks great, but I'm distracted. "Charlie, does Gekas usually pop into The Sugar Dough Stop?"

He sets his plate in the microwave, and while it spins on the platter, reheating, he ponders my question. "Not usually. She'll sometimes come by to check on me, make sure I'm staying out of trouble, but that's about it."

"Was that why she was there today?'

"Didn't seem like it. She hung out with you more than me."

"She did ask us about whether we were staying out of her investigation—"

"Yeah, she's probably worried about us screwing up her life." He pulls his food out of the microwave and takes it to the island. He shovels a big forkful in, relishing the flavours, before adding, "Or maybe she just came for my tasty doughnuts!"

He's only trying to be raunchy for a laugh, but I'm not in the mood.

I dump some food of my own on a plate and set it in the microwave.

"I think she wants our help," I say

"For what?" he asks through another mouthful.

"Her case."

He waves his fork at me. "Why would you even think that? Did she ask?"

"No, but—"

"But *what*? She wouldn't— Hell! She *can't* ask a couple of teenagers to snoop around in an ongoing investigation—!"

"But she didn't ask!"

"Exactly!"

We're talking in circles and Charlie's making the obvious points. There was never a moment when Gekas actually requested our help. But that doesn't stop me from thinking that she wanted to.

I change tactics. "She can't, right?" I say, taking my plate of leftovers across to the island. "Like you said, it would break all sorts of rules."

"Rules, man. That's why I could never be a cop," he says, slicing his meat up and smooshing it together with his potatoes. "You can't just jump in and look for the bad guys. You've got to follow procedure. Document everything. Make sure everything's backed up, quantified, and qualified." He shakes his head in frustration.

The thought of him in law enforcement makes me want to laugh, but I stifle it. "That's what I'm saying, Charlie. She *can't* ask for our help, but when we did it our way—the Shepherd and Wolfe way—" I see Charlie's eyes light up— "we uncovered a lot of things that might otherwise have gone unnoticed."

"Because we say 'screw procedure!'" he declares.

I nod, smiling.

Charlie cocks his head, thinking about what I'm suggesting. "Nah, she wouldn't... Especially not us. Look at the trouble we've caused." He pushes his empty plate away. Not a crumb is left. "Is there dessert?"

Having a teenage metabolism has its benefits.

I sigh, leaning back. "Probably ice cream in the freezer."

He hops off his chair and puts his plate in the dishwasher before grabbing a bowl out of the cupboard.

"I'm honestly stuck. I just feel so certain she was asking for our help without actually asking, and I can't help but think that we should do something."

"No," he says, serving up two huge bowls of double fudge ice cream.

"No?"

"Look, Shepherd, in living here I made a promise to your parents—hell, to your sisters too—not make any stupid mistakes. Chasing killers is *numero uno* on that list. I'm trying my damnedest to live a normal life."

For once, Charlie's moral compass seems to be stronger than mine. And I understand where he's coming from, but I'm surprised by how frustrated I am at his resistance. Am I addicted to the rush of these adventures? I don't want to be. They don't always end well for everyone. And while we've gotten out alive, it's been just barely.

Still, I can't deny that I'm disappointed at not being able to help. And I must not be able to hide it well, either.

"Oh brother, really?" Charlie says.

"What?"

"You're sitting there with a tasty bowl of ice cream and all you've got to give me are those great big brown puppy-dog eyes. It's pitiful." He shakes his head, shovelling a heaping spoonful into his mouth. "Tell you what," he says, swallowing. "We can have a look around."

The edges of my mouth twist into a grin.

"But," he cautions, "if we find something, we tell Gekas, and then that's it. Deal?"

When did we fall into this mirror universe where I want to chase killers and Charlie wants to talk to the cops?

"Yes. Deal," I say.

"But do me a favour. Work on your poker face, okay? It really is freakin' pitiful."

part 2

Jack stands high above the city, watching the twinkling evidence of life below through the floor-to-ceiling windows of his condo. Rachmaninoff's *Symphony No. 2* plays from the sound system in the distant corner, quiet enough not to wake the neighbours but filling the space with romantic peace. The reflected light of the full moon glows through the windows.

There'd been a hitchhiker and he'd come to the condo to shower.

Killing wasn't new. He'd been killing every full moon since that night on the beach, the night he'd met his beloved.

In the first year, he'd drawn strength from the full moon's illumination; the moonrise initiated his monthly ritual. It didn't matter who he killed or where. It only mattered how. By the second year, he'd fallen into a comfortable habit and had branched out, testing new tools, and new ideas. And now, in his third, his skills were taut, honed—he could deal with anyone.

The hitchhiker had yielded to the ritual. But it had slowed him down, and he was no longer on schedule. He'd had to hide the body in a field—putting it with the others would have taken even more time—then contend with the blood and muck on his shoes. His whole suit had had to be tossed. Then there was the shower, followed by the cleaning afterwards to rinse, wipe, and obscure any hint of himself that the condo might hold.

But the hitchhiker is of no consequence.

Storms are forecast for later in the week. This is a good sign. The thaw is almost over. There's barely any ice on the creek, its water levels are high from the melt, and all the ugliness of this place will soon be washed away.

More importantly, his work from November has been revealed. Soon his beloved will appreciate his third and final gift. Not that lowly hitchhiker. Something more. Something special.

And he only needed three. *Omne trium perfectum*: Everything that comes in threes is perfect.

And as he was once transformed by the moon, so will she be. His soul is as deep and true as the blood that flows through her body. His purpose is her purpose. His life is her life. And as she was part of his transformation, he must be part of hers. His work is an offering to her, a conveyance of his strength, to lead her back to herself. To realize the power she has.

And soon, because of him, she will be strong again.

He's aware of the subtle lies he's telling himself—this is *not* all for her. He knows that he covets. He knows that he feels jealousy. He knows that he hates the impostor in disguise amongst the sheep.

The music ends, and in the silence of the night he hears a siren in the distance. It's not for the hitchhiking man or the countless bodies of the rituals to come.

It has nothing to do with him. But it will soon.

It's time to return to the streets and to her. And to the work he has ahead in the world below.

chapter 36

Charlie and I drive to school the next day with a plan to check out the three murder sites later on—because, of course, that's what a couple of ordinary teenagers do.

We get to school with fifteen minutes to spare, and Charlie and I part ways. I run into Mike on my way to Statten's class. His backpack looks like it's full of books, which I doubt—he's not much of a reader.

"Hey," he says, happy and out of breath.

"Looks like someone's ready to learn." I indicate the load he's carrying. "What you got there?"

"Stuff," Mike says defensively. "Mind if we take a detour?"

I walk with him to the library where he dumps his bag on the counter, unloading colourful picture books and early readers with large print. He ignores my stunned look and says, "Did you know our library has a whole children's section, even though it's a high school? Crazy, huh?"

As the library assistant starts processing the huge stack of books he's returning, I casually pick up *The Adventures of Captain Underpants* from the pile.

"Now *that*," he points, "is an awesome book!"

"Geez, Mike, *Catcher in the Rye* too wordy for you?" I kid.

"Holden Caulfield? Actually, yes. Who wants to read them that boring shit."

"Wait? Them? Who're you talking about?"

He leans in. "Hey, while you've been playing crimefighter, I stepped up and became a Big Brother. My little dude is in a reading group with, like, twelve kids and we take turns reading to them. They're good kids and it's fun…and I like it, so shut up."

I wrap an arm around him, trying to get him in a headlock. "Aww, Mike, you friggin' softie."

The librarian shushes us out of the library.

I laugh as he wrestles out of my hold. "This is why I don't tell you things."

I can't stop and as we step into the hall on our way to class, I yell out, "Yo, Mikey! Can you be *my* Big Brother? Hey, how about reading me a bedtime story?"

He responds promptly with a solid, aching punch to my arm.

chapter 37

Psychology crawls by at a snail's pace. Statten's saying something about nature and nurture, and how socio-something-something influences human development, and that's about all that sticks. I know I took notes, but I'm going to have to reread them to process any of it.

English isn't much better—King Lear has now torn off all his clothes and things are looking bleak for a guy named Gloucester—and I stumble out of class thinking Shakespeare was really good at capturing the level of batshit crazy that people can achieve.

Charlie's already in homeroom by the time I get there—talking with Charity in the corner. I grab a desk and wait, and am surprised to find her eyes on me when he comes over.

She actually looks a little humbled.

"What was that about?" I ask as he sits down.

"Turns out her university boyfriend might be cheating on her."

"And she wants you to look into it?" I say, maybe a little too snarkily.

"Geez, Shepherd, we all have crap to deal with," he responds sharply.

Now I feel bad for the attitude. No surprise that Charlie occasionally has to remind me of people's complexities, especially since he's one of the most convoluted people I know.

I try to move the conversation along. "So, you're back in business solving mysteries?"

"Well, I figure if we're going to start chasing serial killers again, what's it hurt digging up a little dirt on a cheating boyfriend?"

Man, when he puts it that way, my decision to help Gekas seems pretty stupid.

He must read it in my face. "Oh, relax, Shepherd. I'm only doing it to gain a little bargaining power in the future. You never know when you'll need a little help from someone like Charity." Then slyly, punching the same arm that took Mike's fist, he adds, "Besides, odds are I won't get stabbed again if all I'm doing is keeping tabs on her boyfriend, right?"

"Dammit, why do you say these things?" I ask guiltily.

chapter 38

At lunch, Charlie convinces Mike and me to go to a diner he knows about. As I should expect of any of his choices, the place is way off the beaten path and looks like it's fifty years past its prime. Behind the counter there's a gruff, super-intense server with thick dark hair, long nails, way too many silver rings, ink from neck to toes, and fishnets under her shorts.

And of course, it's clear Mike's caveman instincts have noticed.

"Mike, she'll make mincemeat out of you," Charlie warns when Mike gives a low whistle.

"Okay. Okay. A bad girl. That's cool."

"Dude, that's not at all what he's saying," I caution.

Mike waves me off.

Charlie reiterates, "I'm saying she's a girl who won't put up with bullshit."

But it's no surprise that Mike ignores Charlie's warning and asks for her number when he pays his bill.

She crushes him. "No, thanks. I'm not into babysitting."

He's quiet as we go out to his truck, and Charlie pipes up, "Don't feel too bad. You got off easy. One time, I saw her just laugh and point at a guy until he left."

This seems to perk Mike up a bit, and as he climbs back into the truck, he says, "Bet he had to ice his balls after that burn," which keeps us laughing all the way back to school.

chapter 39

It's biology, the last class of the day, and Mr. Hall is talking protists and fungi.

I'm ready to fall asleep when the intercom crackles. "Can the following students come down to see Mrs. Blacker—"

Mrs. Blacker is our guidance counsellor and, sure enough, my name is called. Mr. Hall tells me to take my stuff with me—I likely won't be back before the final bell—and I head down to her office. I'm not sure what this is about, but I'm guessing it has something to do with my scholastic future.

When I arrive at her room, I find nine others sitting in a line—all Grade 12—and my suspicion is confirmed: Mrs. Blacker wants to know what we plan on doing after school. Her job is to help contact universities, gather transcripts, and make sure we've filled out all the forms correctly. And, well, I've been slacking.

Or, in truth, avoiding it altogether.

She calls us into her office one at a time in alphabetical order, so I have to wait around for a while. I rarely spend time in Mrs. Blacker's office. Even after everything that happened last year, I never felt the need to sit down and talk things through with her. She's a kind enough woman from what I've seen, but she also expects you to be open and share your thoughts and feelings, and I do enough of that at home.

When my name is called, I take a seat across from her.

She's middle-aged, with a short, bleached, trying-too-hard hairdo and glasses, and although she has a kind smile, she seems like one of those people who worries 24/7.

Behind her is a corkboard, a crowded patchwork of printed memes. Dead centre is the grouchy old guy from the movie *Up*—the caption reads: "This *is* my caring face."

"Anthony, you haven't requested any college applications yet."

I drag my answer out, knowing she won't like it. "Well, I'm still trying to decide—"

"We're into April. It's time to make some sort of decision." Then, realizing her tone, she consciously takes a breath before going on. "What fields are you looking at?"

"Maybe medicine or public policy?" I'm not really sure of either, but she takes it at face value.

She flips through my transcript, nodding, "Okay, okay. That's good. Of course, you've missed most of the deadlines, but I could give you some pamphlets, choices for schools? Do you know where you'd like to go?"

Since I'm only trying to appease her, I haven't really considered any place except here. I have plenty of options—Vancouver, Calgary, Winnipeg, Toronto—cities where I could stay with family members until I found a place of my own.

I've always known that one day I'll leave my parents' house, but it hadn't occurred to me how close that day was. Now that I'm thinking of it—*really* thinking—I realize I could go almost anywhere.

Of course, I don't say any of this to Mrs. Blacker, and she doesn't care what my answer is. She's scooping up applications, program brochures, and academic calendars out of her files and stacking them in a pile in front of me. I feel a little guilty that I'll probably just toss them all into the recycling.

I'm not sure what I want. And everyone wants an answer: Mrs. Blacker, Mom, Dad—I'm pretty sure even my sisters are getting impatient with me. I don't know why I'm being so indecisive. In fact, I had things figured out perfectly until a year and a half ago, and then my life capsized and I never quite recovered.

But this isn't just about Sheri. After meeting Charlie, I've started doing things I'd never have imagined I was capable of, and despite worrying how often our actions cause more problems, I think I've done good in this world—maybe even saved lives.

It's given me a feeling, a sense of purpose, that I haven't been able to shake. Of what, I'm not sure, but once I figure it out, I know it's going to tell me what I'm supposed to do.

Until then, I'll continue to listen to everyone's advice, take all the applications and brochures they hand me, and wait patiently for my answer to come.

chapter 40

I step out of Mrs. Blacker's office. With only a few minutes left before the bell rings, I leave early and find Charlie waiting at the car.

"You ready to investigate some murder sites?" Charlie asks, all nonchalant.

It bothers me that the horrible act of murder has become so casual and commonplace for the two of us.

Charlie notices. "C'mon, Shepherd, don't get all mopey about it. We're not being disrespectful, so get that out of your head right now. We're doing a job and when we're done, we're handing it over to Gekas. Then our hands are clean."

I appreciate what he's saying, but before I can respond, Mike jogs up.

"Where you guys headed?"

Aw, shit. I don't need him tagging along, for a thousand different reasons.

"Charlie's picking up a couple of hours at the bake shop," I lie. "I was going to drive him over and then do some homework."

Charlie shoots me a look of disapproval, and I feel like an ass, but I don't know what else I could've done.

"That's a bummer. I thought maybe we could hang," Mike says.

"Actually," Charlie cuts in, shaking his head, "they cancelled my shift."

"Oh," I mumble. What the hell is he doing?

Mike brightens. "Ah, cool. So what's up?"

With Charlie basically inviting him along, I see no other option but to tell him the truth. "Well, we're heading to the park—"

Charlie interrupts me. "Shepherd and I are heading to park, but *you've* got a date."

"I do?" Mike blinks. "With who?" He's barely finished the sentence when his phone rings. "Hello?" he says, answering it. "Sorry. Who? Carrie? Carrie who?"

I glance at Charlie and he winks.

"Oh yeah...*Carrie.*" Mike looks at Charlie and me, raising an eyebrow before turning away from us to talk to her.

I put my hands in my pocket, resigned to what I know will happen next.

Mike turns back toward us, still on the line with the girl. "No, that's totally cool. Hang on." He drops the phone and whispers, "Sorry, guys. It's Carrie from social studies. Looks like she may want to hang out." He gives us a thumbs up and walks away.

"Aaaaand there he goes," I say out loud.

Charlie shrugs. "I felt bad for the guy after lunch and it turned out that Carrie's had her eye on him for a while now."

"Aww, aren't you the nice guy."

"Hey, no harm, Shepherd. Who knows? Maybe the stars will align for those two lovebirds."

"Just needed a Cupid like you to help it along," I say.

"Ooh, Cupid…," he says, rolling the idea around in his head.

"Are you going to start using your superpowers to match-make now instead of fighting crime?"

"Well, it's better than lying to your best friend," he scolds, and I shake my head at the slight.

"Relax," he says. "I'm not that honorable. It's simply a diversion. Carrie and I worked together at The Sugar Dough Stop, and she owes me a favour."

"Do I even dare ask *what* sort of favour?"

"Ask only questions you want answers to, Shepherd."

I shake my head as we get into Dad's car, and he gives me the finger-guns ahead. "Let's roll."

We have a lot of ground to cover, so I drive to the furthest discovery site first.

Charlie's got his phone out and is researching news articles.

"Haven't you already read everything about these murders?" I ask.

"Not really, Shepherd." Off my look, he adds, "Seriously, I really have been trying to avoid all the nefarious goings-on."

"Did last summer mess you up that bad?" I ask, trying to be as blunt as possible.

"Well, waking up in a hospital bed with a zipper in my gut and you crying over my bed certainly was traumatizing."

"Hey, I didn't show up until later—"

"Oh yeah, what was it you were up to while I was suffering? Swimming?"

"Gotta get my exercise in," I counter. "But you still haven't answered my question."

"Listen, I made a promise to your folks, and I'm going to try my best."

That still doesn't explain the months where he was under no obligation to behave but still stayed out of trouble. I don't push it—yet; he's got to be avoiding it for a reason.

Charlie directs me to the west side of the city, taking us past the RCMP barracks. "Kind of ballsy to dump a body right under the cops' noses," Charlie says. "Turn right here."

We pull past a cul-de-sac with an old community centre at the end. It looks like it's been closed for several years, its windows and doors shuttered with plywood, colourful graffiti sprayed over the orange brick. There's an empty playground behind it, weeds stretching up through the cracks in the cement.

"Keep going," Charlie says, studying his phone.

We roll past house after house. Butting up against their backyards is a bike path that runs along the edge of a park.

"It's all residential," I say. But I keep going until we come to another street that leads into the parking lot for a baseball field.

"Pull in here," he says.

I stop the car in an empty space and we climb out, surveying the area. We can see into every kitchen and living room window of the neighbouring homes. There's no easy way for anyone to do anything secretive—especially something like dumping a dead body.

"Whoever this guy is, he's not scared," I say.

"That's what worries me," Charlie says, wandering up the embankment of the bike path and into the park. "This place would have been pretty busy back in October."

"What are you talking about?" I ask, racing to catch up.

He doesn't answer me directly, looking up and down the long, winding pavement instead.

There are still enough puddles and piles of snow to keep most people from enjoying a bike ride or a run. Beyond the park is the creek and the small island in its centre, connected to the bike path by a couple of bridges.

We start walking toward one of them.

"Think back to when you first asked for my help with Sheri."

I had almost begged Charlie for his help to find her. "Yeah, what about it?"

"And right after asking, I tested you by getting you to cut through someone's backyard to get to your car."

"Wait? That was a *test*?"

"Of course it was. I had to see what you were capable of."

"What's that got to do with this guy?" I growl, getting frustrated. I hate when he's not straight with me.

"Well, eventually, we broke into enough houses that you quit being a pussy—"

"Charlie!"

He sighs, happy he's finally got a reaction out of me.

I swear, I think he lives for this stuff.

"Gekas's guy isn't a pussy," Charlie says. "He's been doing this for a while."

I feel a chill run down my spine. "Which means he's capable of almost anything,"

Charlie nods, grim-faced. "This guy is comfortable with killing."

chapter 42

The island where the second body was found has been left undeveloped as an ecoregion of mixed-grass prairie. Dirt paths weave between tufts of grass, flowers and small, low bushes. Ducks and geese have returned from the south and waddle around on the remaining ice along the edges of the creek. I don't know which species they are, but I'm sure if I asked Charlie, he'd be able to name them all. His understanding of flora and fauna and the natural landscape is impressive.

His mind, however, is elsewhere.

"The body was found by a woman out walking her dog—hey, kind of like Ollie helped us—"

"Let's not even talk about it," I interrupt. That whole incident last summer was disgusting.

"Fine." He goes back to his notes. "The woman came out here in the early morning—about 6:20 a.m., to be exact—and found the body.

"Stop saying 'the body.' Who's the victim?"

"A guy called Rudy Hopper."

"The name sounds familiar. Do you know anything else about him?"

"Just that he was a student at the university," Charlie says, checking his phone. "You know, it'd be great if Gekas could just give us her case files—"

"She's not even supposed to be asking for our help!"

"If she really did," he says skeptically.

I try to ignore Charlie's uncertainty, but it stings a little. "We'll be done soon enough. No harm, no foul, right?" I say, trying to sound like I believe this line of BS myself.

"We really need to talk about your morals, young man," he says, grinning.

I need us to move off the subject of me and focus on the murders. "So, Rudy was a university student?"

Charlie flips through web pages. "Says here he went to the gym but didn't come home. Parents report him missing. Three days later, the woman finds his body."

No matter how many times I hear these stories, the thought of families torn apart by murder is horrible, and I have to shake off the memories of my own experience in order to keep to the task at hand. I can see Charlie's turning the details over in his mind. "What's up?"

"He lived at home, which means he's from here."

"Yeah, so?"

He shrugs. "Nothing, I guess. Just trying to make connections between the bodies." He sighs and looks around.

"So Rudy goes missing for three days, which means the killer held him captive for a couple of days before killing him. Or he could have been murdered the night of his workout, and the killer held onto his body for awhile before dumping him here."

I shudder at the cold nature of Charlie's words—but I'm betting he's accurate about the murderer's mindset.

"Which makes him patient and methodical," I say.

Charlie looks toward the grove of trees at the north end of the island. "Once he gets out here, though, he's got enough cover to take his time," he says.

"But he's got to get out here first," I counter.

"Which makes him fearless and comfortable in killing and clean-up."

This back and forth is natural. It's less about answering each other's questions and more like talking out a problem.

We fall silent and stare at the view until Charlie looks over at me. "You good?"

I feel like we haven't accomplished much, but I know Charlie wants to continue the process at the next location.

"Yup."

"Then let's twenty-three skidoo!"

Honestly, I don't know where he comes up with this stuff.

chapter 43

The first time I drove with Charlie anywhere, he was a bundle of nervous energy. He rummaged through every single slot and console, and pushed every button in my dad's car before choosing the music. Now, as we travel to the next location, he's much more relaxed. Sunglasses on, leaning back in his seat, window open to let in the cool spring air. He even lets me choose the music.

"Beverage?" he asks.

I nod in agreement and take a quick detour to a chain restaurant with coffee and doughnuts. I pull up to the drive-thru speaker and order a couple of coffees, then move ahead to the window and take out my wallet.

"You're buying?" he asks.

"Sure."

"You know, I have a job," he states.

"Yeah. And so do I!" Why's he bothered by this?

"Point is, you're not treating me like some charity case, are you? First you take me in, then you pay for all my stuff."

"Nope. Not at all." I pause. "You'll return the favour at some point."

"Good," he says, nodding.

When the woman comes to the window, he calls out to her, "Can you add a half-dozen assorted doughnuts, please?"

I glare at him, but he's grinning. "Hey, if you're going to be my part-time sugar daddy, then I'll decide the kind of sugar I'm trading."

chapter 44

Charlie's halfway through his third doughnut by the time we get to the city centre.

"Let's get the location of the most recent discovery out of the way first," he says. "Pull down this side street."

I follow his directions and turn onto a quiet little street with large homes. We're actually not far from my house, which is across the creek but only a five-minute walk away. We cross the busy street that bisects the city, and enter the park.

The victim's body was found down by the water landing along a busy road, and not far from the provincial Legislative Building. Even though we're still a good distance away, we can already see the buzz of activity. Yellow caution tape flaps in the wind, and even though a day has passed since the body was discovered, a police cruiser is parked on the path and a boat is anchored nearby. There are divers in the water beside the hull of the boat.

"They must still be processing the area for evidence," Charlie says.

"Gekas is probably over there somewhere."

"We should go over and ask for the case files," he proposes, blinking at me innocently.

I chuckle. "Nope. Not doing that."

To be honest, I'd be surprised if we could get any closer than we already are without drawing the attention of the officers on the scene. Charlie already has something of a reputation with the city's cops, after all.

"Fine, " he says, nodding at a television van parked along the treeline. "Maybe I can get us the next best thing." He plops on a bench and taps away at his phone, then stretches out, turning his face to the sun and closing his eyes.

I could ask him what he's up to, but I'm guessing he knows someone in the press. When you spend your time dealing in secrets, those kinds of connections are probably fairly reciprocal.

He doesn't get to rest for long before his phone buzzes, and he sighs, leaning forward to check it.

"This latest victim's name is Tyson Martz."

He looks over at me to see if I recognize the name the way I did Rudy Hopper's, but I shake my head.

He goes on, "Looks like he was maybe in his forties. The news says he worked construction. He's been missing since November, and cops have just been waiting for him to show up."

"November?"

"Yup. The early freeze must've trapped him under the ice."

I shudder. "I can't even imagine what he must look like."

"You'd think he'd be bloated, right—?"

He's probably researched *exactly* what the body looked like. "Charlie, I don't want to know!"

"But the tissue breaks down and turns into something like soap—"

"Stop! Please, just stop!"

He grins at my discomfort before looking back at his phone. "Anyway, what was left of him was found by an early morning runner. Oh, *this* is interesting. The bag he was in was anchored to a weight."

"Anchored?"

Charlie nods.

"What the hell is this guy up to?" I ask.

chapter 45

When we're done, we walk to the last site, following the curve of the lakeshore along the Albert Street bridge.

"Remember when they deepened the lake when we were kids?" Charlie asks.

"Yup. Heather used to have nightmares about the scary stuff she thought they'd dredge up."

"I guess she didn't know how prophetic she was—if you believe in that stuff." He tosses his coffee cup at a garbage can, swishing it in. He raises his arms in victory. "You know, it's actually strange they didn't find anything."

"Maybe they weren't looking hard enough," I say, knowing full well I never knew half the crazy things going on in this town before hanging out with Charlie.

"I bet they did, and totally kept it all hush-hush!" he says devilishly, pulling out his phone again to research this victim.

As we cut through a wooded grove, I can't help but notice how much quieter it is here. "This place is a lot more private."

"Maybe not as many prying eyes, but still lots of traffic," he says. As if to make his point, a man and a boy appear along the road and bike past us. "Besides," he adds, "park cops drive along here all the time, looking for shady folks doing shady things."

Why do I think he knows this from personal experience?

Charlie checks his phone and points ahead. "The body was found over there, down by the lake."

Seeing my expression, he pauses. His tone changes. "The victim, Paul Gulley, was found by a young couple." He looks over at me. "How about this guy? You recognize his name?"

I shake my head.

"He's about the same age as Mr. Martz, our construction worker," Charlie says, "only Paul Gulley was a loan officer. He'd been missing for nearly two weeks."

"Why'd the killer take so much longer on this one than Rudy Hopper, do you think?"

"Oh, he didn't take longer. The victim just wasn't found right away."

I shake my head at the thought. I don't even want to imagine stumbling across a corpse again.

We walk up a small path to a circular concrete platform that overlooks the north shore of the lake. There's a small tree-covered island across a narrow channel of water, maybe half a football field away. He pauses, looking out across the lake at the Legislative Building on the south shore, then down to the base of the overlook we're standing on.

"Based on the news photos, I think they found him somewhere down there."

We descend stairs that lead to a small dock beneath the outlook. The back wall is covered with colourful graffiti, and Charlie pauses to admire it. "Beautiful, huh?"

I nod. I've always loved urban art and the idea that someone risks making it without permission, but I wish I understood it better. I'm guessing a guy like Charlie can probably interpret every swoop and swirl.

He turns back, looking out at the water again. "Also a nice place to cuddle and make out," he says.

"It's too damn cold." Out of the warmth of the sun, a shiver runs through me. "Besides, you're not really my type."

Charlie grins. "I meant the couple who found Paul Gulley, dumbass. Came down here for a little lovey-dovey, not expecting to find a body floating in the water. With all the caraganas and lilacs hanging in the water, he probably got stuck somewhere and was overlooked until late September."

"Wait. September? This was the *first* body?"

He looks up at me. "Yeah. Why?"

I step back, studying the scene. Not answering a direct question is something I'm used to Charlie doing, but I feel like I'm onto something. I just need a minute.

I nod to the large docking posts sticking out of the concrete. "In the summer, there's a ferry that runs between here and the island. But after the September long weekend, the ferry would be closed and no one would be coming down to the dock."

Charlie picks up my line of thinking. "Except for horny teens trying to find a place to get to second base—"

"Exactly."

"But how many would actually be coming down here?"

"I don't know. Probably not a lot."

"Likely very few," he agrees.

I'm enjoying this back-and-forth rally. "It'd be easier to find a quiet place to make out in the trees—"

"*Much* more romantic, what with all those fall colours—" Charlie says with a smirk.

"And warmer," I throw in, suppressing another shiver.

"So," Charlie says, "the killer stages his first victim here."

"But the body doesn't get found right away."

"And it's a giant pain in the ass. Cops patrol the area—"

"You've got to drag the body up the path, down the stairs, and into the water—"

"And even after all that, it floats away!"

"Exactly!" I remark. "So he leaves his next victim on a running path near the RCMP training depot—"

"Which *still* takes three days because no one finds it—"

"So he leaves the last one in the most public place he can think of—"

"The lake right in front of the Legislative Building where it's *sure* to be found—"

"With excellent access to location—" I gesture to the roadway that runs along the lakeshore.

"And anchors it to make sure it *doesn't* float away—"

"Except we get an early winter and the body doesn't show up until spring!"

"Shit," Charlie says, "this guy's balls keep getting bigger."

"No, it's worse than that," I say, feeling another chill run down my back, this one unrelated to the weather. "This guy wants his work to be found."

As we walk back toward the car, Charlie keeps looking at all the traffic and pedestrians in the park. "It would be great if one of these people had seen something."

"Charlie, the murders happened almost a half a year ago— the latest victim has literally just surfaced five months after the fact," I wave across the lake to the taped-off landing in front of the Legislative Building where a diver is coming out of the water.

"But if they're regulars at the park—people from the government buildings, say, or runners, or folks walking their dog—I bet someone saw *something*."

"If they did," I say, "they probably didn't realize it."

"Hell, they likely don't even remember it," Charlie adds.

I can tell he's not done, though. "What's up?" I ask, knowing the direct approach is sometimes the only way to get him to talk. Otherwise, he'll stay stuck in his head.

"I want to check one more thing," he says.

We walk back along the wide, curving concrete path that follows the shoreline toward the bridge.

"Uh, Charlie?" I say, "I can't help but notice we're headed back toward the active crime scene."

He grins.

"You're not suggesting we go over there, are you?"

"Nope, not today." He's moving fast now—not running, but going at a quick enough pace that I have to push myself a little to keep up. "I'm thinking that although this killer has some pretty messed up ideas, he's not stupid, right?"

"Okay...?" I say, not quite sure where he's going—in either thought or direction.

"He wants his work to be seen without giving himself away."

I'm starting to understand. "Meaning, he's dumping bodies at night, not in the middle of the day when everyone's around."

Charlie finger-guns me. "Right. So, if we're looking for a boogeyman who lurks in the nighttime shadows, we need to find out who else might be lurking in them."

He cuts across the grass and down some stairs to a short tunnel that goes under the bridge and connects the park to a path that follows the creek from the lake to the city's northwestern edge.

There's an inch of water on the passage floor from spring flooding, and I stop at the last stair.

"What? You scared of wrecking your shoes?" Charlie asks, splashing through it. "You got to plan ahead and get a waterproof pair. Functional, stylish, and—" he gives the cement wall beside him a good kick, "steel-toed."

"You'll never be normal, will you?" I ask.

"Hope not."

I grab a seat on the steps while Charlie does his thing, grateful I don't have to wade in too. Both sides of the underpass are filled with more graffiti, and he walks the full length, studying every inch.

"The city always comes down here, pressure-washing it off, and in a week, the artists come back and start all over."

He reaches the end and turns back, pausing halfway to study one large creation. Colours flow in huge zigzags, spelling out the word STRAY.

"That guy's style looks like the one at the overlook," I say.

"Not guy. Gang." Charlie's on his way toward me, on his phone, tapping away.

"Are they marking their territory?" I ask, staring at the wall.

I turn and realize I'm talking to myself. He's already out of the tunnel, walking across the grass back toward the car. Man, this guy!

"Hey, Charlie! Yo!"

He ignores me and I have to run.

"Hey, it's off season for me. At least give me some warning so I don't have to chase after you!"

"Pay attention and you won't need any warning."

"All right, Buddha, thanks."

He pauses. "Ooh, spiritual guru. I like that. That's what I'll tell them at career counselling!" he snickers.

His phone *bings* and he checks it.

"Do we have time for a few more pit stops?" he asks.

I check the time. Supper won't be ready for a bit yet. "I guess. Where are we going?"

"Downtown."

Charlie guides me as we travel downtown.

"So, where we going?" I ask.

"Take the next one-way."

I take the turn, but I'm not done. "No. What are we *doing*?"

"I know who left that graffiti tag."

"And you're hoping they were there last fall around the time of the murders?"

He nods.

"And they're downtown?"

"Nope. Left down this alley."

His vague answers piss me off. "Will there ever be a time it won't be like pulling teeth for you to tell me what the hell's going on?" I snap.

"All right, Uptown Funk, gear down. The only way we're going to get information is to trade some of our own. Now, squeeze through there." He directs me into a brick breezeway that leads to what appears to be a dead end.

"Where are you taking us?"

"The alley is not the destination, dude. It's the journey. "

"You should teach self-help classes," I say.

Still, when Charlie hops out, I follow. He walks to a keypad I didn't notice on the wall and punches in a number. Turns out the dead end is actually a heavy metal gate, covered in peeling green paint. It slides open to reveal a small covered parking area. In four of the six spots are very small, but very beautiful, luxury cars.

He waves me into an open spot at the end. "Cram in there. Don't scratch anyone's paint."

As if I needed the warning. Dad's car looks like a clunker compared to the others, and I can't even imagine how much they cost.

He points to a video camera up in a corner of the sheet metal ceiling. "There's eyes everywhere."

I pull into the spot, but I'm pretty sure I don't breathe until I've turned the car off. "What is this place?"

"The most expensive parking lot in the city."

"Why here?" Although the cars around us are high end, the odd location and grungy exterior sure don't make the lot seem worth whatever money it might cost.

"First, the spots are auctioned off and it's become a whole status thing, so the prices are outrageous. Second, security's tight. From what I've heard, anyone who tries messing around here ends up broken the next day. Third, the best for the best. Whatever you ask for—booze, drugs, caviar from the Caspian Sea, doesn't matter what—will end up in your car by the end of day. And last," Charlie points at a door on the opposite wall, "that door leads all over downtown, including some pricey exclusive club high above the city."

"Really? What's so special about it?"

"No clue. All I've heard is that it's the size of a small apartment but has a waitlist long into next year—unless you own one of these spots. Of course, I've never been closer to it than right here."

"And you know all this how?"

"Lucas, the guy whose spot we're parked in? He told me."

"Won't Lucas want his spot?"

"He's out of town at the moment. We're taking advantage of that."

"So we're not here to meet him?"

"Lucas? Nope, not this time. We're here to see someone far less interesting."

chapter 48

The gate closes behind us and we walk down the alley. Charlie's back on the phone, but I only catch the tail end of what he's saying.

"Yes—brief. Should I remind you that— No? Okay, much appreciated. See you shortly."

Charlie guides us through a back loading bay door filled with workers rolling trolleys of filing boxes to a service elevator. He takes a side door that leads to a concrete and steel stairwell that opens to another door.

Suddenly, we're in the middle of a very new, very shiny glass building. An old security guard sits behind a fortress of a desk, seemingly preoccupied with his newspaper, but as we approach, I notice a bank of high-end monitors tracking our every movement.

We step up to a turnstile with a swipe card-reader, but Charlie's not fazed.

He waves at the security guard. "Hey, John."

The security guard looks up. "Afternoon, Charlie. Keeping well?"

"Always. Heading up to the twentieth floor."

"Sounds goods," he says, buzzing us through.

We cross to the elevators and Charlie hits the button.

"You good friends with John?"

"He had some problems over a gold pocket watch. I helped him out."

As usual, I don't want to know. "So, what's on the twentieth floor?"

"AE and Associates."

"What's that?"

A glass elevator descends to our level and we shuffle in.

"A property management firm that owns a sizable chunk of real estate in town. It used to be called Adam Everness and Associates, and its founder was known for handshake deals and keeping his word. That was a century and a half ago, and their standards have fallen considerably—now they should just be called Assholes and Egos."

Charlie snickers at his comment, but I just shake my head.

"Seriously, Shepherd, who needs something like this?" He waves his hands at the chandeliers, the shining white marble floors, and the polished chrome accents of the lobby we're rapidly being transported above. "You can do business from anywhere. This is just showboating for the public and clients, saying, 'Don't mess with us; we're big and powerful,' but in the end, all it means is a lot more rent. Or maybe they're just compensating for really small—"

Ping!

The doors open and we're on the twentieth floor. A long hall takes us to a receptionist behind a very modern front desk, the letters A and E in brushed metal behind her on the wall.

Charlie doesn't wait to be greeted. "I have an appointment—" he looks at his imaginary watch, "right now with Joseph Lock. Tell him Mr. Wolfe is here to see him."

The receptionist shows no emotion—not annoyance, not obligatory pleasantry, nothing. She merely presses a button on her phone and speaks into it. "Mr. Lock, there is someone," she grits her teeth, giving first Charlie, then me, the once-over before continuing "—a Mr. Wolfe—here to see you."

As she waits for an answer, she stares through me. I smile, trying to get some kind of response, but there's nothing.

"Are you sure? You don't want me to offer them a seat?" She sighs and against her better judgment, raises her hand to direct us where to go—but Charlie's already walking down the hall.

chapter 49

The way Charlie navigates these offices, he's definitely been here before. I'm right on his tail until we arrive at an impressive closed door. He walks straight in without even a knock.

The office is a cliché of the corporate world. Big windows face south over the city. Dark leather furniture and expensive wood panelling contrast the thick white carpet. There's a mini-bar beneath the large flat-screen on the wall behind us, shelves sparsely decorated with sculptures and masks, and a large tropical plant in the corner.

Mr. Lock stands in front of an oversized mahogany desk, in the middle of a practice putt. He's a well-groomed, good-looking man in his late thirties. Though he's wearing a two-piece suit, he's shoeless; his leather Oxfords have been set aside.

"It's real," Lock says, before sinking the putt in the practice mat.

At first I think he's talking about his shot, but he's nodding at the plant. He needs to validate it? That's weird. Really weird.

"Well done, Mr. Lock," Charlie commends.

"Thank you, Mr. Wolfe."

And then they shake hands. Visually, they're complete opposites, but they're behaving like business partners.

"It's been a while. I was getting worried. How've you been keeping?" Lock asks.

"I've moved."

"Is that right?"

"Yes. It seems like—" Charlie considers, "a good change for me."

"Well, don't wander too far," Lock cautions as he lines up another putt.

Something about this guy makes me think he likes Charlie kept tight in the box he's put him in.

"Would you mind catching that door, sport?" Mr. Lock says.

He's talking to me, I realize, though he hasn't looked at me once.

I bite my tongue, say nothing, and swing the door shut.

Charlie takes a seat in one of the plush leather chairs and waves a hand in my general direction. "This is Anthony Shepherd."

Lock extends his hand but doesn't break concentration on his shot. I shake it but feel an incredible need for hand sanitizer after he lets go.

"So, how goes your day?" Charlie asks.

Huh? Suddenly we've got time to shoot the breeze?

Lock sinks another shot, then takes a seat behind his desk. "Aw, you know. Livin' the dream: shithole office, robot assistant, miserable dick of a boss. It's a blast!"

I wonder why he stays if he hates it so much, but strangely, Charlie's sympathetic. "You've definitely got golden handcuffs, Joseph."

"Don't you know it, Charles. Money's too damn good to say goodbye."

How long's Charlie been dealing with this guy?

"What are you looking for this time?"

"I need something to trade," Charlie tells him.

"What sort of thing?"

"Material."

"Big or small?"

"Hmm. Moderate," Charlie says slyly.

Joseph Lock shakes his head. "Talk about being chained to something—"

Charlie tosses up his hands. "Hey, *you're* the one who keeps asking for my help."

"True, true."

It's surreal watching Charlie operate in this rich corporate office. Somehow he's the one with all the power.

"All right, all right," Lock mutters. "I might have just the thing for you." He clicks on his keyboard and scrolls around. He glances over, cold eyes drilling me. "Why don't you take a load off, sport?"

The sooner we're out of here, the happier I'll be. "I'm fine, thanks," I say.

"Suit yourself." He leans in to study the screen, then waves Charlie over.

"Here! Take a look at this. Should be good enough to piss off the old douchebag boss."

Charlie crosses to the other side of the desk to look at Lock's monitor. "This is his?"

"Yup."

"Nice. That'll do just fine." Charlie takes photos of the screen with his phone. "Reciprocity is a great thing in a relationship, isn't it?"

"Hey, don't I still owe you for last time?" Lock asks, leaning back in his chair.

"Nope, it's just good business," Charlie says.

If there's one thing I know about Charlie, it's that he's all about being fair. He hates the thought of being indebted to anyone.

Having others owe him, however...

"And don't worry. It won't be a disaster," Charlie assures him.

Lock shrugs. "Do what you have to do."

chapter 50

We walk out of Joseph Lock's office and past the robot receptionist. I don't say anything until the elevator doors close and we're on our way back down.

"What just happened?" I ask.

"We traded information."

"We did? What exactly did we get? And what, exactly, did we give?"

"A while ago, Mr. Lock had me digging up dirt." Charlie sounds pretty blasé about this.

"Uh. What sort of dirt?"

"You know, the usual. Weaknesses, addictions, who they're hooking up with—"

"Who?"

"Competition or co-workers. Whoever's in his way."

"Charlie! That's just wrong."

"I know, I know. I kind of feel bad, but really they're all greedy, rich douches just screwing each other over, so..."

"Wait. Have you helped his competition too?"

"Hey, it's a dog-eat-dog world. Besides, they've all got gobs of money and insurance; they can afford to buy their way out of most things."

"That's disgusting."

"I know," he shrugs, "but it's all about the connections. It never pays to be too selective. It's like investing: it's always good to maintain some diversity."

I shake my head. "We really *are* all pawns on your personal chessboard, aren't we?"

He grins but doesn't answer.

"So, what did we get?" I want to know.

Charlie holds up his phone, showing me the photos he took of Lock's computer.

All I see are the blueprints of a house.

"What's that?"

"The layout of his boss's multimillion-dollar home."

I'm still confused. "You're failing at communication again," I say.

Charlie sighs. "Remember, Shepherd, it's all about the information."

"So we're giving it to who? The people who tagged the wall?"

"Exactly. We need something of value. What do people want and what do people have? The boss is a dick, and Lock wants a bit of petty revenge."

"So the house is just collateral damage?"

Charlie shrugs. "It's the high cost of doing business."

I shake my head. "Unbelievable."

"You can say that again, *sport*!" Charlie's dig finds its mark.

"Oh, don't you even—!"

"Okay, okay. Just messing with you. Relax," Charlie laughs. "Lock is usually an asshole, but he was being extra disrespectful to you today."

The doors open with a swish, and we walk out the lobby, Charlie raising a hand in farewell to the security guard. "But don't hold a grudge against Lock for too long. I'm pretty sure the old karma wheel will spin back around on him soon enough."

"Never thought you were the type to believe in that kind of thing."

He grins. "Only when my hands are on the wheel."

Sometimes I'm really thankful Charlie's on my side.

chapter 51

We leave the gloss of the city centre behind and head to the low-income working class neighbourhood between the railyard and the industrial part of town. There's the occasional home that's been cared for: exteriors freshly painted, lawns raked and mowed, yard blossoming with flowers. But many others are neglected—*really* neglected—windows lined with tinfoil, paint peeling off siding, weeds sprouting up around broken fences, garbage littering the front lawn. It's the opposite of what I recognize as familiar in my own neighbourhood.

Charlie's got his own take. "You know, people from newer neighbourhoods pass through here and judge, but hell, they've got their fair share of shitty-looking homes too. And I bet there's just as many people dealing and using in the suburbs." He pauses for a second. "Ever notice how lots of these homes have open doors, though? You won't find that in the 'burbs."

I have to admit I've never noticed. "Why's that, do you think?"

Charlie shrugs. "Maybe it's just that there's nothing to steal. But maybe it's for safety, like way up near Churchill, Manitoba."

"What are you talking about now?"

He rolls his eyes at me, as if what he's about to say is common knowledge. "It's the polar bear capital of the world and no one locks their car doors up there, so if a polar bear shows up, you can just jump into any random car to save yourself. No bears to worry about around here, of course, but people are way worse."

"You're a regular ray of sunshine, Charlie."

"Always preaching the truth!"

We pull up to a three-storey house, cream-coloured with brown trim around the windows. There's grass in the front yard, but it's long and unkempt, still flattened from the snow.

"We're here," Charlie announces.

I park the car and wonder exactly where *here* is.

Charlie gets out of the car and I follow him up the walk.

"Is anyone home?" I ask.

"Of course. What did you think? We're going to do another B&E? Seriously, Shepherd, you need to quit being such a thrillseeker."

I shake my head. Despite what he's said, nothing's outside the realm of possibility with him. "You know, Chuck, we do what we have to do."

"Yeah, well, not here." His tone is suddenly serious.

As Charlie often does, when we get to the front door, he walks right in, no knocking.

The main floor has a living room that opens into a dining room, and through a doorway it looks like there's a kitchen. A girl and guy, maybe fifteen years old, are playing a co-op game on two super huge television screens that are way too big for the space.

The floor is sticky and gross, and the whole place smells like smoke and dust. The coffee table in front the teenagers has several ashtrays on it, each stacked with cigarette butts, and none of the furniture matches. In the corner, a box of empty beer cans perches atop three pizza boxes.

Now that I've seen the inside, I'm actually surprised that the window has a curtain.

From somewhere upstairs we hear yelling.

"Get out of the bathroom!! You've been in there forever!!!"

"Screw off! It's my turn."

Something crashes upstairs, and I flinch. Footsteps race above us and someone else yells a distant "Oh shit!"

Charlie chuckles. None of this bothers him in the least.

I, on the other hand, am totally uncomfortable.

"Where's Fran?" Charlie asks the gamers.

"Kitchen," says the boy without looking up, but he dies in the game anyway, his screen flashing a neon YOU LOSE. "Son of a—"

The front door kicks open and a young man backs into the front hall behind us, dragging a green leather sofa. Another kid is pushing it through on the other end.

"Hey, ease off for a sec, will ya!" yells the guy who's halfway in. He hollers at the two on the couch, "Give us a hand!"

The boy who just lost his game scrambles to help, but the couch goes nowhere.

"It's stuck in the doorway," the kid yells outside before looking at us. "Gah! Are you two just gonna stand there?"

Charlie and I jump in to help, me on one side and Charlie shimmying between the couch and wall on the other.

The kid outside expresses his appreciation with a "God! Thanks! Finally!"

We're all reefing on it, trying to twist it around to ram it through the entryway.

The kid from the game says, "This thing weighs a ton!"

"We've been carrying it since First Avenue," says the guy inside.

I calculate quickly. "That's ten blocks away!"

"Duh! But when you see an opportunity, you take it."

"Especially when no one's around to say otherwise," snickers the kid outside.

"It's stolen?" I try not to sound surprised. "And you walked away with it in broad daylight?"

"What'd you expect? We should steal a truck too?"

They all laugh, and Charlie joins in.

We give the sofa one final, solid jerk, and yank it through the doorway.

The kid from outside tumbles onto it and takes a drag off a vape cigarette. "Besides, it's a Natuzzi."

"Nice," Charlie nods with approval.

I hit his shoulder to remind him that we don't need to steal leather furniture, and we don't want trouble for helping those who do.

"What?" he asks, glaring.

"What are we here for?"

"Oh, right."

We leave them to rearrange the front room and walk to the back of the house.

In the kitchen, a heavy-set redheaded woman sits at the table, smoking a cigarette and scrolling through her phone. She's maybe in her early thirties, quite a bit older than the rest of them.

"Hey, Fran," Charlie says.

The woman looks up, registers Charlie, and her expression changes. She stands and comes over to him, turning her limp into a graceful sway, to give him a hug. "Charlie Wolfe, you handsome boy."

"Fran, this is my friend Tony Shepherd."

"Ah, so *this* is Tony. Nice to meet you, finally."

"This is Fran's house," he tells me.

I put out my hand and Fran takes it.

She grins. "Isn't he formal."

A young girl with a bad green dye job in a ponytail and all sorts of facial piercings walks in and drops two bags of groceries on the counter. She looks me up and down, then walks out.

"Is Donny here?" Charlie asks.

"Yes. He's upstairs." Fran turns and shouts through a door, "Channy?"

Silence.

"Channy!"

A voice hollers back. "What?"

"Come here!" Fran yells again.

We hear clomping down the back stairs and another girl appears. She's wearing a uniform from a fast food joint and looks about my age. She's sporting a tattoo on her neck and a *lot* of black eyeliner. When she sees me, her lip curls and she folds her arms, giving me a look of absolute disgust.

"Oh, calm yourself, Channy," Fran says. "Just take the boys up to Donny."

Channy mumbles, "Whatever," under her breath.

"When you're done, come back down if you have time for a visit," Fran says, starting to dig through the grocery bags.

"Will do. Thanks," Charlie replies, and we follow Channy up.

We take the stairs to the third floor, manoeuvering around a couple more kids as we do. As we pass the second floor, I glimpse yet another teenager passed out on a mattress on a bedroom floor.

I can't wait anymore. "What *is* this place?" I whisper to Charlie.

Channy beats him to it. "It's home."

"Home?" I ask.

"Yeah," Channy says, stopping mid-stairwell to turn around and pin me with another glare. "Fran owns the house and Donny pays her rent. But she'd likely let him live here for free if he asked because she likes the company. Some of us have jobs and help out when we can. And some of us s'kids—street kids—come and go. You know—" she looks at me, "actually you probably don't—some of us are throwaway kids. Hitchhikers, drug addicts, dropouts, petty criminals, pickpockets, hiders. Kids who come from shitty homes or violence, drugs, or foster families. We need a place to crash and she lets us. No judgment." She looks at Charlie. "But next to your trailer park shithole, this place is the Hilton."

Charlie doesn't say anything.

I want to jump to his defence, but this isn't my world, these aren't my people, and I don't know what Charlie would think, so I keep quiet.

We reach the dark attic to find an older guy—I can't really guess how old, but he's definitely not a teen—sprawled out in an over-padded moon chair at the far end of the room. The windows have been painted dark, and a lava lamp glows on a table. Incense and candles burn on a shelf on the wall, making this the only semi-pleasant-smelling room in the entire house.

A couple of people are asleep on another floor mattress. Cats wander in and out.

"Boys, Donny. Donny, the boys," Channy says, dripping with condescension. "Introductions are done. I'm out."

"Thanks for the help," I say, a little too smugly.

She gives me the finger as she goes back down the stairs.

chapter 52

Donny stares at us. He's rough-looking and skinny, and I'm pretty sure he's stoned.

"Hey, man," he says, recognizing Charlie.

He doesn't get out of his chair but waves us over.

Why do I get the weird feeling he thinks he's the king and we're his peasants?

"You want a hit? I can get someone to wrangle something up."

I've never known Charlie to do any of that stuff, but I quickly say, "No, I'm good," hoping it'll stop things from going any further.

"Who's the shiny boy?" Donny asks.

Guess I'm a little too clean-cut for this house.

"A friend," Charlie answers.

"Is that right?" Donny takes a longer look at me, and I stand a little straighter without getting too cocky.

"Don't seem like your type of brutha," Donny says.

Is he making fun of my skin colour, or does he actually think he's a gangster?

"Well, he is," Charlie says, his face tightening.

Donny nods, still assessing me, though his words are for Charlie. "So, what's got you crawling back to the old digs?"

Another cheap shot, this time at Charlie's expense, but he's all business. "I've got something you might like."

Donny doesn't respond immediately. He leans back in his chair, deciding.

Charlie waves him away. "Hey, I can go find someone else—"

"All right, all right," Donny says. "Show me what you got."

Charlie crosses to him and flips open his phone.

Donny's leaning in close, smiling wide enough to show the gap between his front teeth. "Not bad, not bad."

"That's what I thought."

"And you got all access?"

"All that's needed."

"And you gonna give me an address?" Donny asks.

"When you give me what I want."

Donny grins. "Always the businessman." He looks at me. "Been that way since I first met him."

He's trying to stake a claim on knowing Charlie longer, but I couldn't care less. Though, for the first time since we got here, I realize that Charlie's uncomfortable.

Donny's smile fades. "So why this house?"

"The guy's a dick. Deserves what he gets."

"No way. That ain't you."

Charlie forces a smile. "Hey, aren't you all about being Robin Hood—take from the rich, give to the poor? Why're you asking questions now?"

Donny laughs. He's missing a tooth, one of his canines.

"That I am, that I am. But you don't come into my house and hand over a potential score without wanting something in return."

"All we're looking for is a couple of answers."

"Ah, see! *There* you are! I thought maybe your new friend over there," Donny indicates me, "had softened you up."

"Enough bullshit," Charlie says now, and there's steel in his tone. "Thought you'd want a fancy house in a gated community, but I guess I was wrong—"

Whatever Donny's been goading him about has finally hit its mark, and Charlie's heading for the stairs.

"Whoa, whoa, there!" Donny calls after him. "Don't be so hasty. We're just talking old times, right?"

Charlie's not having it. "I'm not interested in old times," he says, turning back. "Either you answer my questions or we're gone."

Donny glares at him. Seems they've pushed each other into opposite corners.

"Okay, whaddya want to know," Donny finally asks.

"You still own the park."

"Most of it. Which part?"

"The pedestrian underpass on Albert Street."

"Yup, that's ours."

"How often you get out there?"

A shrug. "Couple days a week."

"How long you been holding that territory?"

"Couple months."

"How about last year, around October or November?"

Donny studies Charlie. "Wait a sec. This about that poor sack of hamburger they just found?"

"Information for information."

Donny stalls, maybe thinking he's got an opportunity. "Last fall? Long time ago."

I tap Charlie's shoulder. "Come on. This is a waste of time."

But he doesn't move. He doesn't even blink.

Donny smiles, the gap in his teeth appearing again. "Seems I can't remember a thing."

A groggy male voice speaks from the mattress on the floor. "What about the suit?"

Donny rolls his eyes, frustrated that all this wheeling and dealing just got upended by Mattress Boy. "Oh yeah. The suit. Almost forgot about him. Good thinking, Benny."

I'm pretty sure Benny's in for a beating, but I'm tired of this bullshit. "What *about* the guy in the suit?" I ask.

But Donny continues to stall, leaning back in his chair, scratching the patch of stubble on his chin, pretending to ponder. "I was working on a mural in the underpass—"

"What time was this?" I ask.

"I told you. Last fall—"

"No, day or night?"

"We own the night, man," Donny says, puffing up his chest.

"What were you doing out there?" Charlie asks, keeping him on track.

"A couple of my people were just hanging out, you know, taking it in, keeping track of who's on our turf and where."

"And the suit was there? Did he talk to you?"

He glowers at me. "Guys like that don't talk to people like us. We're invisible to them. We don't exist. Unless they want something."

I suddenly realize why all the hate's directed my way.

"What did he want?" Charlie asks.

"He asked them where he could score some weed."

"Them? He didn't talk to you?"

Donny sighs, unhappy that he's no longer part of the story. "Nah, he talked to Benny and Granite."

"And all he wanted was weed?" I persist.

"At the beginning. Then he started asking for harder stuff, which we're not gonna get into with some guy we just met in the park."

"You don't think he was a cop?"

"Nope. Cops can't afford the clothes he was wearing."

"You said he wore a suit. How nice a suit?" Charlie wants to know.

"You know." He looks over at me. "Shiny."

I ignore it. "And that's it?"

Donny nods.

Charlie gives him a look. "Bullshit. What else?"

Donny sighs, shaking his head. "You know me too well, brutha."

Charlie ignores him. "What're you not telling us?"

Donny smiles. "Something was off."

"Like what?"

"He wasn't, I dunno, *rigid* enough, and his questions were weird. He started asking about us, about how busy the park was, about how often cops patrolled the place. Questions that shouldn't matter. And then that was it. He left."

"Do you remember what he looked like?" I ask.

His smile turns my way for the first time. "*Hell*, no. My best art comes when I'm high, y'know what I'm saying?" He waves a hand at me. "Pshh. 'Course you don't."

I feel like I'm back on the playground.

He points to Charlie's phone. "Is that enough for the trade?"

Charlie nods and has started to jot down the address on a scrap of paper when good ol' Benny calls out from the mattress again. "You should give him the wallet."

Charlie stops writing and looks at Donny. "You got the guy's wallet?"

Benny mumbles, "Granite picked it when the guy wasn't looking."

Yup, I'm positive poor Benny's getting a shit-kicking later.

Charlie scowls at Donny. "You still holding out on me?"

He shrugs. "Well, it's empty now. Didn't think it was relevant."

Charlie sets the pen down. "Would you mind getting it?"

Donny looks at the half-written address, knowing he's not getting the rest until Charlie's got the wallet. "Benny!"

A scrawny-looking kid appears from under the blanket, his ribcage jutting out from beneath his skin. I don't know what he's on, but it's not doing anything for his health. He grabs a black garbage bag from a pile and dumps hundreds of wallets out on the floor.

"What's missing?" Charlie asks as Benny rummages through them.

"The only thing we took out was sixty bucks, cash. No credit cards, no useful ID. The rest is as is. Whoever the guy was, he didn't want to be found," says Donny.

Benny continues digging for a while and pulls out a leather wallet with a tiny silver dolphin on it. He offers it to me with a lopsided smile.

Poor Benny.

The leather is soft and of good quality and I open it up. There isn't much in it: a punchcard for a coffee shop, a business card for a flower shop, and a library card with a bar code and an illegible scrawl on the signature line. There's no name printed on any of them.

I turn the wallet over and check every compartment.

Nothing else.

"You got what you wanted," Donny nods at the address, "Can we finish this?"

Charlie writes out the rest, then emails the floor plans.

Donny's phone *bings,* and the stone-faced, missing-tooth grin returns. "So, what's gonna happen when your new family figures out who you really are, huh? How long they gonna let you hang around?"

Charlie turns me toward the stairs. "Let's get the hell out of here."

But Donny's not done. "Don't worry, *brutha.* When they're done with you, when they kick you out, you'll always have a place. We'll always take you in. You always gonna be a part of our family. And, God knows, you never turn your back on family!"

chapter 53

By the time we get out of Donny's, I've gotten several texts from Dad asking where we are. We're late for supper.

I hustle us to the car. Unfortunately, it's still rush hour and I hit every light.

"What's the deal, Shepherd? Aren't you hungry?"

"I'm not doing this on purpose!"

By the time we walk in the house, supper's growing cold on the table, and I can see the frowns on my parents' faces.

Charlie intervenes. "Sorry, Mr. and Mrs. S. It's all my fault. I wanted to swing by the mall."

"Why didn't you let us know you were running late?"

"I really thought we'd be quicker," he says.

"And what's your excuse for not replying to your dad?" Mom asks me.

I give her a meek shrug, knowing Charlie's taking it all in, so I throw myself under the bus. "Well, there were these girls—"

"So?"

She's obviously learned not to trust me when Charlie's involved, but I'm ready. "Seriously? You think I'm going to start texting my parents while I'm trying to wheel the ladies?"

I know she'll hate that last part—and I'm hoping it'll distract her from our lateness.

She proves me right.

"You better be treating those young ladies with respect."

"Of course, Mom!"

She shakes her head at the thought of me doing otherwise.

Charlie wanders off to the dining room and plops himself down at the table. "Hey, Mr. S., supper looks great!"

"We're having *maque choux* and ribs," Dad responds. "I thought I'd take advantage of the warmer weather and fire up the barbecue again."

Charlie takes the lid off a ceramic dish filled with some kind of corn concoction. He takes a deep breath. "Mmm. Can we please eat?"

I don't know if he does all this intentionally, but it seems to dissolve the last of Mom and Dad's irritation with us.

Mom motions for the rest of us to sit down, and Charlie immediately takes it as a cue to start dishing food onto his plate. He grabs a sweet corn biscuit, and helps himself to ribs. He takes a mouthful of the corn and swallows it in one bite, giving Dad a look of *Oh my God, delicious!*

I feel bad because I rarely gush over the food my parents make, even though I've enjoyed almost every bite. I guess, having grown up with it, I've taken it for granted.

"Glad you like it," Dad says.

"Definitely!" Charlie's enthusiasm is catching, and Dad returns his smile.

"How was school?" Mom asks.

I can see she'd still like to reprimand us, but we both know the moment has passed.

"Seems good. Too early to tell," Charlie says between big mouthfuls. Mom and Dad give each other a look, and he picks up on it. "Don't worry. I'm sure it will continue to be good. I just don't want to mislead you, saying it's great and then running into a glitch later."

Dad nods. "Well, we appreciate your transparency, Charlie."

"Oh, and I joined the golf—team? Club? Whatever it is, I joined it!"

We're all surprised, and Charlie chuckles. "Yeah, well, I thought I'd take advantage of opportunities I've never gotten before. Of course, there's a small fee—"

"No worries, Charlie—" Dad says.

But Charlie interrupts. "Hey, I've got a job; I can pay for it. You don't need to cover my extracurricular activities. Besides, they supply the clubs and lessons. It's pretty golden."

Mom smiles. "Imagine not having to pay for someone's activities!"

"That'll be a relief," Dad agrees. "Pretty sure we had to take out a second mortgage when Tony joined hockey," he adds.

"Hey!" I say.

"Wait, you were in *hockey*?" Charlie asks.

"One season," I say defensively.

"Thank goodness," Dad chuckles.

"It was like watching a giraffe on skates," Mom says.

Charlie laughs out loud and corn shoots onto his plate.

"Okay, enough," I grumble. I don't need to be reminded of how much I sucked.

Mom rubs my shoulder. "Hey, don't feel bad, son. Remember that one time I went golfing with your dad?"

"Let's not bring that up," Dad says.

"One time?" Charlie sets down his fork and leans in. "Now *this* sounds good."

"You don't want to know," I warn.

Dad jumps in before Mom can tell her version. "She suggested we do a couple's activity and go golfing. I thought it was a great idea—until I started offering suggestions on her swing."

"Hey, just don't tell me what to do," Mom laughs.

"As you know," and here Dad speaks in a loud aside to Charlie, "Keya is, well, just a *little* bit stubborn."

Mom holds up a forefinger and thumb, showing a small amount.

Dad gives us a conspiratorial wink. "She's very protective of the way she does things."

"Only when it comes to taking poor advice," Mom laughs.

"Learning is all about finding your own path," Charlie offers.

"Exactly!" Mom says.

I'm sure she's aware of the irony of agreeing with Charlie on that point.

"And you haven't golfed since?" he asks.

"Of course I have. Just not with Ben."

"Oh, Mr. S., that's a heartbreaker!"

And now Dad really does lower his voice. "Not if you knew what golfing with her was like!"

chapter 54

Once we're done supper, Mom and Dad leave the house for some alone time with Ollie. After the long winter, everyone wants to get outside for fresh air. My parents are no different.

Charlie and I finish doing dishes quickly and start thinking about homework.

"Should I make coffee for us so we can work down here?" Charlie asks.

"Sure."

While Charlie preps the French press, I drop my iPhone into the dock and queue up a random playlist of Dad's music selections—it still kinda blows my mind that Charlie and Dad have the same taste—with a little bit of mine mixed in.

Charlie fills his radio station mug, pours another for me, and sits at the island, digging textbooks out of his backpack.

I should do the same, but I can't focus. "What do you think about what we found today?"

Charlie dumps the rest of his bag on the table. "Homework, dude."

"Come on, man. You ID'd a tag and we traded someone's address for a wallet—"

"Shepherd! Study time!"

"But—"

"Not now."

"When?"

"Later."

I surrender. I can't make Charlie Wolfe do anything he doesn't want to, and I admire his ability to compartmentalize the different aspects of his life.

We work quietly for a while, but I can tell something's bothering him; despite his intention to focus on homework, he can't quite settle into doing it. He must be thinking about the murders. I'm wrong.

"So, this is your normal life?"

"Sorry?"

"You're not making all this," a broad sweep of his arm takes in the tidy kitchen, the cozy house, and me, "look like a Disney movie on purpose, are you? This is your *actual* life?"

"Yeah. This is my life."

"Huh," he says. "You know, I've been popping in from time to time for the past year and a half, but I just assumed you've all been putting on a show whenever I'm here. But this really is the day-to-day deal, isn't it?"

I'm sort of stunned but try not to show it. "You think we'd put in that much effort for you?"

Charlie shrugs. "Maybe?"

"You give us—and yourself—far too much credit."

Charlie says nothing more and goes back to work. But his question reminds me of a certain aspect of today's events.

"Mr. Lock and Donny—?"

"Homework," Charlie mumbles, ignoring me.

I persist. "They didn't seem to like the 'new' you."

He looks up. "What do you mean?"

I try to put it into words. "Neither seemed too thrilled that we're friends."

"Well, not to get all mushy on you, Shepherd, but a good friend never holds you back from growing."

I know he does think of me as a good friend, though he rarely expresses it. "You're saying they like having you in their little box."

There's growing strain on his face, like he's getting a headache. Like he's been holding something back. He closes the textbook and lays down his pen.

"For a long time, I needed them, because, well, things happened. I was on my own and I needed a place to stay, and Fran took me in and Donny gave me jobs to run to earn my keep. It didn't take long to realize how much people value information, and I worked my way through downtown until I met guys like Lock. People like him are everywhere, and I understood I could leverage them against each other."

He pauses to sip his coffee, savouring the flavour. He sets the cup down and I think he's going to go back to work, but he finishes his thought. "Look. People like Donny and Lock don't fit into this way of life," he waves a hand at the house in general. "And they don't like to lose a good thing. But I made a promise to your folks, and I'm going to try and honour it." He picks up his pen and flips open his textbook again. "Now can we quit talking about this? I've got to study for this trig exam, and you keep leading me astray.

chapter 55

Eventually, the coffee pot is empty and the binders are closed. On the way up to our rooms, I ask Charlie, "Mind if I look at the wallet?'

"Really, Shepherd?" he protests.

"Hey, whatever, man," I say, raising my hands in surrender.

He relents. "Fine, I'll bring it to you."

I dump my books in my room and text Mike to see if he had any success on his date with Carrie, but he doesn't respond.

Charlie appears at my door and tosses me the wallet.

I've barely caught it when he gestures at the PS4 collecting dust on my shelf. "Why don't we set that up, play some Rocket League?"

But I have a better idea. "How about we set up your Nintendo and play Mario Bros.?" I know he hasn't touched his moving box; maybe this will finally get him to unpack.

He just stares at me.

I give in. "Fine. We'll play PS4, but after I kick your ass, we play Mario."

"Big talk, little man," he says. "You mean *if*—"

I'm much taller than Charlie, so this makes me laugh. "No, I mean *when*—"

I open up my closet and dig out the small twenty-one-inch TV tucked away in the back.

"Of course you've got a spare TV just lying around."

I never really thought about how indulgent this must seem to a guy who barely has anything.

He shakes his head. "Oh, don't start crying on me now, princess. Just givin' you a hard time." He points to the guitar I have in the closet too. "How come you never drag that out?"

I pause. "Uh, it's just been a while—"

"Wait. Is this a Sheri thing?" Charlie asks.

I don't answer right away.

He sighs. "Aw, Shepherd. Maybe it's about time you start playing again."

I stare over at it, remembering when I used to play it at parties or take it up to the lake and strum away by the campfire. The last two years have made a big difference in my life, but maybe it's time to not let it hurt so much.

"All right then," Charlie says. "Can we stop sharing our feelings now so I can destroy you?"

We set up the TV on the shelf beside the console and turn it on. The game starts up and we choose our cars. I take the Breakout, while Charlie picks the Octane. We play viciously.

It doesn't take long before Charlie's jumping off the bed, yelling, "No! You didn't! Shit!"

I smile to myself. "Hell, bro. I've never seen you like this."

"It's 'cause you cheated!"

"No way."

"I had first touch on that last ball!"

"Doesn't mean anything."

"You've had more practice!"

Now I'm laughing. Seeing him lose control is great—I love it. "*Now* who has to gear down!"

"Two out of three!"

I'm not going to push my luck. "Nope."

"If you win, I'll unpack!"

"What about if you win?"

He smiles. "You have to play me your best badass version of 'Wonderwall.'"

I think it over. "Okay, but I don't care about you unpacking. If I win, you sit down with me and we talk about the wallet."

"Fine. You start."

We play again and I'm severely kicking his ass, so much so that we don't even notice Mom and Dad at the door until Dad speaks. "Homework better be done."

Charlie doesn't look away from the game. "As always, Mr. S."

"How long have you been there?" I ask.

"Not too long," Mom answers.

"You two are weirdos," Charlie says, but his tone is affectionate. "How was the walk?"

Mom ignores the question. "Charlie, come with us please."

He looks at me, but I have no clue either. We pause the game and I follow the three of them into his room.

On his bed is a large wrapped gift. "We got you something. Consider it a housewarming gift."

Charlie pulls off the bow and paper to find a large framed Pink Floyd tour poster from the '70s. It's signed by the whole band.

"It comes at a price," Mom says before Charlie can speak. "It's time to unpack. This is *your* room. You chose to be here. If you're serious about staying, then you should begin acting like it. Put things in drawers. Maybe leave a book out on the dresser. Keep it clean, but start living here."

Charlie looks at me and I give him the smallest shrug. He sets the gift on his desk, leaning it against the wall. He steps back and studies it.

"Ben and I went to their Division Bell concert in Winnipeg in 1994," Mom says, continuing in her kind, persistent way. "It's our way of saying welcome home."

Charlie surprises all of us when he wraps Mom in a hug, brief but warm. He turns to Dad and gives him a hug as well, albeit an even shorter one. Dad gives him one solid pat on the back before Charlie quickly steps back.

"Thank you," he says.

chapter 56

We leave Charlie in his room and go downstairs to turn on a brainless Netflix movie. Dad's struggling to stay awake within the first ten minutes.

"You're too hard on the poor man," I joke to Mom. "You've tuckered him out." But she doesn't pick up the banter. I can see in her eyes that she's got something on her mind.

"What?" I ask, coming off ruder than I intended.

"You two are behaving yourselves, right?"

Damn.

I hate it when she calls me out on this stuff. It always puts me in a corner, and either I'm honest and get yelled at, or I lie to her face and my conscience makes me feel like crap.

"I think so," I say, trying to bend my answer around the truth.

"You're not looking for trouble?"

"Nope, not this time." I really don't think we *are* actually trying to find any, and if any happens to show up, we're dumping it on Gekas.

She takes a minute to decide whether or not I'm lying, and I turn back to the movie. Sometimes it's best to keep my mouth shut and not dig myself a deeper hole.

She's quiet for a bit and I think she's done with me when she mentions off-handedly, "Barb and Irene want you to go by after school tomorrow and check on the Rogers' house."

I know what she's up to.

She's telling me, *Go do your part-time job so you don't have time to do something you shouldn't.*

"Sounds good," I respond.

And that's my way of saying, *Sure, because I've got absolutely nothing to hide, except the fact that Charlie and I are snooping around the dump sites of an active serial killer.*

Unfortunately, I'm pretty sure Mom's certain she knows exactly what I'm saying as well. And she's likely not too far from the truth.

chapter 57

After the movie, I grab a glass of carbonated grapefruit juice and head back upstairs, pausing at Charlie's room.

He's unpacked his box. I guess he finally feels this is the real deal, and I'm glad. He's on his bed, listening to his headphones, and I think he's fallen asleep until he opens his eyes.

"Hey," he says.

"Hey," I say, going in. I set my drink down on his desk and take a seat.

He's glaring at me.

"What's wrong?" I ask.

"What are you? A hillbilly?" He tosses me a coaster from his nightstand.

"Sorry," I say, laughing. I use the sleeve of my shirt to wipe the wet ring left by my glass then slide the coaster underneath it.

He stares at me. "Want to talk about the wallet?"

"Really?"

"Hey, fair's fair. You were winning before your folks interrupted."

"All right," I say, jumping up to grab it from my room. I open it up as I walk back across the hall, studying the three different cards inside. "Doesn't give us much direction."

"And Donny's gang probably contaminated the hell out of it."

"So not much chance Gekas could find fingerprints or DNA."

"Nope, not really. But I don't think it's a complete dead end."

"Me neither. I'd say the flower shop card is useless, though. I mean, how many people order flowers?"

"And the coffee punchcard? That's even tougher. It's local but also a franchise, so who even knows which one it's from. Another needle in a haystack."

Then it dawns on me. "Wait, that library card—" I pull out my phone.

"What's up?" he asks.

"You're not the only one with connections."

"Oh?"

"I have a friend at school, Elaina, who works at the central library." I grab the library card and tap out a text:

Hey. Favour?

Can you check this library card number?

Found a wallet

Thx

I get Charlie's approval before sending it.

"The thing about being a do-gooder," I say, "is that everyone assumes you're not up to anything. Elaina will think I want to return the wallet to John Doe and be happy to help me out."

"Wait, are you telling me we're playing good cop/bad cop?"

I laugh. "Have we ever been anything else?"

The next morning, I wake to find a text from Elaina, asking to meet before class. We set off for school a little earlier than normal, and once we've dropped our bags at our lockers, we head to the common area.

The space is small but so crammed full of kids that I can't immediately see any sign of her.

Charlie doesn't wait, opting to stroll over to the vending machines that line a wall. He had a good breakfast at home—Dad made him a plate of *maque choux* leftovers on a bed of spinach with a couple of eggs on top—but he still stops to purchase some gross processed sugary treat.

I continue the search and finally spot Elaina across the room—or rather I see her tousled, wavy boy cut sprouting above the book she's got her face buried in.

She's kind and self-assured—not one of your cliché pretty girls—and doesn't try too hard to meet anyone's ideal. Her bag's on the table in front of her, her feet are up on it, and she's munching what I first think is a muffin, but then realize is actually a cupcake with a thick layer of frosting on top.

Charlie's beside me, holding his post-breakfast chocolate bar. "Go on. I'd like to eat this baby in peace."

"Here's hoping that one day my parents will wean you off your bad food habits."

He shrugs, unwraps his snack and chomps down. "Mmm… nougaty goodness."

I shake my head and join Elaina.

She doesn't look up right away, so I ask, "What're you reading?"

"Thomas King," she says, trying to finish the last few sentences of the chapter she's working on. "It's for Advanced English. *So* much reading. But seriously, if I had known about him sooner, I probably would've read him anyway."

I have no clue who he is, but it doesn't matter.

When she finally looks up, she gestures to the seat across from her. "Take a load off."

I sit. "Thanks for doing this, Elaina."

"No problem."

Elaina reaches into her bag and pulls out a folded piece of paper. "I printed off the user information of the library card number you gave me. Don't tell anyone—you owe me."

"No problem," I say, tucking it into my pocket. I want to look at it, but now is not the time.

"Can I ask if it's for one of your cases?"

My *cases*? Ugh! I really don't want to answer that.

"Don't worry," she adds. "No need to bullshit me, Tony. Your secret's safe with me."

I nod. "Thanks."

"Is that your friend Charlie?" She points toward the vending machines where he's chewing on his chocolate bar and staring at members of the swim team.

How is it he can be completely cool in the most dangerous places with the most marginal people, but drop him in a regular school with regular kids and he sticks out like a stain on your new jeans.

"Yeah, sorry. He can be a little weird."

"No worries." She keeps studying him. "He's not the usual type of guy you see around here."

"Yeah, he's…different."

"Kind of cute, though."

"Excuse me?"

She ignores my question and continues, "If you need anything else, don't sweat it."

It's nice of her to offer, but I don't ever want to drag anyone else into our troubles.

I thank her again and head back to Charlie, who's finished his chocolate bar and is just standing there awkwardly, hands in his pockets.

"They're up to something," he says, indicating the nearby group of students.

"The swim team?"

"I'm thinking anabolics."

"You sound like a crazy old man."

"Hey, you're the one who asked me to help."

"There's no in between with you?"

"Nope. Either I trust everyone or no one." He nods toward Elaina. "What's the deal with her?"

"What do you mean?"

"Why's she really helping?"

"I told you."

"Pfft. No, really, why?"

"Because she's a good person."

"That's it? Seriously, what's her angle?"

"She doesn't have an angle. She likes me and wants to help."

"Wait. She *likes* you?"

"Oh, good grief. Not like that." He's tried in the past to convince me to ask girls out and I don't need him up my ass about this. "Can we get off Elaina and focus on what she gave me?"

"Right."

I dig out the paper and hand it to Charlie. He unfolds it and reveals the name, address, and phone number of our mystery man from the park.

Charlie scoffs. "Theodore Thompson? That's a fake name if I ever heard one. And that 912 at the front of the address? Got to be a condo or apartment."

Without hesitation, he pulls out his phone and dials the number on the slip. He hits the speaker so I can hear too.

Somehow I'm not even fazed that we're standing in a crowded school calling a potential serial killer; I'm too amped up by how close we may be to answers.

"This number is out of service...," says an auto-recorded voice.

"Surprise, surprise," says Charlie and swipes his phone off. "Well, Shepherd, looks like Teddy's address is calling our name."

"I can't. Barb and Irene want me to check a house out."

"The ladies from your parents' party? Fine. We'll visit our suspect's place, then I'll come help you with your job."

As he hands back the paper, I feel the excitement building. I'm not sure if it's good or bad—but it's there and it's loud.

chapter 59

When the bell sounds at the end of the day, I step out of Mr. Hall's biology class and Charlie's waiting. We're ready to go—until we see Mike bounding toward us like a happy-go-lucky Labrador retriever.

What terrible timing.

"Hey, guys!"

"Hey, Mike."

"Need your help."

"With what?"

"There's a girl—"

I shake my head. "Isn't there always, Mike?"

His smile is huge. "I know, right?"

"What happened with Carrie?" Charlie asks.

"Who?"

"The girl I set you up with yesterday?"

Mike actually pauses, trying to remember. "Oh shit! Yeah, Carrie. Right." He doesn't answer, though, and Charlie has to gesture for him to keep talking. "We-e-ell, she and I never really worked out."

"Really? Why not?"

He half shrugs. "We just didn't gel. But see, this *other* girl—"

Charlie cuts him off sharply. "Nope. Can't help you with that."

"Aw, come on, Chuck!" Mike says playfully, and I wince.

But Charlie just takes the nickname in stride. "No way, Mikey!" he says sarcastically, but Mike doesn't seem to register it. "I delivered you a date, and if you couldn't seal the deal…"

"Hey, I didn't—!"

Charlie raises an eyebrow, and Mike backpedals, trying to defend himself. "Look, I tried but—" He sighs. "Fine. But can't you guys just help me?" He points at me. "You! You're Mr. Charm. Girls just flock to you, and I need some of that."

"Like the man said, Mike," I say, indicating Charlie, "I just can't do it."

"Why not?" We're in the parking lot now and he clues in. "Wait, are you guys doing your thing? Are you chasing—? Whoa, shit! Are you after that *serial killer*?"

"N-no…," I stammer. Every time I hear people talk about us this way, it makes me cringe.

"Let me come—"

"No!"

"Come on. I can be your muscle."

"Mike, you don't want to be part of this."

"Why not? You don't think I can hang?"

"It's not that."

"Why?" He points at Charlie. "You think *he's* going to watch your ass better than your best friend?"

"No, it's not like that—"

Charlie turns on him quickly, blocking his path. "Mike, you're not coming with us."

Mike's a little shocked.

I think I am too.

Mike stiffens. "Yeah? And why not?"

"Because you weren't invited."

Damn, Charlie, you're stone-cold.

Mike looks pissed, and I step between them in case he decides to throw a punch.

"Let it go."

"Wait? Are you siding with *him*?"

I stammer out another no, but I can see he's already hurt.

"It's not like that at all," I say, taking him by the shoulder, trying to turn him away from Charlie, but he shrugs it off.

I'm kind of worried he's going to start swinging at me soon, so I add, "Let's plan something another day, all right? How about tomorrow? We'll play some pick-up. Just me and you. Just not this, please. I need to do this without you."

I'm not sure he's going to let it slide until his face softens and he surrenders.

"I don't like you messing in this stuff, brother. If you can't take me along, you know you shouldn't be part of it," he says.

I nod. "I know. It's just— Look. We're doing this for a friend."

He looks at Charlie, then back to me. "I trust you, and I trust your judgment—" he eyes Charlie and adds, "but you need to be careful."

"Hey, I'm all about being careful," I say.

"But *you*—" he turns on Charlie, "if you mess with *him*, then you mess with *me*."

Charlie offers his hand. "Wouldn't have it any other way."

Mike shakes it, but I can tell he's not feeling the love.

I offer him a big bro hug and he pulls me in for a solid back pat.

"I'll be okay. Relax," I tell him.

"I will when you're no longer involved in this crap," he says as he releases me.

I know he's still not happy, but he's doing his best not to show it.

He stalks away and jumps in his truck, peeling out and kicking up gravel as he goes.

"He's going to be pissed at you for a while," I say.

Charlie nods. "That's all right. I don't mind playing the bad guy." He walks to the car, waiting for me to let him in. "Besides, we don't need him getting mixed up with a couple of hoodlums like us."

"Stop saying that."

"He's being a solid friend, Tony. Be happy about that. Now, let's go and look through some people's homes."

I sigh, popping the locks. "You really have pulled me to the dark side, haven't you?"

chapter 60

We drive downtown, parking a few blocks away from Theodore Thompson's address so no one sees Dad's car. The less we're connected to this place, the better. I pull onto a side street under a tree and plug the meter.

"Do we have a plan?"

"Do we need one?" Charlie chuckles. He reaches into his backpack and pulls out a couple of ball caps.

"What're they for?"

He pulls one on. "Well, if we end up at a crime scene and have to send Gekas in, we should at least have the courtesy to reduce the obviousness of our presence."

"What? Cover our faces from any surveillance, you mean?"

"That and deal with any stray hairs," he says, stuffing his shaggy mop into the hat.

"What? No hairnets?" I joke.

"Nah, too conspicuous. We'll keep them for when we get inside," he says, grinning.

We go to the front door, walking up like we belong here—one of the many lessons Charlie has taught me over the last eighteen months. The condo's front yard is well-groomed and clean—I'm guessing this isn't a cheap place to live. A camera peers down at us from a corner, so we keep our faces low and hidden beneath our hats. I can't see a front desk or a security guard through the windows, and while that's good for keeping a low profile, I'm not sure how we're getting in. The door has no intercom and only a keypad for a lock.

"Doesn't seem like the friendliest place," I say.

Charlie ignores me and digs through his bag. He usually has some sort of electronic device for these sorts of problems. Then I realize there's a couple standing behind us waiting to go in, key fob in hand.

They buzz themselves in—and hold the door for us! I'm in disbelief.

We join them in the elevator and exchange awkward, forced smiles. They press the button for the sixth floor and Charlie hits eleven. The elevator hums along, the four of us standing uncomfortably beside each other until—*ding*—we arrive at their destination and they exit.

The doors close and Charlie immediately hits nine.

"What the hell was *that*?" I ask.

"They assumed we lived here."

"That's what you were hoping for?"

Charlie nods. "I figured pretending to look for a key was just as good as having one."

"But we could've been anybody!"

"Yeah, well, you know, it's the usual," Charlie says, watching the floor numbers rise to the top. "People are just dumb."

I want to point out that most people would say they were being nice, but I don't get the chance. We're at our floor.

We step out into a dimly lit hallway.

I check the address Elaina gave me. "Apartment 912."

We walk down the hall, the only sound the crunch of carpet bristles beneath our feet.

I can't even hear a muffled TV or stereo blaring through a door. "This place is a tomb."

"These suites must be soundproofed out the wazoo."

I laugh at his old-man sayings.

We arrive, and I figure Mr. Lockpick will pull his magic. Instead, he knocks on the door.

I grab his hand. "What the hell are you doing?"

He uses his other hand to ring the bell.

I smack that one away too. "Are you nuts?"

"Is that a rhetorical question?"

"Seriously!" I expect someone to answer any minute.

"First of all, it's normal to knock on a door but not to act all sketched-out about it." He nods at the door across the hall. "You never know who's watching."

Fair point.

"And second," he adds, "if anyone *is* home, they'll now come to the door and we can get the hell out of Dodge." He looks at the imaginary watch on his wrist before announcing, "Guess no one's home."

I exhale slowly to contain how exasperated I am.

He leans in and whispers, "Would you mind taking a step back behind me."

"Why?"

"Because I need your big head to block the nosy neighbour's peephole from what I'm about to do."

I move over as Charlie reaches into his backpack, pulling out his lockpick set. "Oh, and I forgot. Take these." He hands me a pair of surgical gloves and a hairnet.

I stare at them. "I thought you were joking."

He shakes his head. "Clean scene, man. We don't want even a hint that we were here." He yanks off his baseball cap and stuffs it in his bag before snapping on the gloves and tucking his hair under fine mesh.

I pull on the gloves he's handed me, waiting until he pops the lock and opens the door before quickly pulling off my hat and slipping on my own hairnet.

He steps to the side and waves me in. "After you."

chapter 61

Anxious excitement bubbles up as I enter the condo. I try not to think about all the places I've gone into without permission since Charlie's been around. I keep telling myself it's not wrong, that our reasons are always to help people, but I know that it's still breaking the law and that we'll have to deal with the consequences if we get caught.

I also know that the thrill of it gives me a buzz.

As soon as we're in, I feel like something's off—I just can't put my finger on it. The place is hardwood floors and open concept, and bright sunlight blazes through floor-to-ceiling windows at the far end of the room, reflecting off every smooth, shiny surface.

There's a closet in front of us and a kitchen immediately to our right. It's a combination of wood and steel and stone, but it feels like there's never been a meal cooked in it since it was installed.

We open drawers and cupboards and find nothing.

Charlie looks under the sink. "Well, the garbage is empty, but he seems to like his cleaning products." He shows me a large container of wipes and enough bottled chemicals to clean away the worst possible stain.

"What are you thinking?" I ask.

He shrugs. "Maybe he's a germaphobe."

I continue the search, checking out the stainless steel fridge. It's bare. Not even a magnet from a takeout joint. I look inside.

"Anything?" Charlie asks, already knowing the answer.

"Empty."

We move around the kitchen island and its immaculate counters into the sparsely furnished living room.

Charlie looks at the brown wrap-around couch and single chair. "Pfft. Why even buy leather? All you do is slide off every time you sit."

"You might be doing it wrong," I kid.

He ignores me and studies the big speakers and the stereo they're attached to. "That's a solid system. Bet you could level this building before you blew the speakers out on that puppy.

He crosses to the glass coffee table, and I'm suddenly worried he's going to try, but all he does is pick through several remotes before using one to click on the gigantic, eighty-inch television mounted on the wall.

The weather channel announces a warm front moving up from the Midwest.

"I was sort of expecting another channel. Maybe half-dressed people and kinky sex," he says before shutting it off.

Nothing else decorates the room—no paintings, no shelves, no end tables, and no carpets. The only lights are the fixtures hanging from the ceiling.

"This place has just a *ton* of personality," I say, letting the sarcasm show.

Charlie walks over to the wall of windows, leaning his hair-netted head against it. "This feels freaky, like the glass is going to break and you're going to plummet to the street."

My gut flips. "Uh. Could you maybe just step away from it, then?"

He looks back at me. "Wait, are you afraid of heights?"

"No—just falling."

He steps away, smiling, and I know I'll hear about this later.

He opens a door in the wall opposite the TV. "Looks like a laundry room."

He disappears inside to look around, and I stroll down a short hall toward two closed doors. I open the one on the right.

Bathroom.

Again, nothing in the drawers or the garbage, but I do find soap and shampoo in the shower. On a hunch, I look under the sink.

"I found more cleaning supplies," I call out.

Charlie appears at the door. "Yeah, and there's a ton of bleach in a cupboard in the laundry room. I'm starting to think this guy's trying to keep any evidence of himself—DNA or otherwise—to an absolute minimum."

I give him a questioning look.

"Well, he's got the basic cleaners, but there's also some heavy duty acids in there too."

"Is he murdering people here?"

Charlie shrugs. "Maybe he's just cleaning himself after the crime." He pauses, then looks around the shower a bit. "I don't suppose you've found any tools?"

"There was a screwdriver under the bathroom sink." I never really thought anything of it. "Why do you ask?"

"Bet all the doughnuts in the world he's unscrewing the drain to scrub chemicals down that pipe to ensure he's covering his tracks."

I stare at him. "What makes you even *think* these things?"

He grins at me. "Oh, I just try and figure out what it would take to outsmart someone like me."

I shake my head, laughing. "You really do think that much of yourself, don't you?"

Across the hall is the master bedroom. Again, the furniture is minimal. A dresser along one wall—I'm certain it'll be empty—and a bed on the other, made smooth and flat with crisp corners.

Charlie leans over, careful not to touch the fabric, and gives the pillows a sniff. "Not a hint of B.O. Pretty sure he's never slept here.

I look inside the closet and find nothing on the hangers, but on the shelves there's a stack of dress shirts and slacks with the tags still on them. "He buys Italian."

"He could get those from any high-end menswear store. Or online. What size does he wear?"

"You going to tell me you can tell his build based on his shirt size?"

"You can't?" Charlie asks as he gets on his hands and knees and looks under the bed, opens every drawer of the dresser, checks every single hiding spot.

"There's nothing here," he says. "He's probably never even lived here."

"So we can call it quits, then?" I ask as we go back to the living room.

He pauses. "What if he really *is* like me?" he asks.

I realize what he's saying.

He goes back to the laundry room while I climb up on the kitchen cupboards to look in all the nooks and crannies of the cabinets.

Nothing.

"I'll check the bedroom closet," Charlie says, disappearing down the hall.

I stand in the middle of the living room, trying to think like Charlie—not an easy thing to do. But if I *were* like him, I'd hide things in an obvious place, in plain sight.

I walk to the TV and feel along the edge where it meets the brick wall. Something catches my finger.

"I got something!"

"What is it?" he asks, rushing down the hallway.

I get a hold of it and yank it out.

In my hand is a boarding pass for Theodore Thompson on a flight from Melbourne to Toronto last September.

"Holy shit!" Charlie says.

Somewhere in the back of my head a warning bell rings. "Why printed? You put them on your phone these days.

"Who cares?" He points to the QR code at the bottom, "Those have everything: personal data, future travel plans, everything. People who don't destroy these things are idiots."

"So we take it to Gekas?"

Charlie shakes his head, pulling out his phone. "All we need is a picture. Let's leave it where we found it." He digs into his backpack and pulls out a sheet of lined paper. He lays it on the ground, sets the ticket on top and snaps a picture.

"Why'd you do that?"

"Best not to link ourselves to this place if we can help it."

It takes me a minute to realize he means that we shouldn't show the hardwood. Plausible deniability is always a good thing.

He hands the ticket back to me and I slide it back in place, careful to arrange it the way I found it.

"All right," he says. "Time to go."

chapter 62

We climb into the car.

"Gekas?" I ask.

"Two seconds," he says, opening up an app on his phone. "Just need to strip all the EXIF data off this to cover our tracks."

"What are you talking about?'

"Every picture has a date, location, camera info, etc. I prefer to be extra cautious."

"Of course you do."

"Remember the good ol' days when our digital signatures weren't everywhere?" he says as he pulls up his contacts.

I'm surprised to see Gekas's name pop up. "You have her number?"

"Hey, you're not the only one with a direct line."

He attaches the picture to a text message and the address of the condo—no "Hello," no "This is Charlie," no context whatsoever—before sending it off.

It doesn't take long before she's calling.

Charlie answers, hitting the speaker icon so I can hear too.

"I'm assuming the two of you are together?" she asks.

I can tell already she's not amused.

"Hi, Detective," I say meekly.

"What is this you sent me?"

"Information."

"Regarding what exactly?"

"Um. Your serial killer."

There is a pause, long enough to be uncomfortable.

I break the silence. "You asked if we had heard anything—"

"Boys—"

"So we asked around—"

"I didn't— Wait, who did you talk to?"

Charlie shakes his head, but I already know I can't share anything about the s'kids.

"Sorry. I can't tell you that," I say.

"Why not?"

"Please, Detective, just listen. They gave us information and it led us to the airplane ticket—"

"They *gave* this to you? You have it?"

Charlie answers. "Let's just say we saw it."

"And this address? Is this where you saw it?"

"We thought it might be of interest to you."

"Wait a second, did you boys commit a B&E?"

"We didn't say that, Detective Gekas," Charlie says.

I notice how he's phrased that answer—even though we committed it, we never actually told her.

Plausible deniability.

She's too flustered with us to call him out on the evasion. "You've *corrupted* a potential crime scene—?!"

"But, don't you realize?" he interrupts, "it's an international flight. You can track his passport. They'll have photos of him. You'll be able to catch him!"

"How stupidly irresponsible can you get?"

She's pissed.

"Detective…" I struggle with what to say and end up with a lame, "we thought you'd be happy."

"*Happy*? Why would I be happy?"

"We gave you information. We helped you out—"

"Anthony, Charles. Stop talking."

We fall silent.

"What you've done is act stupid and reckless. You shouldn't have been anywhere *near* this."

We stare at each other quietly. Could we have misread her so completely?

"If this screws up any chance of us catching this guy—" She sighs. "Stop pretending to be something you're not, all right? Leave this to me. Let me catch him. Do you understand? Both of you?"

I'm speechless, but Charlie pulls the phone close.

"Look, Detective, we were just trying to help. *You're* the one who came to us with all your useless dead ends. You can check the address or not. I don't really give a rat's ass what you do. But don't worry," and he's nearly shouting now, "because we're absolutely *done* doing your job for you!"

And he hangs up on her.

chapter 63

We drive home in silence.

Whatever I'd thought was going on, I was absolutely wrong. Gekas didn't want our help. She didn't want us anywhere near the case. And now she's pissed at us and Charlie's pissed at her and I feel like the shit's been kicked out of me.

By the time we get home, however, Charlie doesn't seem fazed at all.

He pauses inside the front door, inhaling the savoury aroma of garlic and sauces. "Ah, Chateau Shepherd."

"Hello, gentlemen," Dad calls from the kitchen.

"Hey, Dad!" I say, doing my best to cover my pissy mood.

It must not be enough, though, because Charlie gives me a sideways glare. He drops it a split second before Dad comes to greet us. "Hey, Mr. S. Need anything from us?"

"Just an appetite."

"I can do that," he says. "I'm ready to feast like a king!" Charlie says as we follow Dad back to the kitchen.

"Keya will be home soon. She had a meeting after work."

"I think we should wait," Charlie says, hopping up on a stool at the island.

"She'll appreciate that." Dad's looking at me. "You all right, son?"

Man. Parental radar never fails.

"Aw, he's fine," Charlie waves him off. "Just stung a bit because I kicked his ass—sorry, his butt—in some one-on-one."

"Ah. Well, let it go, son. You can't win all the time."

Charlie pulls over a bowl of homemade tortilla chips that Dad's prepared for tonight's meal, and grabs a handful. "I'm not going to lie, Mr. S. I'm impressed that you got to see Pink Floyd when they were on tour," he says, changing the subject.

Not obvious at all, Charlie.

But Dad seems to go for it.

"It was amazing." Dad pulls the bowl of chips back toward himself and takes a few. "Of course, we couldn't afford it, but we maxed the credit cards anyway. Took us forever to pay them off."

"Wait, you made an irresponsible choice?" Charlie asks. He's handling the conversation for both of us.

Dad shrugs. "Well, sort of. I was working for the provincial park service at the time, so I had money coming in, but we definitely had to stretch our dollars. Shared driving costs with four others and picnicked on PB & J en route."

Charlie's grinning, enjoying the story. "And I looked it up. They opened with "'Astronomy Dominé'?"

Dad's eyes light up. "Absolutely. Oh, and 'Shine on You Crazy Diamond.' Talk about a sound experience."

"Was that your only 'experience'?" Charlie hints.

"What? Are asking if I partook in the pot?" Dad pauses for effect. "No! Never!" he smirks. "Besides, Keya would kill me!"

This shakes me out of my head. "Dad!"

He smiles. "I knew sooner or later I'd get a rise out of you."

"Hey, you're my parents first, Pink Floyd groupies second."

"All right, all right," he says, but continues the reminiscing. "I stayed clean. But we stayed until the very last notes of 'Run Like Hell,' then hit a couple of pubs. By the time we were done, it was 4:00 a.m., we were exhausted, and nothing was open, so we decided to sleep in the car."

"Nice!" Charlie says. He likes that this side of my parents exists.

"We were sleeping like rocks when someone tapped on the window and scared the hell out of us."

"Cops?"

"Nope. A street person looking for bottles. We gave him what we had, plus a sandwich, and a thermos full of coffee from the gas station down the street."

Mom happens to walk in at this point and joins the conversation. "I always liked that thermos. Sort of sad I gave it away."

She gives Dad a kiss.

"You boys must be starving," she says, lifting saucepan covers. "It smells delicious, Ben."

"I'm famished," Charlie agrees.

"Well, then. Let's eat."

chapter 64

After supper, Charlie and I borrow Dad's car so we can check on the Rogers' home for Barb and Irene.

Mom gives us a hard time, saying that I should have prioritized homework and my part-time job over playing basketball—seems Charlie's story stuck—but thankfully, she doesn't make a big case out of it.

It's not until we're travelling north that I finally ask Charlie, "Why aren't you upset about Gekas?"

"Wondered when you'd bring that up."

"She reamed us out, man."

"Yup."

"Doesn't it bother you?"

"Sure. But who cares? It's out of our hands."

And that's when I get it. He's happy we're done. For the first time in a very long time, he's got a normal household: home-cooked meals, hot showers, and people who care. Chasing serial killers can only mess that up. And sooner or later, no matter what, I'm going to have to let it go too.

Then Charlie casually says, "So, the library girl—Elaina?"

"What about her?"

"What's her story?"

"I told you. She's nice, smart, a little bit different— Oh, wait a minute! Chuck, you ol' sly dog, you got a *thing* for her."

He gives my arm a swift punch, hitting so hard that the car swerves a little.

"Settle down, man!" I yell, arm throbbing.

"Quit making this difficult," he says. "Does she have a boyfriend?"

"I don't think so, but I can ask around."

"Aw, Shepherd, that's okay. I'm a big boy. I'll pass my own notes in class."

One thing about Charlie is that he never shies away from doing what needs to be done—even if it's asking someone out.

chapter 65

The Rogers' house is on the edge of an older neighbourhood, along one of the central streets that runs through the heart of the city. When we pull up, Charlie climbs out and stands in the middle of the road to survey the area.

Across the boulevard there's a small park with a spray pad where kids play in the summer, and an outdoor hockey rink for the winter. Right now it's empty, but there've been times when I've come by here and the place is bustling, no matter the weather.

"This place has a nice feel," Charlie says.

"Really good community around here. Mom and Dad always say it's like a small town."

"I've never seen so many free libraries." He nods to the small house-shaped boxes filled with books on a few front lawns.

"The area's packed with hippies."

"I can almost smell the pot."

It wouldn't surprise me, actually. I've stopped by this house more than once and been certain the neighbours were getting blazed in their backyard.

"Betcha they've got a lot of swingers around here too!" he says.

I shoot him a look, and he gets defensive. "What? It's all about the free love, man!"

"Let's go inside," I say, gently nudging him up the sidewalk.

The Rogers' house is a small two-storey with a covered deck on the front. A stained glass window decorates the front door.

Charlie whistles. "That's some fine craftsmanship."

"Let me guess," I say. "You've done it in the past?"

"I wish. But I don't have the patience. I'm better at breaking them than building them," he says with a grin.

"Well, not now," I say, pulling out a key from my pocket. I unlock the door and we step inside.

Charlie takes his shoes off right away, poking my shoulder until I do too. "We can't be savages, Shepherd. Someone's paying you to look after their place. You've got to respect that."

The first floor of the house is filled with huge painted canvases, many of which are stacked in rows along the walls. A small bedroom contains even more, while the kitchen has been converted into a space for paint supplies and cleaning brushes. An office in the back corner is a combination sunroom—there's a whole jungle of potted plants—and library; wall-to-wall shelves are filled with books on subjects ranging from art theory to philosophy and history, and everything else in between.

Charlie whistles again. "There's a whole other something going on with *this* family."

"Actually, it's just one person. An art professor at the university."

He thumbs through some of the artwork in a stack. "She was married though, right?"

"Yeah, her ex was from Italy and decided to run back home. Wait, how'd you know?"

He shows me one of her art pieces, a mix of blue and red and black streaks. "I don't know when this period's from, but it's showing a lot of resentment toward someone."

Of course Charlie would pick up on something like that.

"So, what do we do?" he asks.

"Check locks and windows, water plants, make sure the basement isn't flooded, switch some lights around—"

"Really, this is your job?" he says scornfully.

"Hey, give me a break. True, this is the easy time of year. But summer? It's all about mowing and gardening. Fall is raking—"

He grins. "Oh man, you've really got it tough, princess."

"Just don't steal anything, okay?" I say as I head downstairs to make sure the sump pump is working.

"I'll try and resist the urge," he yells. "But I could probably sell some of this artwork for a couple thousand to some of the assholes downtown."

There's no water on the cement and no one's broken any windows, so I go back upstairs.

Charlie's nowhere to be found. He's likely gone up to the second floor, so I wander up.

The upstairs is the size of a small bachelor suite. There's a kitchen with a big window looking out into the backyard on one side of the main room, and a sofa, chair, and TV on the other side.

Charlie's down the hall, looking at framed pictures in the bedroom. "Any of these Ms. Rogers?"

I point to a couple of pictures of her on beaches in far-off places.

"Pretty good-looking for an older woman."

I'm about to comment when my phone hums in my pocket. I pull it out and see Gekas's name flash on the screen.

"Answer it!" Charlie says.

I swipe and hit the speaker. "Hi, Detective."

She cuts to the chase. "I didn't know if you'd listen to me, boys, but I thought I'd let you know that the information you sent me was a wild goose chase."

"What do you mean?" I ask.

"Theodore Thompson? It's a fake ID."

I can hear the frustration in her voice.

"But what about the plane ticket?" Charlie asks. "It could be attached to a profile."

"All of which are dead ends. A mishmash cobbling together of stolen identities."

Charlie grabs the phone out of my hand. "But it was an international flight! He must've needed a passport, a certified photo—"

I can tell he's grasping at straws.

"Unfortunately, it's easier to fake an ID than a passport."

"So it was stolen?"

"Correct. He was able to book the flight, but it would've been flagged if he'd tried to use it—"

"So he never got on the plane."

Gekas's silence confirms Charlie's guess.

"But the condo?" I ask.

"Paperwork was all done online. No one ever met him in person."

"But there was stuff inside—"

"A furnished rental."

"But he *had* to have been there. We found his ticket."

"Oh, the neighbours saw a man coming in and out of the apartment, heard him blasting operas and symphonies, but so far I've been given three different descriptions of what he looked like."

"Disguises?" Charlie asks, but Gekas doesn't respond.

"What about the cleaning supplies?" I ask, knowing that doing so tips our hand that we were inside.

"Doesn't prove anything, Anthony. They could've been left by the last tenant or brought in by a cleaner—"

"And I'm betting there's no DNA or fingerprints because he destroyed it all with bleach," Charlie splutters.

Gekas pauses. We know she can't share anything more.

"Boys, Theodore Thompson is nothing. He doesn't exist. He's a ghost. You need to let this go."

chapter 66

After Gekas hangs up, we stand in the silence of Professor Rogers' home. For the first time today, Charlie doesn't seem content with the outcome of our actions.

"I thought we had him. I was *sure* we were done," he says, shaking his head.

I had been too, except...

My thoughts drift back to Theodore Thompson's condo and the warning bell ringing in my head. Something's still bothering me, and I'm trying to grasp it, to understand it. My eyes search the room, trying to make the intangible real. I stare at the television in the corner—

"Why'd he print out a ticket?" I ask. "Hell, why leave the ticket there?"

"Huh?" Charlie asks, caught off guard.

"Of all the places he could have put it, why there?"

"Because he's weird like me."

"Maybe," I say, ignoring the cheap shot I know I could make. "But it doesn't make sense. The condo was pretty well empty.

Why leave that one piece of incriminating evidence in the whole place?"

"He forgot it…" Charlie trails off, and I can tell by the tone of his voice that not even he believes it. "Or he wanted it to be found."

I tap my nose, knowing we're onto something.

"But why?" Charlie asks.

"I've got a better question: How'd he know we'd find it?"

Charlie pauses, thinking it through, until he tosses his head back and I know he's come to the same answer that I've come to. "It's all part of his plan."

"He *wanted* the bodies to be found," I say. "And at the start, when they weren't showing up, he had to change where he was leaving them so they *would* be."

"He didn't just *happen* to talk to Donny and his people—"

"He did it intentionally. How good are Donny and the gang at picking pockets?"

"Not bad," Charlie says.

"But if this guy's as careful and cautious as we think he is—"

"He'd've protected himself. Unless he *expected* to be robbed."

"He's been guiding us the entire time, leading us to the condo."

"But why?" Charlie wants to know.

I stare at him and I suspect we're thinking the same thing.

"We're all just pieces on his big ol' chessboard," Charlie says, clicking his tongue.

"Not so fun when you're one of the pawns, is it?"

"Nope, not really." He shakes his head. "So, what do we do then?"

"I'm afraid we have to wait for his next move."

chapter 67

The first rains of spring arrive.

Droplets speckle the third-floor window of the house, flowing down in haphazard tiny rivers. And somewhere hidden behind the clouds high above, the moon is waning gibbous.

Jack sits in the centre of the room, twisting his beloved's purple ribbon around his fingers, the one he took from her the night they met. The one he's kept, a symbol of the love that binds them, regardless of place or time. And as he's bound to her, he's bound to the moon.

But now it's all unravelling.

The boys have upset the balance. They have made connections and found his condo. They've been inside. They're close.

He knew they would come, but he didn't expect it to happen so quickly. They were good…maybe too good.

He quells a sudden flash of anger. Such weakness will not help.

Time is speeding up, rushing forward. Things are happening quickly, and for him to achieve his goals, to deal with the impostor and the boys, and to protect his beloved in her weakened state, he must take control. And the only way forward is to let go.

He must untether himself from the moon.

But if he lets the ritual go, what change will come? Will he be able to move the pieces and guide the course of events? Will he maintain his strength and ability?

Will she understand his sacrifice?

As the storm builds, he knows his answer: *If you love something, you must set it free.*

Without *his* risk, without *his* sacrifice, she will never become truly strong again. Not only must he untether himself from the moon, but also from her.

He knows what he must do. He must kill again. And he must do it very soon.

But not for her. Not this time.

This special gift will be just for *them*.

chapter 68

The next morning my phone rings, waking me up.

Oh God, it's 5:00 a.m. Who'd be calling me at this hour?

Gekas.

Shit. We're going to jail for B&E after all.

I answer.

"Anthony?"

I try to shake off the sleep. "I'm here."

"Sorry to wake you but I wanted to tell you personally. There's been another murder."

Why's she telling me? Didn't she just bitch me out last night for sticking my nose where it didn't belong?

"They found him—they found another body. He was on the running path…where Sheri disappeared."

Oh Jesus.

My whole body tightens, but that isn't the worst of it.

"It's Mike," Gekas says. "Your friend Mike is dead."

part 3

chapter 69

There is nothing but pain.

With Sheri, I never knew what happened. I had time to wish and hope and deny. I had time to process. But here, there is no question: Mike is dead.

My friend is gone.

Some cowardly asshole had snuck up, shot him in the head, dismembered him, and stuffed him piece by piece into a canvas bag.

My chest aches and my ears ring and I want to vomit. I will never understand how someone could do such a cold, senseless, brutal thing to my friend.

I stumble into Mom and Dad's room to tell them, but they're already up. Gekas called them before me.

Mom puts her arm around me, and I barely feel it. My brain is somewhere far away, replaying Gekas's phone call again and again. I don't remember hanging up or saying goodbye. Shit, maybe I just dropped the phone and walked away.

Dad comes back into the room. I don't even remember him leaving. He's got a phone in his hand and through the dizzying fog, I wonder who he's calling.

"Shirley and Bill are on their way down to the station," Dad says.

Mike's parents. God, what must they be going through?

"News will likely start reporting it in the coming hour." He sits beside me, his hand on my back. "Gekas is going to do everything she can to find out what happened—"

The more he talks, the more the anguish hits, a dull throbbing building behind my eyes in wave after wave.

"Dad, please stop."

He falls silent. My parents sit on the edge of their bed, their arms around me.

I should feel safe. I should. But I don't.

All I can think is that I'm responsible.

chapter 70

I wait until Charlie wakes and finds his way into the kitchen for coffee before I tell him. He barely knew Mike. They sure as hell wouldn't have met if it weren't for me.

But Charlie surprises me.

"Shit, man. I'm so sorry."

"Charlie, don't give me any bullshit—"

"No, Tony, seriously, just stop. Mike was your friend. What happened—how it happened—it just really sucks."

He's right.

It does suck. It sucks in the absolute worst way.

chapter 71

Although Mom doesn't want me at school, I decide to go anyway. It'll help me get out of my head. Being around people, listening to teachers, having to do homework—hopefully all of it will help. I just know that the more I sit around the house, the more it'll hurt.

Charlie makes himself a big breakfast, but I can't imagine forcing food into my mouth. A dull, solid headache pumps away at the base of my skull, and I grab a couple of Tylenol before heading upstairs to dress. By the time I come downstairs, Charlie's waiting by the door.

Dad offers to drive, but I tell him we'll walk.

The morning air is cool on my face and crisp to breathe. Charlie pulls his jacket up around his neck. My head starts to clear.

I can't stop thinking about Mike. Dumbass things he said or texted. The way he made a fool of himself at parties trying to pick up girls. Oh God, his stupid pick-up lines! Or how he'd steal my food all the time.

Once in Grade 4, he decided to stick his feet into the front tire spokes of his own bike. In Grade 9, he tried to forge a detention slip because a girl told him she wanted to fool around with him one day after school—

Did my stupid decision to help Detective Gekas cause this? Did *I* do this to him? There's no way Mike crossed paths with Theodore Thompson, is there? Yet somehow he caught the killer's attention.

It just doesn't make sense.

Mike wasn't part of our investigation. He never went with us to the crime scenes or to the lawyer's office or to see the s'kids. And he sure as hell didn't break into the condo with us.

So if this was retaliation for any of it, why go after Mike?

"What's on your mind, Shepherd?" Charlie asks as we wait to cross Albert Street.

"Nothing...," I say unconvincingly.

"Stop blaming yourself for this shit."

I hate that he always knows what I'm thinking. "Is there anyone else?"

"Yeah, the asshole who did this to Mike!"

"But it wouldn't have happened if we hadn't been messing around. Gekas didn't even want us—"

"Oh God, stop it, Shepherd. We tried to *help*. Don't go blaming yourself for that.

"You don't think Mike died because of us?"

"No," Charlie states emphatically. "No, I don't."

But he doesn't look at me when he says it.

chapter 72

By the time we get to school, the news has broken, and there's an eerie familiarity about it. Radio and television vans line the street in front of the school. Students stand in small, sobbing huddles. And when people see me coming, there are darting glances, hushed whispers, and awkward, forced acknowledgments.

Grief counsellors are on hand, and I understand the need—in fact, I appreciate it—but the pain is too raw to talk about. I just want to keep moving. I've lived this before—once was too many times for my liking—and it isn't any easier now.

But I find myself asking how genuine some of these people's feelings are. Charity Pelton's bawling in the middle of the hallway near my locker, and I wonder if she'll miss Mike or just his fawning over her at parties. I catch the mean-spirited thought and force myself to empathize. Perhaps I'm misjudging her; maybe she did actually care for Mike.

Mike was a good guy who played hard and was liked by a lot of our fellow students. He was all about the team and sportsmanship, and although he might've been a little over-infatuated with the opposite sex, he was like a big ol' puppy dog everyone liked having around. And now—well, it feels like another gigantic hole has opened up in my universe.

I say bye to Charlie and go straight to Psych 30. No one's there and I sit in my desk, but as soon as I see the empty place beside me, the dull thudding behind my eyes picks up the tempo and I struggle to roll through it.

"Tony?" Statten's at the doorway, moving calmly into the room.

"Sorry." I struggle to speak. "I just needed a place to hide."

"It's all right, but can you take a deep breath for me?"

"I'm fine," I lie. My forehead feels like it's stuck in a vise.

"No, you're not." She's beside me now. "Start with one small breath."

I'm not interested in her help, but she's not going to leave me alone until I do what she asks. I inhale, hold it, then let it out. Something in my head loosens.

"Good. Take another."

I make more of an effort this time, and after a couple more deep breaths, the tightness in my temples diminishes a bit.

"Better?"

"Yes. Thank you."

She sighs, staring at Mike's empty desk. "I'm going to miss him." She smiles sadly. "God, he could be such a pain to deal with—" She catches herself, realizing how her words might sound. "Mike was a good kid. Such a big heart." Now she's looking at me. "Should I ask why you're at school today? Or are you just going to ignore my advice?"

I smile meekly.

"A lot of people are going to want to talk to you."

"They've already tried to offer their condolences—"

"Not just that. They're going to turn to you for help."

"Me? Why?"

"Because you've gone through this before."

I shake my head. I'm a mess—I can't help anyone else.

"Anthony, they look up to you."

I look at her. "Why?"

"Because you're a leader and a good friend. And because you try to make things right."

I don't respond. If I had just left things alone, if I hadn't tried to "make things right," maybe Mike would be sitting here, telling me about his latest conquest.

I sink down in my chair, wishing I'd never come to school.

She kneels down beside me. "Whatever's going on inside your head, don't hold on to it too tightly. It's not your fault."

I hear what she's saying.

I'm just not ready to listen.

chapter 73

When the intercom crackles during English that feeling of déjà vu settles over me again: "Can Anthony Shepherd come down to the office, please?"

All eyes are on me as I gather my books, but I'm neither surprised nor concerned by the call. Somewhere in the back of my mind, I expected it. Just like with Sheri, they'll ask me what I know. I doubt I'm a suspect, but I try to ready for myself for anything. I'm halfway down the hall when Charlie trots up behind me.

"They called you too?" I ask.

He shakes his head. "Nope, just figured you could use the support."

I didn't really expect this from him, but I'm glad he's here.

"Do you know what's up?" he asks.

"Figure they'll have some questions. See if I know anything."

It's not a shock when we see Gekas at the front desk in a discussion with our principal, Mrs. Johnson. Nor do they care that Charlie's tagging along with me.

"Anthony, Charles, can we talk?" Gekas asks.

Gekas leads us into the principal's office.

Mrs. Johnson follows, and there's an awkward moment when I think Gekas is going to ask her to wait outside, but then she changes her mind.

The two of them take their places almost exactly like they did last year when I first met Gekas. Mrs. Johnson settles into her chair, while Gekas pulls out the folded leather case containing her ID and badge to set it on the desk before leaning against its corner.

"How are you doing?" she asks, and I hear the concern in her voice.

Charlie doesn't say anything and I only shrug. Really, what are we supposed to say?

Fortunately, she doesn't try to make us share our feelings, and gets back to being a cop.

"I called Keya—" She's a little too familiar with our family and glances at Mrs. Johnson to see if she's caught on.

Mrs. Johnson has definitely taken notice.

Gekas starts again. "I told your mother I had a couple of questions for you—"

"The last either of us saw Mike was right after school yesterday," I say, trying to be helpful. "He was talking about hooking up with a girl, but he didn't mention anyone specifically."

"You don't know where he went?"

"I didn't think to ask," I say. "I wish I had."

"And he—" Gekas pauses, looking over at Mrs. Johnson again before continuing, "he wasn't with you *at all* after that?"

She's asking if he was with us at the condo.

I catch sight of the badge beside her on the desk, its smooth black leather surface, the finely stitched corners. Somewhere on her identification will be her first name: Margaret. It never sticks in my head how strange our relationship with Gekas really is.

"No. Nowhere close," I say, trying my best not to say anything that would raise a red flag for our principal.

Gekas nods, considering what I've said. "Was he with you before that? At any point?"

It's clear Gekas wants to get as much information as she can while it's fresh in our minds. It's often little things people don't think are important that can be the biggest breaks.

But before I can answer, Charlie interrupts. "Detective, do you think there's some connection between Mike's murderer and the guy who went after Sheri?"

I never considered the possibility.

Mrs. Johnson shifts a bit in her chair. She seems uncomfortable that Charlie's addressed Gekas in this manner, but it doesn't seem to bother the detective.

"What are you getting at?"

"I mean, why would this guy choose the jogging trails? Seems like too much of a coincidence."

"Charles—" she says.

He persists. "Have you talked with the scumbag who took Sheri? Checked into any correspondence he's had? Maybe someone's a copycat."

"You know I can't answer that," Gekas says. And although she does nothing to encourage Charlie's treatment of her as a colleague instead of an authority figure, the way her lips twitch upward briefly makes me think she's impressed.

"Could he be some sort of obsessed fan of serial killers?"

"We're checking all avenues."

Now it's my turn for questions. "Could this be some sort of message?"

Gekas glances at Mrs. Johnson, worried I might incriminate myself, so I clarify my meaning as carefully as I can. "Maybe a threat to those investigating to say, 'Back off'?"

"It's highly improbable."

"But it's a possibility?" Charlie persists.

She frowns at the thought. "I don't believe so, no." She leans forward in her chair and I realize we're about to be reined in. "I do, however, think it would be best if you stayed close to home for the next little while—"

"Oh, come on, Detective!" I mutter.

Charlie, though, is strangely quiet.

"The fact is, we don't yet know what's driving this individual, so we all just need to be cautious."

"What are you saying?" I ask. "We're under house arrest?" My voice is pitched higher than I intend. Louder too. I can't believe this—we've got to get this guy and she's *benching* us?!

Gekas pauses a little too long before forcing a conciliatory smile. "No, not exactly. But perhaps a little less wandering around. For now. For your safety."

I can tell she's not going to relent, no matter how much I plead, and when Charlie still doesn't speak up, I realize I'm on my own.

chapter 74

After Gekas is done with us, Mrs. Johnson sends us back to class.

Why did I think coming to school today was a good idea? Every class or spare or lunch period I ever had with Mike, every moment spent by my locker talking, every corner and hallway, is filled with memories of him. By the time the final bell rings, I feel like absolute shit.

And it only gets worse.

My phone *bings* as I pack my bag to go home. It's a message from Dad:

Out front.

"Looks like Gekas told your folks to keep us on a short leash," Charlie says, walking up, holding his phone out with its identical text.

"Yup."

And this won't be the last time, either. Until Gekas says otherwise, Dad will be our personal chauffeur to and from school.

As we climb into the car, he informs us that we're expected to stay on a set schedule. School during the weekdays and close to home on evenings and weekends. Any deviation from this plan and we need to call Gekas with our whereabouts. They've even kiboshed taking Ollie for a walk unless we have parental accompaniment.

I know everyone's trying to protect us, but it really feels like we're being treated like children.

I didn't think I could feel any more restricted, but as we pull up to the house, Charlie states, "Looks like she's decided to put us under surveillance too," and points to a nondescript navy blue car across the street.

A man and woman are sitting inside, looking our way.

"Does she really think we're in that much danger?"

"She's only being cautious," Dad says.

I don't care what Gekas's intentions are. I hate it.

Feels like we're the ones who've been thrown in jail, while Mike's killer is running loose.

chapter 75

After supper, I want to disappear upstairs, but I'm betting that's not going to happen.

"Anthony, can you please put on the kettle?"

Shit.

Mom has us gather around the island for teatime, and I'm hoping that it'll be quick and painless. But when Dad asks the first question, I realize it won't be.

"How are you doing, son?"

I shrug. "Fine, I guess. Under the circumstances."

"We know it's tough. Sheri. Now Mike. And, after Maggie's request today,"—ha, "request," nice one!—"a lot is being dumped on you."

"Everyone just wants to make sure that the two of you are safe," Mom adds.

"Why is Gekas so concerned about us? She said it was highly improbable that his death has anything to do with us. And Mike has other friends. Are any of *them* being watched by the cops?"

They glance at each other, then Charlie, then me.

"No, it's just—" Mom stops.

"Considering what you boys have done in the past, the connection to Sheri, and Mike being your close friend... It just seems personal."

I'm irritated. "And nothing to do with anyone thinking it's our fault?" I look at Charlie for some sort of support.

Charlie isn't saying anything, which bugs me more.

"No, Anthony. Not at all—" Dad counters, but Mom cuts him off.

"*Are* you?" Mom asks.

I glare at her, feeling angry but also guilty, knowing I should tell her about how we were trying to help Gekas.

"It seems like an awful coincidence that such a tragedy occurs less than a week after you two start living together under the same roof."

And that's when Charlie finally decides to step in. "Well, Mrs. S.—"

Mom shuts him down immediately. "Thank you, Charles, but I'm talking with Anthony."

I'm pretty sure Mom has no interest in, or patience for, whatever lie he was about to tell.

He falls silent and I'm on my own.

Do I tell her the truth? That we thought Gekas wanted our help; that despite promising my parents that we'd behave, we broke into the home of a potential killer; that Mike paid the price because of it?

"No," I say finally. "I don't think so."

"You don't *think* so?"

She's going to keep hounding me until I spill my guts—then I realize she might already know everything anyway, and I just need to find out. "You talked to Detective Gekas. Does she think Charlie and I are responsible?"

Mom leans back in her chair, the crease in her brow deepening in frustration. "Well, she's worried you might be indirectly connected. She said she was exploring the possibility of a copycat killer."

Ah, Detective, do you feel so guilty that we misunderstood your intentions that now even *you* aren't telling my parents the whole story?

Before I can argue further, Mom adds, "For your sake, Anthony, I hope you have zero connection to whoever's responsible."

So do I, Mom. So do I.

chapter 76

My head is pounding by the end of the discussion, so I skip homework and go to bed early.

I dream of floating deep in the water of a lake. The moon is above, ripples shining down on me. I need to breathe and I try to swim, but I can't seem to get my hands and legs to work together. My lungs are about to explode and I think I'm going to drown, but I bust through the surface for a big gulp of air, happy to be alive.

That's when I see Mike, far below me, wrapped in purple ribbons, dead eyes staring up at me. There's nothing I can do. I call out to him, but he can't hear me.

I wake up screaming, bedsheets soaked in sweat.

chapter 77

When I wake the next morning, there's a dull ache where my heart used to be, and I figure I'm so numb I can stand anything, even school. I'm thankful that it's Friday, though.

I get ready, and wait for Dad and Charlie downstairs. I put my phone on Do Not Disturb and remove all notifications. I learned last year that social media after a tragedy like this is best avoided.

I'm quiet on the car ride, and Dad and Charlie don't push me to talk. I keep my head down through my classes and my teachers let me be. The only person who actually stops me in the hall is Elaina.

"That information I gave you the other day? That has nothing to do with Mike, does it?" she asks. She has dark circles under her eyes—how much stress has worrying about this put her through?

"No," I try to say as convincingly as possible.

I don't blame her—it's not her fault—but I sure as hell wonder if she's right.

"If I—" she breaks off, unable to finish the thought, wincing in mental anguish.

I use the words that Charlie used on me, "Elaina, the person who did this to Mike—he's the one responsible. Not you."

She nods, accepting the idea, and I think we're good.

I turn to go, but she touches my arm. "Then will you do me a favour?"

"What's that?"

"Can you and Charlie do what you do and stop this asshole?"

chapter 78

A few days later, Mom, Dad, and I go to Mike's parents' to pay our condolences.

We gather in the living room, where I have memories of Mike's birthdays and sleepovers and the occasional high school housewrecker, and stand helpless now, watching his parents struggle against waves of sorrow and anguish.

They're an odd pair—his dad, Alex, is tall and big like Mike, and his mom, Jocelyn, is only a bit more than half his height—but as the two of them huddle together on the couch, crying over the loss of their son, they're almost the same size.

Grief can do that to you, make you shrink into yourself.

Mom consoles them, and Dad tries to keep the conversation going with happy, funny stories about Mike, but it's rough. Only a few weeks ago, if our parents got together, Mike and I would've bolted from the room and gone to play Xbox or basketball in the backyard.

Jocelyn keeps running through Mike's last days over and over, like a song stuck on repeat. "He was home so early the night before and then off to school the next day. If only I'd known that was the last time I'd see him…our last dinner…our last hug…our last chance to say 'I love you…'"

I can't imagine what they're going through.

Charlie said that considering what the killer did to him, the cops likely wouldn't have asked his parents to come in to identify his body and would instead have used some other distinguishing detail, like his wallet or school ring.

To not be able to see your son. To have him torn out of your life so suddenly and unexpectedly—

I ask to be excused and stagger to the bathroom, the crushing weight of grief making it difficult even to move.

I stop at Mike's bedroom. The door's open and it's a disaster—either his mom has chosen to leave the space as he left it, or it's simply far too painful to go in there to tidy up. Clothes are everywhere, dresser drawers wide open and half empty. There's a poster of a '64 Austin-Healey Sprite convertible, like the car his uncle owned and promised to sell to him when he turned twenty-one.

I remember that he's got a stash of porn mags under his bedside table. As his best friend it's my duty to dispose of them—although now is not the time.

I stand outside the bathroom, not really needing to use it, eyes closed, waiting, before reluctantly trudging back to the living room.

Mom is looking at photo albums with Jocelyn, and Alex is on the floor by the television, digging through home-recorded DVDs, telling Dad about an old basketball game that Mike scored twenty points in.

Suddenly, Mike's mom asks, "Anthony, you don't know what happened to my baby, do you?"

Mom and Dad look panicked, like I'm going to say the wrong thing, and although I've been running the question through my mind all week, I still don't have an answer.

"No, Mrs. Raynor," I say, and then, as an afterthought, add, "but I wish I did."

And although she may not be satisfied with my answer, I truly mean it.

chapter 79

Mike's funeral is the next day.

Half the school shows up, filling the church. A lot of faces are here, many I don't know or didn't expect to see. A lot of girls are crying, and the bittersweetness of their tears makes me want to smile; I know Mike would appreciate the impact of his loss on the ladies.

Although Mike's parents ask if we want to sit with the family, I tell Mom and Dad that I want to stay a few rows back. All of it—this place, this reason—it's all too much and I need my own space to grieve. Mom and Dad sit beside me but leave me alone. Even Charlie is solemn and quiet.

I don't cry during the service—I've had plenty of time beforehand—and I think I'm beyond it, until we're at the cemetery and Mike's casket is lowered into the ground. My throat starts to swell, and as I watch the coffin descend out of sight, I close my eyes and let the tears flow.

chapter 80

When we get home, I go into the backyard and sit in one of the lawn chairs. The clouds pass in front of the sun and I pull my coat around me. Ollie lies at my feet.

"Mind if I join you?" Charlie stands at the patio door, holding two cups of coffee.

I nod and he plunks down beside me.

"Figured it might help warm you up," he says.

"Thanks."

We listen to the sounds of the neighbourhood: the birds in the trees, the flow of traffic on the main thoroughfare several blocks over, someone practising saxophone a few houses down. A passenger plane passes overhead, coming in for a landing at the airport on the west end of the city.

"I don't know if what we did has anything to do with Mike," Charlie says. "We may never know. But I think you need to stop beating yourself up over it."

"Thanks, Charlie," I say, taking a sip of coffee. Its bitterness feels good on my tongue and warms my belly as soon as I swallow it.

"But, I've been thinking...," he says, though he doesn't finish the sentence right away.

His pause is so long that I complete his thought.

"It's time we get off our asses and find the guy who did this to Mike."

"Better than feeling sorry for yourself, right?"

I don't say anything for a minute.

The birds keep tweeting and the cars keep buzzing along nearby. The saxophone player stops—practice must be done for the day. The sun comes up behind the clouds, and I start to warm up.

"Look. I didn't know him very well," Charlie says. "But I think we owe Mike that, at least. Don't you?"

"Yeah, you're right, Charlie," I say, nodding slowly. "I think you're absolutely right."

chapter 81

By Thursday, we have a laundry list of people who may have crossed paths with Mike over the last few days of his life. As soon as Dad drops us off at school, we go our separate ways to cover more ground. I walk to the gym while Charlie sets off for the library. We agree to meet back at my locker before the first class starts.

I run into a lot of dead ends.

One guy saw Mike last Wednesday using the weight room in the morning, but he was going in just as Mike was leaving. A couple of other guys from the team shot hoops with him the night before, but all they did was trash talk each other's game. I head back to find Charlie, and he tells me that the librarian hadn't seen Mike since I was there with him the other day, and a girl from his homeroom said he was his usual self.

We proceed to the senior hallway, hoping to find the one person we're hoping may have more info about Mike's last days.

"Hey, Carrie," Charlie says as we approach a cute blond girl sitting against the wall with a few of her friends.

Although I recognize her, we never really hang around in the same social circles, so I don't really know her.

She glares at Charlie. "I was wondering when you'd come nosing around my way."

"Aw, don't be like that," he says. He's relaxed and casual despite her tone, and I remember that Charlie works with her at the doughnut place.

"I should've just listened to everyone and stayed away from Mike," Carrie says.

"Why?" Charlie asks. "You couldn't stop talking about him last time I saw you."

"Yeah, well, maybe it's because I'm an idiot." She looks over at me for the first time. "I'm sorry for what happened to your friend, but he was a dog."

Sadly, this doesn't really surprise me—I know exactly the type of guy Mike is. Was.

Charlie shrugs, not even trying to make an excuse. "All we want to know is what happened between you two."

"Why would I tell you that? It was embarrassing. He acted like a complete ass."

Ouch! He's barely been gone a week. I want to get mad, but he must have done *something* to piss her off so much. I need to find out what.

I kneel down so as not to tower over her. "Will you tell me what happened, exactly?"

"The nitty-gritty details? You a perv like your friend?"

I think she's talking about Mike, but her eyes are on Charlie when she says it.

"You might've been one of the last people to be with him."

"So? You think *I've* got something to do with his death?"

"No. But you might've seen something that could help."

"And you think your perfect smile and silky voice is just going to charm it out of me?"

Wow. Now she's dumping on *me*! What the hell is going on?

"Did I do something to you?" I ask.

"Yes... Well, no. It's just that people like you—"

People like me? What the hell does *that* mean? I must be amping up because I feel Charlie's hand tighten on my shoulder.

"What are you talking about, Carrie?" he says calmly.

"What do you mean 'what do I mean?' Him—" she points at me, "and his chiseled abs and perfect parents—"

"Hey, you don't know anything about me!"

"Yeah, well, I'm probably right." She looks at Charlie. "Right?"

Charlie's grinning at me. "Your abs *are* pretty decent, Shepherd. And Ben and Keya are pretty fantastic parents." He looks at Carrie conspiratorially, like they're sharing a big secret. "His dad makes supper every night, and they sit around the table and talk about how their day went."

"What's wrong with that?" I stammer.

"Gah, that's what I mean—you're *clueless*!" Carrie shouts. "You probably even have brothers or sisters that you get along with and a big, adorable dog, and it all just comes so easy for you."

"Wait, a second. Do you not like me because I'm...," I struggle to find the words, "I'm *normal*?"

"No. I don't like you because you're *perfectly* normal. You never have to put in any effort, you never struggle with confidence. You're all good genetics and proper upbringing, and it pisses me off."

Wow, I never expected any of this, and I have to take a deep breath and focus on why I'm here. "Look. I'm just trying to find out what happened to my friend."

"And then what? What exactly do you plan on doing if you find out?"

"I'm only looking for answers."

She sticks her hand in my face. "Nuh-uh! I'm not saying anything."

This is frustrating. "Why does this matter to you?"

"It doesn't." She looks at her friends. "But I know what you're up to. We all do. Leave it to the cops."

"Please," I plead. "You only hung out with him the one time—"

"Barely that."

"—so why is this such a big deal?"

"God, you really *are* just a dumb jock, aren't you? Look at this—" she waves her hands around herself.

I give her a quick glance, not understanding what she's getting at. "Yeah? And?"

"Do you realize how *hard* it is for someone like me to get a chance with a guy like Mike? He's way out of my league! But then Charlie gave me his number and says he's interested and that I should call him." She gives Charlie the finger. "*That's* what I should have done, but no, I heckin' called him! And he heckin' said 'yes!'"

She's a mix of anger and self-doubt, but she keeps talking so I stay quiet, hoping she'll continue.

"And *then* what the hell happens? He picks me up in his truck and that's all he wants to do! Park in a heckin' parking lot, and—you know—in his truck!" She points at Charlie. "I blame you! You set me up! You probably told him I was easy and he thought he'd get something!"

Unfortunately, I know this is all Mike.

"So you got out of there?" Charlie asks.

She sighs, shaking her head. "I should've. I really should've. But, like I said, what were the odds I'd get this chance again, so I tried to save it."

"How?"

She sighs. "I suggested we go to the Belmont Café."

I know the place. It's a regular hangout for a lot of kids from school.

"Anyways, he agreed—which, of course, was my second mistake."

"Why?" I ask.

She scowls at me. "Because, jackass, he bailed on me after twenty minutes—"

She holds for a dramatic pause and doesn't go on until Charlie asks, "Why?"

"He hit on the barista. I'm pretty sure she gave him her phone number while I was in the bathroom."

Aw, man, Mike! You really can be a jackass sometimes.

chapter 82

At lunch, Charlie and I walk over to the Belmont. It's close to the school but also gets some spillover from the university crowd. The staff is young and hip, and although it's not really my type of music, they usually have some funky bands playing on Friday and Saturday.

"The service is shit here, but the coffee is fantastic," Charlie notes. "They source some of their beans from Sulawesi. Grown at a really high altitude. Creates a silky body, smells like chocolate, and at times has hints of pepper."

Typical Charlie.

"Do you know the flavours at *every* coffee shop?"

"Somewhat. Some of these places change suppliers so much, or don't give a crap about mixing their beans, that they aren't worth my time."

A skinny guy with a beard, not much older than us, greets us at the till. "Suh, dudes? What can I get you?"

Before Charlie can be a smartass, I step in. "Just wondering if you happen to know who was working here last Tuesday afternoon?"

The guy shakes his head, like I just blew his mind with the most profound question in the universe. He reminds me of a surfer from an '80s movie. "Why you want to know something like that, dude?"

I don't really feel like sharing any information with this new "dude" and Charlie senses it, so he takes over, grabbing a comment card from a plastic holder by the till. "We had some awesome service from a girl the other day and we wanted to know her name."

Again, the guy shakes his head like Charlie's slapped him with another truth bomb.

"Well, I'd have to look at the schedule," he responds slowly.

"Ah. Right on, dude. That'd be cool if you would," Charlie says, with no hint of sarcasm.

Suh Dude's brain turns over the decision a few more times before he finally replies. "All right, but you two need to do something for me."

"Sure," I say. "Whatever you want."

He reaches beneath the counter, pulling out a canvas drawstring backpack that's been designed to look more weathered and older than it actually is. He opens it up and takes out a CD.

"Here's my mix tape. Regular price, I would charge you ten, but I'll give it to you for five, long as you tell your friends about me."

"Deal," Charlie says. "Pay the man."

I pull out my wallet and Suh Dude goes to the back to grab the schedule. While we wait, Charlie flips open the CD to read the liner notes.

"Ooh, his first song is called 'You're My Only Angel,'" Charlie whispers. "Oh, then he gets down with 'In and Out.' I hear that one's lit."

"Shut up," I hiss.

"Also on here is 'Your Body Washes Over Me' and "Come Back to My Heart.'"

"If you ruin this—"

Suh Dude comes back out and sees Charlie looking at his CD. "You like the artwork? My ex, Cheryl, did it for me."

By the look on his face—and some of the song titles—he may not have been ready to say goodbye to her.

Charlie nods. "I'm definitely looking forward to listening to it."

Again, not a hint of sarcasm.

Suh Dude leans over the counter and flips through the schedule. "Looks like Autumn was working most of last week."

"Autumn? What's her last name?"

Again he pauses, thinking over how much he should divulge.

Charlie goes back to the liner notes; that seems to decide him in our favour.

"Flettner."

Autumn Flettner. There's a familiar ring to it, but I can't put my finger on why.

"And when does she work next?" Charlie asks.

"She's off for the next few weeks."

Crap. Dead end.

"What's she doing? Holidays?" Charlie's nothing if not persistent.

"Uh. Thought you guys were just filling out a comment card?"

"Just curious, man," Charlie says, but it's obvious that Suh Dude is slowly—very slowly—realizing that we're up to something.

Charlie changes the approach. "So, the honest skinny is my friend here has a small crush on Autumn."

Thanks, Charlie, for throwing me into your lie—except Suh Dude doesn't seem to care, so Charlie hunkers down beside him over the counter, all confiding-like. "See, my man's been feeling down for the last month. His girlfriend of two years dumped him. Can you imagine that? Two years!"

Charlie looks over at me, waiting until the idea sinks into the brainpan of our coffeehouse friend before continuing. "Well, I had to get him out, and I brought him here for some fine coffee, and then afterwards—" Charlie drops his voice really low so that only the two of them are involved in this intrigue. Even I have to strain to hear. "Well, all he did was talk about Autumn, and I thought, 'If I can help my friend move on from Zoey—that's his ex—then, hell, I'll do whatever I can.'"

Suh Dude looks at Charlie, then me. He's still not convinced.

"I don't need her home address or phone number," I put in. "Just tell me if she works somewhere else now or—"

"She's studying."

"Which school does she go to? Ashworth Comp? Guthrie High—?"

"No. Adult school."

A quick glance at Charlie and I can tell he's as confused as I am as to what—or who—Mike had gotten himself messed up with.

chapter 83

We get back to school before anyone—especially Gekas or my parents—notices we're missing.

"The Adult Campus is across town. We'll never get there and back to school over lunch tomorrow," I say.

"Not unless you take your spare."

"But you have Native studies. You planning on skipping?"

He shakes his head. "Hell, no. I've got my documentary on Louis Riel to finish up."

"Documentary?" He's only been here two weeks—and what a very long two weeks it has been.

"Yeah, well, everyone else was doing commercials, and Statten told me I could do something smaller, like a brochure, but I was like 'hell, no.' So I started researching for the commercial, and, well, it just sort of grew into something bigger."

Who *is* this guy? Every time I expect him to zig, he zags.

"So you want me to go alone?"

"Sure, why not? You've done this long enough. You're a big boy."

My heart beats a little faster. The thought of going out on my own and doing something against my parents' wishes—it kind of freaks me out. I've always had Charlie as my fallback excuse for when I misbehave.

If something happens this time, I'll have no one to blame but myself.

chapter 84

The next morning we do a low-key planning session over text while we eat breakfast, not that we're given any other choice. My parents hover—Mom at the house, then Dad on the ride to school. I'm certain they're keeping close tabs on us so we don't try to stage a breakout on them and Gekas.

Suh Dude told us that Autumn worked at the library at the school, so Charlie wants me to check there first. He hands me a little USB stick drive in the event I can't find her there. "Find a network office computer and plug this in. Should help me enough so I can at least find her home address."

I hate the legal complexities of this business, but it's clear that if I want to find out what happened to Mike, I'm going to have to cross a few lines I'm not usually willing to step over.

I try to focus on Statten's psych class and English 30, but I'm running through the plan over and over before I get to homeroom. I feel over-prepared. I've dug up enough change and double-checked the bus schedule several times, but I'm still nervous that something'll go wrong.

As soon as homeroom's done, I rush out of school to the bus stop. It's been forever since I've taken public transportation. As soon as I got my license, I pretty much said goodbye to long, cold winter rides and weird, stinky strangers. Fortunately, the ride downtown goes smoothly, with no need for transfers. From there, I have only a five-block hike.

The Adult Campus is in an old three-storey building downtown, not far from the office of Charlie's "buddy," Mr. Lock. It's a drab, boring structure on the outside, with a lot of red brick and no real sizzle or flash. It was likely a series of shops and offices at one time, but now every window is covered in plastic blinds, concealing the educational institution inside.

I go in the front door and follow the signs to the library on the third floor. I arrive at a plain door, with a torn piece of paper taped on it: QUIET. LIBRARY.

I step inside.

chapter 85

The library is small. I mean really, really small.

There's a desk by the door, but no one's sitting at it. Behind it are five rows of shelves, double-sided but maybe only an arm-length or two long. There are maybe a couple hundred books. Past the shelves, the room opens to reveal a bright workspace with four tables in the centre and a half-dozen small cubicles against the far wall. Several people look up when I enter, distracted by my presence—except for a woman not much older than me, wearing earbuds. She continues to work, head down, in one of the cubicles, and I immediately realize why I recognized the name of Mike's barista.

Autumn Flettner was a year ahead of me and Mike. In fact, she and Heather hung together in the same social circles back in grade school. But when she got to high school, she quickly became a known badass, hanging with a crowd that enjoyed shoplifting and joyriding in stolen cars and, of course, my sister avoided her completely.

I'd almost forgotten about her until this moment.

She seems not to have forgotten me, though.

"Tony Shepherd?" she exclaims loudly when she looks up. "Holy crap, look at you, all grown up!"

The other students glare at her, but she doesn't give a shit.

"Hey, Autumn," I whisper, pulling up a chair and hoping that getting closer will encourage her to lower her voice.

It doesn't.

"How's your sister?" The tone of her voice, you'd think she looked up to Heather a little.

"Good. In university, taking law."

Autumn rolls her eyes—obviously not too enamoured by my big sis's choice. "Of course she is. What about you? You taking classes here?"

"Uh, no. Still in high school."

"God, tell me about it. I'm trying to finish my Grade 12."

"You're not done?" I ask, hoping I seem surprised.

"Nah, I got suspended near the end. Who knew arguing with teachers and picking fights would get me kicked out of school."

I think she's actually shocked by this.

"So, what brings you here, then?" she asks.

"My friend, Mike."

Her smile fades, and I wonder if Gekas has already been here. "There's nothing to talk about."

I proceed with caution. "Well, some people at the coffee shop said you'd given him your number."

"Ha! People! You talking about that skinny-ass chick he was hanging out with?"

I can tell a guy at the next table wants to hush her, but he decides not to risk it. I wonder how many run-ins she's had with her fellow classmates here.

Likely a few.

"Look, it's not my fault. He'd tried hooking up with me for a while and I kept telling him no."

"Was he coming around a lot?"

She shrugs. "Once or twice. Why's everyone so interested in this guy? I know he's younger than me, but seriously, it's only a year!"

I suddenly realize something. "You don't know he's been killed, do you?"

chapter 86

After I tell her, Autumn needs to step outside for a smoke.

It's cool in the alley, and she paces back and forth, one hand tucked tight in her underarm to keep warm, the other holding the lit cigarette. "Jesus, *that's* why that cop kept calling. I thought she was ragging on me about my probation."

So Gekas had followed the trail at least this far.

"How many times were you with him?"

"We weren't together!" she hollers.

"Okay, okay." Sheesh. "How many times did he come around?"

"Just a few. Once at the coffee shop and then a few times at my old job."

"Where's that?"

"The sandwich shop."

Wait! The sandwich shop? *Mike's* sandwich shop? "The one in the mall downtown?"

"Yeah, Fresh Buns. Why?"

Mike had been a fan of the place ever since it opened last year. More specifically, he'd had a huge crush on one of the girls who worked there.

"You ever have shifts with someone named Haley?"

"Oh God, that slut? Yeah, she tried to get me fired!"

Oh, Autumn, you're so eloquent.

Then something else occurs to me. "Didn't you say he'd been only coming around the coffee shop recently? Mike's been going to Fresh Buns for nearly a year. You must've seen him."

She glares at me before finally relenting. "Okay, fine. I knew he'd been around and had a thing for Haley." She's already eyeing the door, ready to leave, but I'm not done.

"So the two of you were interested in him at the same time?"

"Hell, no. I tried to piss her off by hooking up with him at some party, but he passed out before we got anywhere. Then shit happened—"

I interrupt. "What shit? His?"

"Do you not listen? I got expelled. I was out on my ass. And then—" She pauses, taking a big drag on her cigarette. "Look, I didn't see him for nearly a year, okay? Then he started coming around again."

"Before last Tuesday?"

"Can you please keep up? Yes! 'Cuz he started hanging with that bitch Haley again, so we started flirting again."

Interesting that Autumn's attraction to Mike only occurs when there's another girl in the picture.

"But it was all innocent," she insists. "We never hooked up. I promise." She finishes her cigarette, stubbing it out on the brick wall. "Listen, I gotta get back to studying."

"Autumn—?"

She gives a heavy sigh. "God, Tony! I haven't seen Mike since last Tuesday, okay?" She pushes past me to the door. "Say hi to your sister for me."

Before I can ask anything else, she's disappeared inside. I stand alone, shivering in the alleyway.

She's hiding something. I just need to figure out what.

chapter 87

I get back to school just as the bell rings for fourth period. I haven't got a chance to track down Charlie—I'm guessing he's on his way to graphic arts already—so I head off to law.

I'm having a hard time focusing on the class. We're discussing contract law, specifically landlord and tenant agreements. The words roll around in my head, but none of it makes sense. Once the bell rings, I head straight to Charlie's locker, only to find him talking to Elaina.

"You don't suppose your parents would be too upset if Elaina came by the house this weekend?" he asks me. "She wants to show me the new Edgar Wright film, but I'm trying to convince her to watch some David Lynch."

"I don't know." I really have no clue what he's talking about—not that his question really matters to me at the moment. I only want a quick word with him about Autumn before the bell rings. "Can we talk for a minute?"

He shakes his head. "No can do. Elaina's taking me across town so I'm not late for work." He slams his locker shut, swinging his bag over his shoulder. "We'll talk tonight, okay?"

Elaina waves goodbye to me as the two of them head down the hall, leaving me standing at his locker, alone.

chapter 88

The last bell rings and I walk out of the school to find Dad.

There's talk in the hallways about a pre-grad mixer, as well as a get-together at a farm outside of town. A bunch of the guys from the team are planning a game of pick-up shinny to grieve and reminisce about Mike, but here I am in Grade 12, waiting on the curb for my parents to pick me up so I can spend the entire weekend being grounded.

On the way home, Dad asks a bunch of question about how my day went, and I do my best to answer them, but I'm pissed about my situation and wishing Charlie could've spared two secs to rehash the conversation I'd had with Autumn.

After we arrive at the house, I take my bag upstairs, hoping to hide in my room, but Dad calls me back down to help him with the pizza he's making for supper.

"You chop vegetables while I finish the dough," he says.

I begrudgingly oblige since he's not giving me much of a choice.

Dad pulls the dough out of the mixer and spreads it out over the rolling board. "I know things aren't easy right now, but all we want is to keep you boys safe."

I'm sure he's trying to be caring and helpful, but when I realize this is exactly the sort of thing that pissed Carrie off, I laugh.

Dad raises an eyebrow. "Want to share?"

"Not really. Just keep on being your perfect self."

It doesn't make much sense out of context, but Dad rolls with it, giving me a quick salute. "Aye, aye, captain."

I watch him work and decide to open up a little more. "With everything that's going on out there... It's just..." I sigh. "I'm not trying to be ungrateful."

"Son, you've faced more in the past two years than I think I've experienced in my lifetime. And it makes me proud to see how you've dealt with it all." He pauses to dust the work surface with flour, and I think he's going to give me a big *however*...

But he surprises me.

"I wish there were more people like you and Charlie. Willing to fight for the good in this world. I know you don't know what you plan to do when you graduate, but I hope you keep pursuing that fight."

He pauses again, looking at me, forcing a smile. I can see the rigidity in it, and the hint of fear in his eyes. "But not quite yet. Give your mom and me just a few more months, okay?"

It's only then that I realize how much they worry about what my future could hold.

chapter 89

Charlie arrives home with Mom and the four of us have another family supper together.

"How was slinging doughnuts?" I ask.

"Tough but good. You know how it is when you're bringing home the bacon." He takes a sip of his carbonated water for dramatic effect. "Oh, wait. No, you don't."

"I work!"

"One house—to check on *plants*?"

"Hey, it's busier in the summer!"

Mom and Dad laugh, and I let the sarcasm fly. "*Why* did I invite you to stay with us?"

Charlie's quick, though. "First, your parents offered, not you. And second, you're a masochist when it comes to me."

"You got that right." It's time to turn the tables. "Sooo, did you ask Mom about Elaina?"

Dad's ears perk up at the mention of a girl, but Mom just smiles. "Yes, we discussed his plans on the way home."

Of course Charlie hadn't hesitated to ask a question that most normal teenagers might find awkward—especially with a family he's just moved in with.

Mom continues, "I thought it might be a nice way to break up the weekend." She looks over at me. "You know, son, if there *are* any girls…ones you respect and treat with kindness—you might want to invite them over too."

"Let's not even go there, Mom."

She rubs my shoulder but is willing to let it go, at least for now.

Mom and Dad talk about their day, and Charlie tells them how his classes are going. I answer their questions as they come my way, but I feel somehow outside of myself, thinking about Mike, and Autumn, and my future.

It's odd how normal it is to have Charlie here; he's become part of our family dynamic, like he's always fit in. If someone had told me a year and a half ago that this is where we'd be now, I wouldn't have believed them.

After supper, Charlie and I are on dish duty. He's washing and I'm drying, but I'm falling behind.

"Yo, Earth to Shepherd. What's on your mind?"

"Autumn."

He sighs. "All right, what about her?"

I tell him everything until he interrupts. "She's chaos."

"And I'm sure she's lying," I say. "I just don't have a specific reason—"

"Call it a hunch. I dig hunches."

"*Dig?* Did you just get zapped out of the '60s?"

"You know, we can't all be 'perfectly normal' like you," he says mockingly. "So, you think she's involved with what happened to Mike?"

"Oh, she's definitely trouble," I agree. "But do I think she killed him? No."

Charlie finishes the last dish and hands it to me before hanging up his dishcloth and drying his hands, thinking things over.

"But…?" He waits for me to continue.

"I can't quite pin down how she's connected. She's not telling us something."

He leans against the counter, head down. "Well, we know she's been tempting him for a while. They had that exchange on Tuesday when he was on his date with Carrie—"

"Not much of a date," I say.

"Hey, he's your friend."

I appreciate that Charlie hasn't put him in the past tense yet.

"He played some basketball, then, according to his mom, was home early Tuesday night."

"So Tuesday's a bust. Wednesday, he was at school with us—before we left for the condo."

I hate thinking about that moment. If he'd come with us, would he have been safer? Was the girl he'd been talking about that day Autumn or someone else? If only I'd talked with my friend a little longer maybe he'd still be here.

Charlie goes on. "I think we need to check out the mall, see if Mike went there after school. There's a few people there who might be able to help."

I shake off my funk and focus on the problem. "And I know some of the people at the sandwich shop. So, sneak off Monday at lunch?" I ask.

"Actually, I have an idea how to get us there this weekend."

chapter 91

Charlie's idea is stupid: he asks my parents to take us.

Of course, he's prepared a story. He tells Mom he needs new clothes, showing her the holes in his socks and underwear, all of which I'm sure she didn't need—or care—to see.

And, surprisingly enough, she agrees but decides to make a morning out of it, starting with the farmers' market downtown.

We call to let Gekas know our plans but only get her voicemail, so we leave a message. Hopefully, she won't freak out that we're going to walk around in a pack in a couple of very public places, but it wouldn't surprise me if we "happen" to bump into her or her officers while we're out.

We get to the farmers' market early—there's a chill in the spring air and some of the booths are still getting set up—but Mom and Dad have an agenda and beeline for the vegetable trucks from the local farms.

"Mr. S., the prices on the produce trucks at the other end of the market are way cheaper than here," Charlie says in front of the local sellers.

It's kind of obnoxious.

"Yes, but they're from BC. These are practically grown in our backyard."

"Fine," Charlie relents, assessing the cabbages and potatoes Dad already has in his basket. "At least barter them down a little!"

Before he can utter another insult, Dad indicates an Ethiopian food truck selling *chechebsa*, a breakfast dish that Charlie's intrigued by. When he goes off to get some, both my parents and the seller breathe a little easier and the transaction runs smoothly from there.

We continue down the rows of shops, hunting though tables full of jams and large tents filled with fruit, as well as a little hippy van whose open doors reveal a display of braided necklaces and other handmade art. I'm sure it's both the proprietors' store and their home.

Charlie buys some honey for Dad from a beekeeper and a set of handcrafted dangling earrings for Mom.

"You know you don't need to buy them anything," I say.

"What else am I going to do with my money?" Charlie asks, shovelling in the last spoonful of his Ethiopian breakfast.

"I don't know. Save it? Buy some scratch-and-wins?"

"Hey, share the wealth, I always say." When I look at him, perplexed, he adds, "Just because I lived in trailer-park squalor doesn't mean I didn't invest a little. Not my fault that Mom had her addictions. I tried my best."

I never know how to proceed after Charlie opens the door a crack on his personal life—especially when he and I are spending Saturday morning out with my parents at the farmers' market, checking out craft beer and artisanal cupcakes.

Afterwards, the four of us head to the mall.

I'm trying to figure out how to get some time on our own, hoping Charlie's got a plan already worked out, but my parents make it easy on us.

"Okay, you've got half an hour to do your shopping," Mom says.

Charlie balks. "I can't possibly get everything done in that short a time. How about an hour?"

"No."

"Okay. Forty-five?"

"Thirty."

Charlie grins. "All right. Sounds fair, boss lady!"

As my parents set off, I turn to Charlie. "Take me to your people."

chapter 92

Charlie's people, of course, are the mall's security guards.

He guides me down a grey cindercrete hallway with several doors that lead to the back rooms of the mall's stores. Some of them are propped open; it'd be pretty easy for someone to just grab a box of stuff from a stockroom shelf and take off. I'm quite certain I'd never have even considered such a thing until I started hanging around Charlie.

We wind down several sets of stairs at the end of the hall until we pop out on the other side of the mall near the parking garage. Charlie stops at a nondescript door and knocks.

"Who is it?" comes a voice from the other side.

"Rocky Raccoon," Charlie replies.

I don't question this, knowing both his love for mystery and for weird cultural references.

"Just a sec." A lock and deadbolt click one after the other, and the door swings open to reveal a skinny, middle-aged guy with short blond hair, and a scruffy moustache and beard. "*Hola, amigo.*"

Charlie introduces us. "Anthony, Brett. Brett, Anthony."

I nod hello as Brett guides us into the room then secures the door behind us. "You can never be too careful. People seem fascinated with trying to get in here."

I look around and realize why. A wall of monitors spy on almost every nook and cranny of the mall. Every entrance, hallway, walkway, galleria, and public space is covered. I'm sure if I looked carefully enough, I'd be able to spot my folks.

"So, what can I do for you?" Brett asks.

"I'm trying to track down some information about a guy," Charlie says.

"And what's in it for me?"

Almost every relationship in Charlie's life seems to be a transaction. I can't help but wonder what bargain I've unknowingly struck with him.

Charlie starts to rattle off the possibilities: "Two tickets to the upcoming concert?"

"Nope. Don't like country."

"4K 50-inch TV?"

"Tempting, but no."

"Might be some jobs opening up with Stonecreek Security."

"Guaranteed?"

Charlie shakes his head.

"Come on, man. You're holding back. You know what I want."

"Fine." Charlie grabs a notepad and pen from the desk and writes down a ten-digit number.

This immediately piques Brett's interest. "Really? Is that what I think it is?"

Charlie nods.

I'm not sure if he'll ever tell me what the number means, but it doesn't matter.

Brett tears the sheet off, folds it up and sticks it in his pocket. "Shit, man, thank you. Yeah, go ahead, ask away. I'll do whatever I can to help."

I pull out my phone and bring up a picture of Mike. "Do you recognize him?"

"He looks familiar, but I couldn't tell you from when or where."

"He probably hung around the sandwich shop."

"Who wouldn't?"

"What do you mean?" I ask.

"Uhh, the ladies are cute there," he says like I'm an idiot. "And that Haley's always giving me extra toppings." He studies Mike's image again. "Yeah, I think I remember seeing him hanging around when she was working."

"Or maybe Autumn?" I add.

"Oof," he mutters. "Now, *there* was a piece of work. Always with the mind games."

"What do you mean?" I ask again.

"Buddy of mine tried to date her and it was all hot and cold. He could never figure out where she was coming from."

Interesting but not immediately useful. I think of something that is. "Do you have any of the tapes from the food court the Wednesday before last, say sometime just after 3:30 p.m.?"

Brett smiles. "Of course I do."

chapter 93

Brett cues up the footage on his computer and hits play. All the screens flicker on, showing us that moment in time across the whole mall, nearly a week and a half ago.

A monitor in the top row shows the food court, full of people. Below it and to the right is a closer view, and I can clearly see the sandwich shop, Fresh Buns. Three people stand behind the counter.

"Can you get closer?" Charlie asks.

"Like 'zoom and enhance'?" Brett laughs. "You've been watching too many movies, son."

"Can you tell who's working?" I ask.

He leans in and squints at the pixelated image. "Nope. Kind of looks like Hulcy, but I can't be sure."

I continue staring at the screen. Customers walk up, order, and wait. Eventually, they get their food and move on. I patiently watch for my friend.

"I can double the speed. You'll still be able to tell who comes and goes."

"Sure."

He twists a dial and the figures on the screen jump ahead, rushing in and out of the frame, scurrying back and forth like ants.

"Stop!" I shout.

Brett hits a button.

"Go back, but slowly."

The bank of monitors flashes, reversing in ten-second skips.

"Okay," I say. "Back maybe another minute? Stop!"

There, standing at the counter of the sandwich shop, is Mike. Seeing him, alive and well, is a gut-punch.

"Go forward," Charlie says. "Slowly."

Mike stands at the counter, rocking back and forth on his feet, but he doesn't stay long before moving off to the left.

"Go back again," Charlie says.

I look over at him. "Why, what did you see?"

He doesn't answer, only watches the screen intently. "Can you loop a few seconds?"

Brett smiles. "Absolutely. This thing can do it all—"

Charlie interrupts, "Go to when the guy shows up and loop when I tell you."

Brett seems a bit miffed by the brusque request, but he must be used to it because he does as he's told.

"Okay, right there."

All the screens replay thirty seconds of the past in minia-ture, over and over.

"You see it, Shepherd?" Charlie asks, finally, directing me to two places on the screen.

I don't at first, then it becomes clear. Mike does a kind of wave, almost pointing to the right. And a shadow bobs past the doorway in the back of the sandwich shop.

"A fourth employee?" I ask.

"Let it run, Brett," Charlie asks, this time in a much kinder voice. He points to the monitor displaying a wide shot of the food court.

Now I can see Mike clearly: he's walking away from the restaurant toward the right of the screen. Just before he steps out of frame, a door opens and he disappears through it.

What are you up to, Mike?

Charlie asks, "Any monitors in that hallway?"

Brett directs us to one on the bottom right. Mike and a girl wearing a Fresh Buns ball cap are walking away from the camera down the cindercrete hallway.

"Where does it go?"

Brett indicates a couple of monitors. "There's a few exits. This one...," we watch a door that looks like it leads out to the parking garage, but no one comes through it, "...now, this one," a second door opens to the street. Again nothing. "And, finally, this one." The last one exits onto an alley between two buildings. A dumpster blocks half the view.

The door swings open, and Mike and the mysterious stranger step out, their backs to the camera.

"Where's that alley?"

"Loading zone behind the department store. Leads to staff parking. A lot of crazy shit happens back there."

I scan the monitors, searching for another viewpoint. "And where's the camera?"

"There isn't one," Brett says. "Beyond my jurisdiction." Like he's some beat cop.

"Go back ten seconds," I say, needing to be sure of what I saw.

Brett rewinds, but Charlie is already whispering, "Nice, Shepherd."

The video plays and we both see it. For a split-second, as she walks through door into the parking lot, the Fresh Buns girl turns and we can see her face clearly.

It's Autumn.

chapter 94

We leave Brett and his security monitors and walk back upstairs.

"So, she *did* lie to us," I say.

"Yeah, but why? What's she hiding?" Charlie asks.

Autumn likes trouble, and I'm worried that happy-go-lucky Mike got himself caught up in something ugly and complicated.

I want to talk to Charlie about it more, but he shushes me. "It's socks and skivvies time, Shepherd."

We walk into the main part of the mall. I start for the department store, but Charlie doesn't follow.

"What? You don't like this place?" I ask.

"Hell, no." He takes me next door to an outdoor sporting goods store. "You might pay a little more here, but this place offers clothes with the comfort and fit that you should expect, and the durability and temperature control that you should demand." He opens a package and pulls out a pair of boxer briefs. "Now, feel the inside of that. How smooth it is. No friction there! And look at that crotch! Cut and stitched and shaped to give your—"

"Okay, enough!" I never thought I'd be getting underwear advice from this guy.

"I'm only saying you get solid support."

"Wonderful. Can you just pay for your magic drawers so we can go?"

"But I haven't told you about the socks."

"Charlie, please."

"Fine."

Charlie grabs what he needs and takes it to the counter. The guy at the till looks at the ripped-open underwear box.

"Yeah, I found it like that. Can I get a discount?"

chapter 95

After Charlie gets ten percent off, we travel up the escalator to meet my folks.

"Mind if we eat in the food court today?" I ask them.

Mom looks at the rows of greasy food joints and I can tell she's about to say no, when Dad interrupts her. "It's been forever since I had a burger and a shake."

I see Mom's disappointment, but Charlie says, "Mrs. S., if you're looking for something a little healthier, try the Thai place. Ask for the vegetarian sauce and bean sprouts instead of rice. Or, if you want to skip healthy and try some adventure, ask for *meekati* or *pad kee mao*. They're not on the menu but they'll know what to do."

She's intrigued by Charlie's suggestions, and she and Dad go off to order their individual lunches.

Charlie looks over at me. "Let me guess: Fresh Buns?"

"Of course."

chapter 96

I don't recognize the girl behind the counter at Fresh Buns. Her name tag reads BECKIE. Charlie and I order a couple of sandwiches anyway, and Beckie looks over her shoulder to call out, "Need some help up here!"

Haley comes from the back, carrying a container of lettuce, and as soon as she sees me, I think she's going to burst into tears. "Tony, I'm so, so sorry about Mike. I saw you at the funeral, but I just couldn't—"

She's more emotional than I would've expected. I always assumed she didn't really care about Mike; maybe I was wrong.

I glance at Beckie before responding, but she's out of earshot making our sandwiches. "That's actually why I'm here, Haley. I heard Mike came by here last week. Just wondering if you or anyone saw him?"

Fresh tears start to stream, and she puts the container down to grab a napkin.

"I'm sorry to bring it up," I say gently. "But it's important."

"Me, Beckie, and Lorna were here," she says, wiping her eyes.

"That's it?"

She nods.

That doesn't make sense, though; we saw at least four of them on the security footage.

Well aware I might be stepping into a minefield, I ask as casually as I can, "How about Autumn? Was she working?"

Haley's face distorts, and her tears stop immediately. She sneers in disgust. "Yeah, she was here. But not to work. Just to pick up her last cheque."

"Oh?"

Haley glances at Beckie, who hands us our sandwiches and goes to serve another customer, before lowering her voice and leaning toward me and Charlie. "I got her fired." It seems like she might leave it there, but then she begins defending herself. "She was crazy, okay? Always bringing drama to work. She'd hit on older married men—even customers!—then try to sleep with your boyfriend. One minute she'd pretend to be your friend, the next, she'd backstab you. "

Wow! Autumn really was all about the chaos.

"And Mike?" I ask, and again sadness crosses Haley's face.

"Oh, that poor boy." There is genuine care in her voice. "She strung him along, all right."

"What do you mean by that, exactly?" Charlie asks.

She gives us a sheepish look. "Look, when he first started coming around, I could tell he was interested in me, but I had a boyfriend. Then we broke up and I was interested, but Autumn got her hooks in him." Haley's tone changes. "When

I ended up with someone else, she dropped Mike and went after my new guy."

Talking about Autumn has made her irate. "Plus, she was always stealing my shifts, doing whatever she could to make my life a living hell. And I liked Mike—I really did," she adds, "but he wasn't interested in long-term so it wasn't worth all the aggravation."

"And so you got Autumn fired."

"Yeah. I was going to quit—I mean, I like the job, but I hated her—except my boss liked me more and got rid of Autumn so I'd stay."

I'm starting to realize what happened—at least part of it. Autumn thought Haley was interested in Mike again and so she went after him once more. When he stopped by the sandwich shop, she did whatever she could to piss Haley off.

"You said Autumn flirted with older men too?" Charlie asks.

Haley rolls her eyes. "Yeah, she was pretty disgusting."

"She sleep with any of them?"

"I don't know. Probably. Wouldn't put it past her."

"Any of them get attached?"

"A few, maybe, but they usually came to their senses eventually."

Charlie's quick. "But not always?"

She sighs. "When I first started, there was this one older guy who came around all the time. Autumn seemed interested—*so* gross—but then one day, she quit talking about him."

Haley pauses, looking out at the food court. I'm guessing Mom and Dad have found themselves a table out there in the sea of people. "Turns out, though, he was still showing up."

She points to a table. "He'd sit over in that corner, just watching us, and when we realized he was there, he'd move somewhere else. And when we figured that out, he'd change where he sat, when he showed up, even how he looked. But we were sure it was him."

"Sounds like he was infatuated," I say.

"That's an understatement," Haley snorts.

"He still coming around?" Charlie wants to know.

She shakes her head. "Haven't seen him in months."

"Did she ever call the cops?" I ask.

Haley shrugs. "I don't know. By that point she and I hated each other, so she wouldn't have told me anyway."

"He have a name?"

"Not that we ever heard. She was pretty secretive about him."

Charlie's thought of something else. "Do you think he was ever around when Mike showed up?"

"Maybe. Like I said, after a while, we never knew when he was watching. We just started to assume that he was always around somewhere."

Shit, Mike, did you get in the way of some psycho stalker?

chapter 97

Charlie and I find Mom and Dad's table and dig into our sandwiches. I don't know about Charlie, but I'm having a hard time carrying on a discussion with my folks while my brain spins through our conversation with Haley. Who's the mystery guy? Is he the reason Mike died?

We drive back home and spend the afternoon doing chores. Dad has us spring cleaning the garage, reorganizing his junk, dragging stuff to the curb for donation, and sweeping the floor. Just when we think we're done, Mom sends us down to the basement to tidy up the storage room.

"Your parents are taskmasters," Charlie says, hauling a box onto a top shelf.

"Welcome to my world."

"So," he says, "that Autumn, hey?"

"Yup."

"What a piece of work."

"That's one way to describe her."

"She lied to us. Let's send Gekas after her."

Much as I'd love to, I have to say, "There's so many reasons why we can't."

He sighs. "I know. But it'd be fun."

True. Though I have to add, "I'm pretty sure she didn't kill Mike."

"No, but that honour might go to her stalker," he says.

Sounds like we've both been trying to figure out who he is. "I don't know anyone who could tell us anything more about him. It seems like Autumn pisses off everyone who knows her."

"Who'd she hang around with at your school?"

"I have no clue. I kind of remember seeing her at parties, but she always seemed to be floating between guys."

"Considering her M.O., that doesn't surprise me. She was also probably scrapping with other girls at school."

Good point. And it gives me an idea. "Maybe we should ask a teacher."

"Who you thinking?"

Besides my coach, there's only one I know well enough to talk to: Statten.

chapter 98

Charlie and I play games most of Saturday night. Sunday is pretty low key, except for Elaina coming over to hang out in the afternoon. They invite me to watch movies with them, but I decline. I'm not interested in being a third wheel, and besides, I can use the time to do some biology homework. Mr. Hall's a lot better than Harriet was, but he still wants the lab experiments written up on time.

I know the presence of a girl in the house makes Mom happy, but I also know she'd much rather have someone coming by to visit me. It's been a year and a half since I lost Sheri and everyone's told me it's time to start moving on.

I'd be lying if I said I wasn't noticing girls, but none of them have come close to what I felt for Sheri. I worry sometimes I'm remembering the past in picture-perfect terms—who knows? Maybe I am—but until I'm ready to move on, I'm happy to wait until the right person comes along.

Monday rolls around, and Charlie and I are anxious to get to school, but Dad's running slow.

"What's the rush, boys?" he asks.

"I'm hoping to work on my documentary about Louis Riel, Mr. S.," Charlie says.

"You can't do that at home?"

I know for a fact that he's been editing it on his phone, but I stay silent. I feel bad we're not being honest with Dad, but I'm willing to do anything to get him to move faster. Mike's murderer is still out there.

Unfortunately, he gets us to school with no time to spare, and I can't help but wonder whether he did it purposely so we wouldn't have an opportunity to find trouble. We clamber out of the car just as the first bell for homeroom rings.

"Too late to talk to Statten now," I say, as we hustle inside.

"Meet me at the end of third period and we'll catch her at lunch," Charlie says.

We separate, rushing to our lockers to dump our backpacks before going to class. I walk into the classroom as the second bells rings and grab my chair. Statten's still teaching the unit on child development, but I struggle to focus enough to take notes. For most of the class, all I can think about is whether Statten knows anything more about Autumn, or worse, if Gekas or my parents have warned the school about us stirring up shit, and whether Statten will rat us out if they have.

The bell rings and I head straight to chem. Although I did my homework this weekend, I'm absolutely stumped when it comes to interpreting solubility curves and hope to find some clarity from Mr. James. By the end of class, I'm slightly less confused, but now we're calculating the solubility product constant for saturated solutions, so I spend most of my spare trying to figure out my homework on that.

I don't realize what time it is until the bell rings, and I have to pack my books up quickly and hustle back to Statten's room. The door is closed when I arrive, and there's no sign of Charlie, so I knock.

"Come in."

chapter 100

Charlie's already there, sitting near Statten's desk, and I take a seat beside him.

"Why do I feel this has nothing to do with Native studies or psychology?" she says, giving Charlie a look. Obviously he's been buying time until I arrived. "What's this about, boys?"

Even asking this simple question seems to make her tense.

I don't see any easy way to approach the discussion, so I jump right in. "What can you tell us about Autumn Flettner?"

Statten stares between Charlie and me, then finally blinks. "Autumn Flettner?"

We nod.

"Why are you asking about her?"

She clearly knows enough to recognize the name. That's something.

"It's about Mike." This might sink the whole thing, but I'm hoping her kindness to me the other week means she'll grant us some leeway—maybe even give us some answers.

"How so?" she asks, looking far more distraught than I'd expected.

I'm not quite sure how to put it. All I can come up with is, "Well, we're worried that she somehow involved him in something bad."

"And you think it could have led to his murder?"

I get a weird twist in my gut. She *does* know something.

"We're not sure," Charlie says. I'm guessing he's where I'm at, trying not to let any of us jump too far ahead of the questions. "Did you ever have to deal with her when she went to school here?"

"This is none of your business."

Shit. We've stepped into it big time.

"Anthony, when I told you to make things right, this isn't what I meant."

"Ms. Statten, my friend is dead—"

"I know. And you should leave the matter to the police."

"And we will," I say. "Whatever we find out, we'll tell them."

Statten studies us, deciding if she'll continue.

"All we're trying to understand is what Mike was up to so that we can help them."

"And what does that have to do with Autumn?" she asks.

"We know she saw him the day of his murder. Mike's not the kind of guy to find himself mixed up with a killer, but the way Autumn causes trouble—"

"You think she may have?"

Charlie and I both nod. I continue pleading for her help, "All we want to know is what you can tell us about her."

Statten picks up a pen, playing with it between her fingers. "She often got into trouble. I saw her in detention quite a bit."

"For what sorts of things?" I ask.

"The usual. Fighting with other students. Fighting with her teachers. Fighting with the administration."

Everything I'd already assumed.

But then she continues, "One time she spit on one of the maintenance staff."

"Wow. She likes to be difficult," Charlie says, and hearing him make a statement like that makes me stifle a laugh.

"Most kids seem to want to get along, but that girl seemed to find pleasure in being the villain."

"Did she ever cause grief for any male teachers?" Charlie asks.

She clicks the pen, suddenly nervous. "What do you mean?"

"I don't know. Hook up with them? Get in their pants? Schizzle their dizzle?"

"Charlie!" she warns.

He raises his hand in surrender. "Don't hate the player. Hate the game."

I take over. "I'm sorry. We've just heard that she had a habit of flirting with older guys."

Click click click. A pained look crosses her face. We seem to have struck close to home.

Statten pauses for a moment. "There *was* a thing, but I'm not sure what it might have to do with Mike." She pauses again. "Last year, she accused a teacher of Inappropriate conduct."

How much, I wonder, not for the first time, have the events of the past year made me oblivious to everyone else's lives?

"A teacher from here?" I ask. "Who?"

"Mr. Harriet."

My old biology teacher.

I'm curious whether this has anything to do with his recent absence, but Charlie's already asking her what happened.

"Autumn accused him of sending inappropriate texts."

"Like, sexy texts?" Charlie asks.

Statten nods. "Autumn said at first she didn't know who it was, but when she figured it out, she reported it immediately."

"Seems like an open-and-shut accusation. If it were true, she could show the texts and he'd get booted."

Statten nods again. "Yes, but like everything about Autumn, it gets complicated. She said Harriet told her to delete the texts. She even said he showed her how."

"Sidestepping blame seems to be her strong suit," Charlie says. "But wouldn't a computer forensics team be able to retrieve the data?"

"They said they could've if she'd come forward sooner."

"Why would she destroy the texts only to turn around and accuse him afterward?" I ask.

"I think at the start she liked the attention." Statten looks out the window as a couple of students run past. "He's older than she is, relatively good-looking. It was exciting."

"So, she deleted the messages. No evidence, no case," I say.

"Yes, but Autumn dragged it out. Said she had screenshots of some of the messages but then couldn't find them, then said the phone containing them was stolen."

"Ah, the old 'destroyed evidence' story!" Charlie sneers.

"The whole thing went on for far too long and dragged Mr. Harriet's name through the mud. He ended up going on paid leave, then paid stress leave. It affected his marriage and eventually his wife divorced him."

"Geez, everything this girl touches turns to shit," Charlie says, and Statten glares at him. "Sorry," he says quickly.

"Did you know him?" I put in. "Did you ever ask his side of the story?"

She shakes her head. "I knew him enough to talk to in the staff room or the hallway, but not enough to ask such a personal thing."

There's only one question left.

"So. Was it true?" I ask.

Statten shrugs, still playing with the pen. "Who knows? There's no proof that it happened. Given Autumn's habit of deception and antagonism—"

"But you think it did?"

Statten doesn't answer.

"You do, don't you?" I persist.

She sighs, unwilling to make an unfounded accusation against a colleague, before finally giving a reluctant nod. "After a while, you start believing there could be a tiny morsel of truth amid all her lies."

chapter 101

We step out of Statten's classroom and walk to the cafeteria.

"Every time I think I've heard the last of Autumn's craziness, she just adds more fuel to the fire," Charlie says.

"Do you think Harriet's the mystery stalker?" I ask.

"Could be. If he is, it certainly gives him motive."

"And if there was any truth to her accusations, it fits Haley's story. They start flirting and he starts hanging around Fresh Buns—"

Charlie interrupts, "Then, things go sour in the relationship and he disappears—"

"Until they go *really* sour and she accuses him of sexting—"

"And he slips into stalker mode."

"*If* any of her story is true."

I catch Charlie glancing at me and we both know that this is a pretty big "if." Autumn hasn't given us much reason to believe anything she says.

But something else doesn't add up.

"Does any of this really lead to Mike's killer?"

Charlie runs a hand through his shaggy hair. "I don't know, man. I never knew Harriet. You did. Did he seem like the killer type? Even the pervy type?"

"I don't know," I shrug. "He taught biology. He was boring. He gave us homework. And occasionally he yelled at kids."

"That could make any teacher a killer," Charlie says.

"Precisely."

"So, let's run through the motive. He gets attached to Autumn. She dumps him, screws up his life."

"He loses his wife, starts creeping on her at work."

"Mike starts showing up—"

I interrupt, "But he's there for Haley, not Autumn."

"At the start. So, Harriet doesn't worry."

"But at some point, Autumn gets petty and digs her claws into Mike—"

"And now Harriet notices."

"So she hooks up with Mike on Tuesday night and—what? Harriet murders him in a fit of jealous rage?"

"That seems like a real slow burn. Why not do it sooner? What set him off this one time?" Charlie asks.

All good questions.

I have another. "And what does any of this have to do with the other murder victims? Are they *all* Autumn's exes?"

"If only we could talk to Gekas," he says, surprising me. He catches my look. "Yeah, yeah, I know. It just seems like we're missing something and it'd be nice to ask for her help."

"I don't want to go anywhere near Gekas until we've got something solid."

Then the bigger question comes into view.

"Why would Harriet leave the body at the running trails? Is this about Mike or is it about *us*?"

Charlie sighs.

It doesn't feel like we're anywhere close to knowing what's going on.

chapter 102

In the cafeteria, Charlie heads directly to Elaina's table, and I follow.

She's surrounded by a bunch of her friends. Most of them are pretty smart—the kind who work their asses off on assignments and keep up with their studies.

"Hey, Laura, Maxine, Gretchen," I say.

They all express their sympathy for Mike, and I'm grateful. It's nice to know he won't be forgotten quickly.

"What happened to you two? In trouble again?" Elaina asks.

By the looks on her friends' faces, this has become a foregone conclusion. I wonder if they always thought I was a troublemaker, or if this is a recent development because of my association with Charlie. Either way, I try not to take it personally.

"Just talking to Statten," Charlie says.

Although he's sitting beside Elaina, they're not holding hands or anything. I've got to give the guy respect for not rushing things.

"Oooooh," Maxine says, rolling out the word.

She's prone to drama, so I'm sure she's got a million ideas of what went down.

"Just homework questions," Charlie adds.

"Yeah, right," Gretchen says. She's the sassy skeptic of the group. I'm pretty sure she and Maxine will end up in a catfight one day.

"Is this homework academic or something more...personal?" Laura asks.

She knows me the best out of all them. Long before I met Sheri, Laura and I hooked up a couple of times before she broke it off because she found me "exasperating." In fact, it was through my relationship with her that I got to know Elaina.

Charlie grins. "Man, you guys are your own interrogation unit. Bad guys would be sweating bullets in no time."

He's avoided the question and I'm not the only one to notice. I don't think any of them are going to let us continue until they get a proper response.

"Personal," I say, hoping that keeping it short will put an end to the cross-examination.

"What about?" Maxine asks. She wants the juicy gossip.

Charlie steps in. "You know. Stuff. Stuff unrelated to school. Stuff that gets us in trouble."

"So if we told Mrs. Johnson or Mr. Barry—?" Gretchen says.

"Sure, if you want," Charlie replies.

Laura looks at me. "Or your parents?"

I shrug—they just want a reaction—but with all the questioning they're doing, it occurs to me that they might be able to help.

"Do you guys know what happened with Harriet last year?" I ask.

Maxine gets a gleeful look and Gretchen rolls her eyes.

But Elaina says, "That was downright creepy."

"How so?" Charlie asks.

"All of it. Harriet for doing it and Autumn for letting it happen."

Maxine pipes up. "No, it was Autumn staying after classes to begin with."

Laura sighs, like this is a disagreement they've had many times. "That's just bullshit. No one saw any of that."

"It wouldn't surprise me if Harriet made the first move," Gretchen says.

"Why's that?" I ask.

"He's gross. Always had an eye on girls in class," she says.

"He'd stare?" The things I'm oblivious to. "Would he do anything more?"

Gretchen glances at Maxine, then Laura and Elaina. "Well, not to me."

"Not to any of us," Elaina quickly adds.

"But you'd hear stories," Maxine says. "Shauna said he once flirted with her after class."

"Supposedly Bianca once found his number in an assignment he marked," Gretchen says.

"It was always just rumours though. No facts. No proof," Laura puts in. She'd be an excellent amateur detective—if it didn't feel like she was so judgmental about what we do, that is.

"The piece of paper with the number?" Charlie asks.

"Never saw it. I don't think anyone did."

"So, Harriet might be a sleazeball?"

Elaina answers this. "It was always just a feeling. Like, you believe he *could* do it, you know? You could believe all the stories had a grain of truth."

"It was enough to make you cautious and want to keep your distance," Laura says.

"But he was married," I say.

Laura laughs. "When has that ever kept a guy from trying something?"

Maxine adds, "Never kept him off of Statten, did it?"

Wait, what?

chapter 103

Charlie and I glance at each other.

"Back the truck up," he says. "What are you talking about?"

Maxine's eyes light up again, realizing she's got goods to share with us. "Harriet and Statten were a thing."

"You're not serious?" I say.

I can't picture it. How out of it *was* I last year?

"Oh, they tried to keep it on the down-low, but we started figuring it out."

"How?" Charlie asks.

"People caught them together in classrooms," Gretchen says.

"Doing what exactly?" He's doubtful too.

"I don't know— "

"Making out? Fooling around? Having sex?"

"Well, no—"

"Then how do you know they were together?"

"Have you ever heard of LockerBuzz?" Elaina asks.

I shake my head, and Maxine says, "It's like Jodel."

"Or Yik Yak," Gretchen adds.

None of this means anything to me, but Charlie seems to get it.

"Anonymous texting. You write whatever you want and share it, but it never tracks you. There's a ton of these apps around."

Laura continues, "LockerBuzz is the best one right now." She swipes opens her phone, brings up an app, and hands it to me.

It's exactly as they've described: a bunch of anonymous messages ranging from

Party this weeknd
I feel the need for weed
wanna hook-up?

to

mrs johnson sucks butt

Beside each, there's a place to vote it up or down, or reply.

"What's this have to do with Statten and Harriet?" I ask.

Elaina replies, "There are whole threads of students outing teachers' possible hook-ups."

Maxine puts in, "Like, if you see two teachers, you hashtag the school and their names with the when, where, and what. After a little while, these things start adding up."

Laura takes her phone from me and types *#stattenandharriet* into the search. Dozens of entries come up.

She passes it back to me and I look through it.

Statten's room spare #stattenandharriet
gym after school #stattenandharriet
saw #stattenandharriet at Mannie's Pizza!
Harriet's room lunch #stattenandharriet
#stattenandharriet PARK!!!

"All that's here are times and places. But no details," I say, handing it over to Charlie. "How do we know they aren't just friends?"

Laura looks at me. "You're saying you don't know *anyone* who was attracted to someone they hung out with?"

She's referring to her and me.

"Fair enough. But it's still not concrete proof."

"No," says Elaina, "But where there's smoke, there's usually fire."

I glance over at Charlie and I know he's not convinced either. Being seen together by students doesn't make them a couple. They could just be friends.

But I can tell by Charlie's look he's also thinking what I'm thinking. If even one of those postings on LockerBuzz is true, why did she deny they were close?

By the time the warning bell rings for period four, Charlie and I know we need to go back and speak with Statten. Unfortunately, there isn't enough time before class.

"You could go on your own in your spare," I offer.

"Nope, Elaina says Statten's got Psych 20 then."

"Then we leave it until tomorrow?" I hate thinking this is our only option.

He pulls out his phone, tapping out a message. "Let me see if I can buy us some more time."

I look over and see him texting Dad.

Can I stay and edit my doc

for an extra 30 minutes?

We wait patiently for a response, knowing the final bell will ring any moment.

Finally, Dad starts typing:

Fine.

You and Anthony be at
the door right at 4.

It's like he knows we're standing beside each other.

The bell goes and we have to split.

"Meet me at Statten's room at 3:30," Charlie says as he backs away down the hall.

I can't get over the irony that the last hour of my day is spent waiting impatiently through what was once Mr. Harriet's biology class. I feel sort of bad that Mr. Hall has to put up with me—he's told me to focus a couple of times now on my notes—but I can feel the rush of adrenaline that comes from closing in on a mystery.

When the bell rings, I don't wait, and slip out of the room quickly. I rush toward Statten's classroom, only to find the door closed and lights off.

Charlie's there, standing still amid the sea of students rushing to get out of here. "She's already gone."

"Teacher's staffroom?" I ask.

He nods and we push our way through the crowd toward the main office, but when we arrive, it feels like everyone is trying to clear out of here too, like the whole school is a sinking ship.

"Is Ms. Statten in the back?" Charlie asks Mrs. Opal.

Mrs. Opal asks the English teacher, Mrs. Dafoe, who says, "She just left."

"I can page her, if you'd like?" Mrs. Opal offers.

Waiting around to see if she'll return the page means we'd risk missing her if she's already left the building.

Charlie and I rush out of the room, with Mrs. Opal yelling at us to slow down.

We race to the teacher's exit and burst outside.

Statten is halfway across the parking lot.

"Ms. Statten? Ms. Statten!" I call out, and as soon as she turns and sees us, her face falls, and we know she's figured out that we've made the connection.

Statten's leaning against her cherry Mini Cooper. Our very presence seems to have kicked the shit out of her; she seems sapped of her confidence.

I feel horrible, but I've got to have answers.

"Why didn't you tell us the truth?" I ask.

It always feels weird demanding answers from an adult, especially a teacher I've sincerely liked over the years. It's a real shift in the dynamics of the relationship and, once crossed, I know we're never going back.

"I don't know. I hoped, maybe, that if I didn't say anything, it would just go away—"

I can see by her grim expression that even she didn't believe this naive thought.

"I knew there was gossip, that people had their suspicions of what was going on. But since none of it was true, I hoped it would eventually blow over." Her face is pained, her arms crossed. She could do a whole psych class on this moment alone.

"Will you tell us what really happened?" I ask.

She shifts against the car, looking up into the sky. It's another warm day. In a couple of weeks, the trees will start budding and spring will be in full swing. I think Statten would like to skip ahead to that moment and avoid all this.

"Tom—Mr. Harriet—and I were friends." She pauses before quickly adding, "But not anymore." The notion seems to upset her.

"Only friends?"

Another troubled look clouds her brow, and she nods.

"What happened?" Charlie asks.

"We started teaching here the same year. Both new, both having taught for only a couple of years. We turned to each other for support, for encouragement."

"Nothing else?"

Statten shakes her head, but it's wistful. "No. He was married. Carol, his wife, was wonderful. Caring, supportive. They met at university, in the education program."

"So she's a teacher too?" I ask.

"Over at Cornwall High."

Charlie asks, "Are they both from here?"

Statten shakes her head. "Not originally. She's from Winnipeg and he grew up on a small farm north of the city."

"Did you know her well?" Charlie inquires.

What's he getting at?

She smiles, reflecting fondly. "The three of us would get together on weekends and drink wine and tell stories. There was never any animosity between us." Statten shakes her head. "Carol even tried to set me up a couple of times, usually with another teacher, but it never worked out. Half the men out there have so much baggage there's no room for a relationship."

"But it was Carol who did the matchmaking?" Charlie pries. "Tom didn't try to set you up?"

Statten's tone is biting. "No, *Mr. Harriet* didn't." Her face softens as she pauses.

I urge her to keep going. "It became obvious he was interested in you, didn't it?"

She nods. "He'd come by my classroom, and we'd visit over spares or lunches, or we'd stay around late, chatting after school. It never crossed my mind—"

"Did he ever try anything?"

She shakes her head again. "No, I never realized any of it until after his divorce."

I feel like she's still not telling us something.

"Were *you* ever interested in *him*?" I ask.

"No—not really," she amends. Thinking about it seems to frustrate her. "I don't think so. Maybe I wondered. But he was married."

"So if nothing happened, why deny the friendship?"

Statten's struggling with something deep, scrutinizing us.

"Did he do something?" I'm really pushing now, but I have to.

She begins to shake her head, letting out a short, sharp laugh. "When I first moved here, I had an apartment downtown. It was a crappy place. There were always incidents. Cars broken into, strangers being buzzed in that weren't supposed to be."

Having taken advantage of this tactic ourselves, I glance at Charlie. He ignores me.

"I knew I was going to move out at some point," Statten says. "I was just trying to get settled in the city."

It hadn't occurred to me that maybe Statten isn't originally from here either.

She's still talking. "Well, eventually, I had a break-in—"

"When was this?" Charlie asks.

"About two years ago, over the summer."

"Were you home when it happened?"

"Oh God, no, thank goodness."

"Did they take anything valuable?"

"My computer, money, jewelry—" Another rueful laugh, another shake of the head. "My complete sense of security."

I get it, all too well. After last summer, I didn't feel safe for a long time. Even though we can lock the doors at night and set the alarm system, it's not enough; if someone wants to get in, they'll find a way. All that keeps a person out of your home is their own moral choice not to enter.

"Anyway, after that I asked Tom to help me out. He was handy that way. We deadbolted the door, added a safety bar, and installed a security camera." She hesitates, considering the past. "If there was a moment when our friendship truly began—and possibly an inkling of interest from him—it would have been that day."

"You grew closer after that?"

She nods. "That's when the work time visits started."

"Do you think Tom's—Mr. Harriet's wife suspected he was growing interested?" Charlie asks.

"Probably. That was about when Carol started inviting me over to the house."

"You said you aren't friends anymore. What changed?"

"You mean *who*," she says, and there's regret in her voice.

"Autumn?" I ask.

She nods. "The accusations hit, and his life went into upheaval. At the start, things were pretty damning, but it was more rumours than facts at that point. He denied everything, yet some teachers pressured the administration to fire him, and eventually he was put on paid leave until they could sort things out."

"But you said you thought there *was* something to it."

"I don't know what exactly happened with Autumn, but I tried to help. Tom and Carol were my friends, for God's sake. Then one night I got a call from Carol, accusing me of sleeping with her husband—"

"Why do you think she did that?" Charlie asks.

I answer with a question, "Autumn again?"

Statten nods. "It seemed the most reasonable possibility. She was stirring up so much trouble during that time. It was like she intended to leave nothing but scorched earth when she was finished with him."

"Why do you think—?" I start to ask.

Statten cuts me off. "Because I think it was true."

"He actually *did* text her?" Charlie asks.

"I think he did it all," she answers. "I think he slept with her. I think they had a relationship, and that he thought he could keep it all quiet and hidden."

"But he didn't know he was playing with the devil," I say.

She agrees, adding, "He was his own worst enemy, though, and Carol used it against him. Credit card bills showing up with mysterious charges. Strange texts to his cell. There were just too many things coming up through the cracks."

She pinches the bridge of her nose and drops her head. She's been holding it in for so long and now she's letting it all out. "People abandoned him. Teachers steered clear. He was always in a miserable mood. Suspicious of everyone."

"Why?"

"Always said none of it was his fault. His anger grew—"

"At who?"

"Everyone. The administration. The women in his life. He didn't trust anyone. He wanted recompense, reparation for everything that had been done to him."

"Revenge?" I ask.

She nods once more, and we stand there in silence. It sounds like we might know who to blame. Not all the pieces fit, but we've at least got the edges of the picture in place.

I think we're done, but Charlie isn't quite finished. "You're still not telling us something."

I look between him and Statten, and it isn't until she sighs that I realize he's right.

"After Carol left, I tried to be there for him. A shoulder to cry on. I tried to do the right thing."

"He wanted more, but you weren't interested."

"The friend I had known was *gone*," she says, with exasperation and regret. "He was an angry, bitter man."

"Something happened," Charlie states. It's not a question. "He did something."

"Once, while we were still close." Her whole body pulls tight at the thought. "I said no. He got aggressive..."

"Did he hurt you?" I ask.

"No," she says quickly, then rethinks it. "Almost."

"Was that the end of it?"

She shakes her head. "It was for me, but not for him. He started following me. Showing up where he shouldn't be."

"You had another break-in," Charlie says, and I look at him, confused.

What's he talking about?

Statten, however, simply answers the question. "The second time was in the fall."

"But you were home this time?"

She nods again. She's exhausted. Our questions have taken everything out of her.

"Was it him?"

"I don't know," she says quietly. "He wore a mask. He seemed taller, but I was terrified. I'll never know…"

"What happened?"

"Charlie, stop."

"Did he hurt you?" he persists.

"Enough," I say.

He glares at me, then changes tack. "Do you think Harriet hurt Mike?"

She considers. "I suppose it's possible."

"Then why haven't you said anything?"

"After the last break-in, I moved. Nice place. Anonymous. Underground parking. Security guard at the door. Ridiculously unaffordable on a teacher's salary."

"But it's safe," I put in.

She forces a smile. "I still don't sleep much without a sedative." She pulls out her keys and unlocks the car door, only to turn back. "If you do find out it's him, be careful. Call the cops. Don't try anything on your own." She gets into the driver's seat. "But if it is him, stop that son of a bitch."

chapter 107

Statten drives away, and we go back into the school.

I look at my phone. "Dad'll be here in ten minutes."

"Perfect."

The school is almost empty. There are a few stragglers standing in the hallway talking or searching through their lockers for missing homework. We can hear the girls' volleyball team running laps in the gym, and the band warming up for musical theatre rehearsal in the concert room.

"Where are we going?"

"One last stop."

I follow Charlie to the far back corner of the school, past the library and the home economics labs. Charlie takes a left and arrives at Mr. Cerva's art room.

"What are we doing here?"

Charlie pulls out a ring of keys.

I can't believe it. "You've already lifted these off a teacher?"

"Actually, I only need one, and I borrowed it from the maintenance office."

"Doesn't matter—!" I'm about to lose it, but he shushes me and opens the door.

We step inside.

"And we're here because…?" I ask again.

The whole place smells of turpentine and clay. Paintings dry on desks. Most of them are ugly blobs of colour, but there's the occasional promise of a budding artist.

"First, Cerva's never around after school. He's usually one of the first teachers out of here."

Charlie leads me to a separate office tucked in at the back of the art room. It too is locked, but it seems Charlie's stolen a master key.

"Second, Cerva's office provides perfect cover from prying eyes." He takes a seat at the desk. "Not that it matters, because the maintenance guy in charge of this area is lazy and often skips this room." He smiles. "Dude's totally going to get fired."

Charlie opens up the computer on the desk and starts typing away. "And third, I figured out five of the teachers' logins by the second day I was here." The screen *bleeps* and shows a window of admin folders. "Including the principal's, Mrs. Johnson."

I can't believe what I'm seeing. Every record and interaction between Mrs. Johnson and the school's teachers, including salaries, performance reviews, and private correspondence.

"Uh? What happened to you behaving yourself?"

"What can I say? You can't teach an old dog new tricks?"

The mouse hovers over a file marked "Grades."

"You want a better mark in any of your classes?" he jokes.

At least, I hope he's joking; I don't doubt he could do it. "What are you looking for?"

Charlie scrolls through the files until he finds Harriet's name. He clicks and the screen fills with Harriet's image, most likely taken for his identification card.

"Always good to have a face to the name," Charlie says.

I forgot that he had no clue what Harriet looked like.

"Born in '83. Huh, he's an Aries. And look at that, he lives only a few blocks from us." He moves to a tab marked "Confidential." A long list of communication fills the screen. "Yikes," he says. "I figured it would be bad, but man, oh, man."

Every meeting, inquiry, and email is listed, and the subject lines alone are pretty damning. Words like *intimidation, harassment, bullying,* and *cease and desist* appear repeatedly.

Charlie scrolls down to the bottom of a page of reports. The first entries seem normal, but then we get to two years ago, and the first mention of Autumn shows up. It's innocuous to begin with, a request for a meeting, then it slowly escalates and the first mention of a hearing appears.

Something catches my eye. "Can you scroll back?"

Charlie moves down the page, and on the first entry is a familiar name: Rudy Hopper.

"Aha!" he exclaims.

"Our second victim," I say. "*That's* why I recognized his name. He went to our school!"

Charlie opens the file. "He and Harriet got into a fight over extracurricular activities. He wanted out of class early, but Harriet wanted him to stay to do overdue homework. He also said Rudy didn't have a signed permission slip to leave early. It was eventually resolved when Mrs. Birch gave permission."

"Birch teaches band."

Charlie nods and reads on. "Seems like things came to a head when Rudy, who clearly didn't like being told what to do, called Harriet a 'three-inch man' and said he was 'ugly and venomous like a toad.'"

"Wow, Rudy certainly had a way with the insults."

"Sounds like someone who read a little too much," Charlie says.

I laugh out loud that he, of all people, would accuse someone of that.

"Harriet freaked, threw a three-hole punch at him, and Rudy reported him."

"Harriet seems to have some anger management issues," I say.

"And Rudy's only the start. There's a couple more incidents in here." Charlie goes back to the top of the page and types in "Tyson Martz," the name of the other victim.

Nothing.

"Damn," Charlie says. "I was hoping we'd find some commonality."

"Like that they're all former students of Harriet's?" I ask.

He nods, then adds, "But it feels like there's more to it than just that."

"I can't believe I'm about to suggest this—"

"Are you thinking we should take a walk in his neighbourhood?" Charlie asks, scrolling back to Harriet's home address.

"Yes, I guess I am."

chapter 108

Charlie and I stay close to home for the rest of the week. There's no way we'll get out of the house and not get caught by Mom's, Dad's, or Gekas's watchful eyes, so we decide to not even try.

This does, however, give us time to strategize and consider the challenges. Harriet's a potential killer, and we don't know what to expect going into his place. We also don't know if he'll be around. From our conversations with Statten and Haley, neither of them has seen him for quite some time, but that doesn't mean he's not at home. We spend a few hours on Wednesday looking at a map app and studying the street view, but what we really need is to get on the ground and scout the place out.

I take a strategy out of Charlie's playbook to get out of the house: we spend all day, every day around my parents, driving them batshit crazy. From Monday until late Friday night, we stick to them like glue. We hang out with them every second we can. Every meal and every homework session is spent hovering in their vicinity. We talk incessantly, telling them every mundane detail of our days. Charlie even has the brilliant idea to have us argue at least once a day. We disagree over who's supposed to do chores or which movie to watch. Eventually, we get so tired of each other that some of the fights start getting a little *too* personal, but we don't care because it's all for the greater good.

By the time Saturday morning arrives, all of us are ready for a change.

"Tony? Can I trust the two of you on your own for the morning?" Mom asks me at the breakfast table.

"Where are you going? Can't we come?" I ask.

Might as well take it to the bitter end.

"No," she says, almost too quickly. "Your dad and I need some alone time. And we're just going to the farmer's market."

"What about Gekas? Won't she have something to say about that?"

"I left her a message. Unless she calls me back, we're going."

Wow, we broke Mom!

"Did I hear 'farmers' market'?" Charlie says, appearing at the bottom of the stairs.

"Not for you."

He looks disappointed, and if I didn't know better, I'd believe it.

"Fine, but do you mind picking me up some maple mustard? It'll be amazing for Mr. S.'s pork roast next week."

They seem convinced that we're not up to anything, but we continue badgering them for the next half hour. Charlie asks them to buy three more things, and I try to get their opinion on two pairs of shoes I'm genuinely interested in purchasing online. By the time they leave, I wonder if they'll come back for supper.

As soon as the door closes and we've watched them drive away, we head to our rooms. We skip showers today, and dress in jeans and T-shirts, tossing on a couple of ball caps for good measure. We head to the back door, only to find Ollie waiting patiently beside it, red leash in his mouth.

"Sorry, buddy. We can't walk you yet," I say.

He doesn't move.

In the end, I have to tell him "kennel," and he sulks away, careful to toss a dejected look my way before he lies down in his bed.

We step out the back door and go straight to the back alley.

No one's on lookout.

"I actually feel sorry for the poor cops who're now sitting outside an empty house," Charlie says.

I have to agree. They're there to keep us safe and we're ignoring their efforts.

Harriet's house is two blocks west and three blocks south. We take the back alley as far from my house as we can before cutting back across the empty street.

I'm hoping we don't accidentally run into anyone we know.

Harriet's house is on a quiet, tree-lined street. It's a two-and-a-half storey character home, grey with red trim, and there's a tall fence skirting the perimeter all the way around.

"Let's try the alley," Charlie says.

We move down the block to the end of the street and trek back down the narrow gravel lane.

"Really private people always seem to build tight, high fences, or slap a garage across their entire lot to feel super secure," Charlie observes.

"I'm guessing you'll say none of it keeps criminals out?"

"Actually, no, it does a pretty good job. Most petty thieves are looking for a quick in-and-out. The more effort required, the less interested they are. Of course, if they *really* want in—"

I realize what he's about to say. "They have perfect cover."

"Exactly. Any place can be broken into, and turning your yard into a fortress with high walls that block your neighbours' sitelines only helps hide anyone who really wants in."

We come to a grey garage with red trim matching Harriet's house. "And as luck would have it, we really want to get in."

He steps up to the garage door, pushing it on the top and bottom, and jamming his fingers beneath to give it a tug. "Pretty solid. Must have a garage door opener. That'd deter maybe half the riff-raff."

He moves to the small fence gate on the side. It's about seven feet tall and built solid. "Man, Harriet put some effort into this place." He peeks through the cracks between the wood, whistling. "Thick wood panels, double-locked gate, welded metal frame." He steps back, studying the construction. "Damn, he even put those pigeon spikes at the top to keep people from climbing."

I look up to see long sharp rods pointing from the top of the fence. "It's like he built it just to stop you," I kid.

"There's no way we're going over," Charlie says, ignoring me. "Tight-knit community. Big windows on everyone's houses. I have no clue how we're getting in."

Suddenly, I've got the solution. "Leave this one to me."

chapter 109

I convince Charlie to follow my lead, and we go back around the front and stroll up the walkway.

"Ah, the frontal assault," Charlie mumbles under his breath. "You better know what you're doing."

"Trust me. Just be ready to pop some locks."

I knock on the front door, taking the opportunity to spy through the window and study what I can of the layout. The front porch is open, clear glass windows letting the light spill inside. There's a second door into the house, but its window is frosted, and thick white curtains cover the front windows of what I'm guessing is the living room. I search for a hint of movement, waiting a few seconds before knocking again.

Nothing.

If anyone's here, there's a reason they're not answering.

Charlie and I go down the steps and follow a path around to the side, where we find another gate. And, just as I hoped, the security is more lax. It's not as tall as the alley gate, though its latch is padlocked.

Charlie already has his kit out of his backpack and nonchalantly works away at the lock while I keep watch. It takes him only seconds to get it open and we slip into the backyard, closing the gate behind us.

There are no easy access points along the side of the house. The basement windows are barred and the ones on the first floor are too high.

We go into the backyard.

"Those are some nice-looking crabs," Charlie says, nodding at the row of trees along the left side of the property. "They're called Spring Snows. They produce some really pretty white blossoms mid-season."

I glance at the trees he's pointing to, then swing my head back to look at him, raising an eyebrow. He's picking locks and talking blooms. Will I ever get used to this?

"Shut up," he retorts, though I haven't said anything.

Along the right side of the house is a low flowerbed filled with wild ferns and perennials that are starting to pop up in the fresh spring dirt, not to mention assorted weeds, some brown and dry from the fall.

"Harriet hasn't been looking after his backyard," I note.

The rest of the yard is paved in patio stones, except for a nicely built wooden deck off the back doors. A brick firepit stands in the centre, and there's a wood stump pulled up beside it.

Someone calls out, "Excuse me. Can I help you fellas?"

We turn to see an older man hovering over the fence above the flower bed. Either he's a giant or he's standing on his deck or a stepladder. However he's doing it, he's got a clear view of everything going on in his neighbour's backyard.

"Go work on the door," I whisper, and Charlie gives me a look like *Are you crazy?*

"I got this," I whisper.

"Hey there," I say, turning to the man, trying to sound as ordinary as I can. I walk over and reach up to offer my hand. "My name's Anthony Shepherd."

Charlie might be critical of the use of my real name, but it's got to be better than flubbing my way through some made-up one.

I dig into my wallet and pull out one of the business cards that Irene's given me to sell their services. "I work for Two Ladies and Your Lawn. We do house-watching and maintenance for homes. Just checking in on one of our clients."

The old guy takes the card and scrutinizes it.

I force myself to stop talking—as Charlie says, less is more.

The guy looks at me, then Charlie, then the card, then back to me. He's already made up his mind about us, and now we just have to wait and find out what he's going to do.

"And you say you work for the fella that lives here?"

"Well, I work for the house maintenance company, but, yes, he hired their service," I lie.

He flips the card over, like he expects it to tell him whether or not to believe me, before studying the phone number again. "And what'd you say your name was?"

"Anthony Shepherd."

The neighbour seems satisfied, and I think we're all good, but he pauses. "I suppose you won't mind if I give this number a call and ask about you?"

Shit.

"Sure, no problem. Better safe rather than sorry, right?" I say, forcing a smile that I think will tear my cheek muscles, I'm straining so hard. "Be sure to ask for Barb or Irene."

The old guy nods, and I think he's going inside to call when he looks at me. "You mind if I ask you another question?"

"Sure!" I say as cheerfully as I can, feeling the sweat roll down my back despite the spring breeze.

He pauses for a moment and I expect the worst. "Do you know if the fella here is okay?"

Not what I expected. "What do you mean?" I ask.

"Well, the way he's been— Well, he's been acting a tad worrisome."

I really wish I didn't have to dig so hard to get answers. "Oh?"

"Putting the house on the market, then off the market, then sitting back here and burning stuff—"

"Burning stuff?" I look over my shoulder at the firepit and that lone stump of a seat.

"Hell, he gets the fire right hot. Flames shooting high as a man."

What are you burning, Harriet?

The neighbour is staring at me, wanting some sort of reassurance about me and my so-called client.

"Well, you know, what with the divorce...," I say, hoping that's enough, but by the look on this guy's face, it isn't.

I continue, "He's been taking things pretty rough."

That's one way to describe it.

The old guy's nodding like he's starting to believe what this teenager is telling him.

"Well, yup, I s'pose so, poor fella. Hope he sorts things out."

He gives a wave and disappears into his house.

I hurry back to Charlie. "Please tell me you've got it open."

"For a little while now. That was your big plan? Draw attention to us and give out your real name?"

"It didn't quite go as I thought. Don't give me a hard time."

Charlie smiles. "Quit worrying. Without busting a window, that was probably the best way to do it. Do you think the ladies will vouch for you?"

"No clue. I'm hoping we can get out of here before we find out."

"Ask forgiveness later?"

"Yup," I nod.

"Boy, Shepherd. I really *am* a bad influence on you."

"Yes," I agree. "You are."

chapter 110

We step quietly into the dining room of Harriet's house and wait patiently, listening for any movement. When we don't hear anything, we move into the kitchen. There's a bare white fridge, a lone microwave, sterile surfaces everywhere. There's almost no sign of life except for a bowl of old apples.

"Feels like no one lives here," I whisper.

Charlie nods, opening the cupboard under the sink. Inside are a ton of cleaning supplies and bleach.

"Could be our guy."

He opens the garbage and lifts out a take-out container, giving it a sniff. "And he likes Chinese."

I walk into the hallway that leads to the stairs. No pictures or decorations, except for a large mirrored wardrobe.

"Do you mind if we deal with the creepy, psycho basement first?" Charlie asks, nodding at the doorway under the stairs.

"Absolutely," I say. "Lead the way."

He shakes his head, annoyed. "Fine, but you get the upstairs."

"Deal."

He pushes open the door and looks into the darkness. A window offers a bit of illumination somewhere in the back. He hits a light switch beside him and it burns bright, then overheats and shorts out.

"You've gotta be shitting me," Charlie grumbles.

"Go on."

"All right already, just don't rush me."

He takes the first step down and peers over the edge of the stair. "Oh, great. The stairwell's open to the back so someone can grab my legs and yank me ass over teakettle."

"Seriously?"

"Hey, you don't get good at noticing things without being a little paranoid."

"But ass over teakettle?"

"What can I say? I'm an old soul!" he protests.

We get to the bottom in one piece.

The basement is a little underwhelming. A few cans of white paint under the stairs, a "for sale by owner" sign leaning against the wall, but not much for hiding places except for a big old freezer sitting in the back corner.

"Nothing suspicious about that! Who's opening it?" Charlie asks, searching for a light but finding nothing.

"Why're you asking me? I'm in charge of the second floor," I respond.

"Fine, but that's the last veto you get to exercise." He pulls out his phone and turns on the flashlight. "If you see anything, you kick its ass," he says, looking over his shoulder.

He crosses the basement, flashlight waving back and forth, the teleposts and an old brick chimney casting long, sweeping shadows over cracked walls and dusty corners.

"Man, it stinks over here."

"Like what? Something dead?" Sadly, I've had more than enough experience to know what that smells like.

"No, like a musty mould. Floor's probably leaking like a sieve from groundwater."

He approaches the freezer. "It's not plugged in. If anything's in it…" He doesn't finish his statement but grabs hold of the handle. "Well, here goes nothing," he says, taking a big breath and yanking it open.

"Well?" I demand. I'm not interested in going over there until I know things are fine.

He doesn't seem horrified or repulsed. Just sort of sad.

"What's wrong? What's in there?"

He reaches in and pulls out a big pail of ice cream. "By the looks of it, I think it went from solid to liquid and back to solid." He shines the light up to it. "Also, it says it's vanilla, but I see green."

"Don't open it," I plead.

"You sure?" he jokes. "We could take it home for dessert tonight."

"Put it down."

He drops it back in the freezer carelessly and cries out, "Shit! It cracked open!"

"What?" I yell, and am immediately hit by the foulest of stenches. "Shut the freezer, shut the freezer," I cry out, trying not to vomit.

He drops the lid on the appliance and scoots back to me. We race up the stairs.

"Oh *man*, that was gross," he says, gagging.

"Of all the crap you've subjected my senses to, who'd've thought a pail of ice cream would nearly kill us," I laugh.

He shakes his head and crosses into the living room, trying to get his breath. I follow him in and look around.

A leather couch and chair sit around a coffee table atop a dark red-and-yellow patterned rug. A television rests against one wall; it's not even plugged into an outlet. A thick coat of dust covers everything.

"There's no way anyone lives here," I say, looking up to the second floor, listening.

"We're so noisy, I don't think there's much surprise left," Charlie agrees. "But you're still going up first."

"Fine."

I climb the creaky stairs, and he hisses, "Doesn't mean you can't be a little quieter."

I glare at him. "And how the hell am I supposed to do *that*?"

He shrugs. "Skip the noisy ones?"

I shake my head and continue my squeaky way to the top to find four closed doors.

Charlie's close behind, and I know he's alert and got my back, so I open the first one to discover a master bedroom that stretches the entire width of the house. Although the bed is made, the top sheets are shuffled about.

"Someone's slept here," Charlie says.

I check the closet. A suitcase lies open, men's clothing inside.

"Whoever's staying here is ready to leave in a hurry—"

"Or just got back from somewhere warm," Charlie adds, nodding at a cool, lightweight cotton shirt.

We exit and move to the next room. It's empty except for a pullout futon and a dresser.

Charlie slides open a drawer and finds it bare.

"Guest room?" I guess, and I can tell from Charlie's look that he has no more clue than I do.

We continue on and find the bathroom. A toothbrush, a tube of toothpaste, and an electric razor in a travel case on the counter. There's a bar of soap beside the sink.

"Whoever's here is travelling light," I say. "There's not even shampoo."

Charlie studies the toothbrush and soap carefully. "But it's got that cracked, dry look, like it hasn't been used in forever," he notes.

We open the final door and find a room filled with moving boxes. I check the writing on them. "This one is 'T–Bedroom.' And this one is 'T–Office.'"

"The neighbour said the house was on the market, then they took it off. Maybe they divided up their stuff after the divorce?" I propose. "Carol took hers and he was going to wait for the place to sell?"

Charlie shakes his head. "And then he backed out? Why?"

We stand at the base of a final set of carpeted stairs. It goes halfway up then bends around so we can't see the top floor.

"Your turn," I say.

He shakes his head. "There'll be one of those giant head-chopping blades up there, right? I'll have to duck, won't I?"

"Absolutely," I say laughing. "Because that's what a biology teacher installs in his middle-class home."

He scales the steps and peers around the edge before taking the rest of the stairs two at a time. His severed head doesn't come bouncing down toward me, so I follow him up.

He's standing in a carpeted attic that's been refinished as an open space. There's a window at each end; both are open. A set of weights and a rowing machine face one wall, and on the other side of the room is an office, with two sets of shelves full of books.

I walk over and study them. "Science, history, some astronomy, some biology. Definitely seems like they're Harriet's."

"But why are the books the only thing that feels like he's been here recently? Why does it feel like he's some transient?" Charlie asks, and I shake my head, not knowing.

"There's nothing here," I say. "Just a big, empty house."

"And no answers."

I stare at the room, considering. I study the low roof, the freshly painted walls, the office space.

Nothing.

Then I notice the vacuum paths in the carpet. Whoever lives here is keeping this room clean. Or is hiding something.

I move to the first bookshelf and look behind it.

"What's up?" Charlie asks.

"Can you help me with this?" I ask.

Together, we pull the first bookshelf away. The carpet catches the bottom, making it difficult to move with ease, but we pull it forward far enough.

"What's that?" Charlie asks, staring at the edge of a doorframe sticking out from behind the second shelf.

"Help me with the other one," I say.

We drag it back to reveal a small door.

"It's a crawlspace."

I unhook the latch and open it. Warm air floats against my face.

"Why's it so toasty in there?"

I pull out my phone and shine the light. "It's insulated, but the heat from the sun still gets in and warms the space up," I say.

He's staring at me, wondering how I know this.

"Mike's old house had something like this," I tell him. "We used to play hide-and-seek, and I hid in there once behind an old Christmas tree. He never found me. It was the middle of summer, and when I crawled out an hour later, I was soaked with sweat, dizzy and dehydrated. My folks said if I'd stayed in there much longer, I could've have passed out and—" I realize where the story is going, realize I'm talking about Mike, and stop myself. "Anyway, not a place you want to be."

Charlie's staring at me.

"What?"

"It's your turn," he grins.

I shine my light back inside the hole.

"Sorry, man. It's the only place we haven't looked, and you agreed to no more veto powers."

I sigh. He's got me.

"Don't worry, man," Charlie says encouragingly. "I've got your back."

chapter 111

I climb into the hole. Spray foam insulation covers every-thing: the roof, the wall, and the floor. It sticks to my jeans and T-shirt, and as soon as I start crawling, I can feel it dig into my palms. It's dry, and I can't shake the thought of in-haling the tiny fibres that float in the air. I try to pull my shirt up to cover my nose and mouth, but after crawling a few inches, it slips off.

I shine the light ahead and see an obstruction about half-way down.

"How's it going in there?" Charlie calls.

I grunt a response. I'm not in the mood for talking. And who knows what I'm inhaling. I try to keep my breaths shal-low. I've already started to sweat and it's dripping into my eyes, soaking into my shirt.

"What do you see?"

"Something's in my way," I yell back.

"Like storage boxes?"

"No. Like a wall."

"It's probably the stairwell. Can you get past it?" he asks.

I'm still a few feet away so I can't be certain, but I shout back, "I think there's room."

I shine the phone light at it when I'm closer. Although it'll be a tight squeeze for a tall, gangly person like me, I can get through.

The light catches something behind it.

"Charlie," I say, breathless, "there's a cage back here."

"*What*?" he says.

I'm in so deep that the insulation muffles my voice. I yell again. "There's bars. Like a jail."

No matter what, I have to make sure there's no one in there. I shine the light toward the back of the cage.

"Tony—?" Charlie's crawled in a little way to hear me better.

"There's no one in here," I call back.

Charlie's quiet for a moment. I don't know what he's thinking—what he's expecting—but my answer seems to have satisfied him.

I need to take a closer look, so I wiggle through the gap between the stairs and the roof. I'm in so tight, I can barely move. I don't have claustrophobia, but if I can't get out of here, I sure as hell *will* get it really damn quick.

I shine the light around. The space is about six feet long. You couldn't stand in it, but could sit or lie down. Thick lengths of two-by-six wood have been fastened into place over the roof and walls with large metal screws drilled hastily into place. Wire mesh covers the other wall, and I realize there must be a false wall on the other side of the carpeted attic to hide this horror.

That's when I see the wrist irons on chains fastened to the wall at the end.

And something else lying against it.

I have to crawl all the way inside the tiny compartment to get close enough. I'm overwhelmed by the strong smell of antiseptic—someone's been scrubbing the wood, and I think it's probably worse than whatever it smelled like before.

I stick my arms through the bars and reach for what looks like a billfold or wallet wedged into a crack between the roof and the floor.

I've got my whole arm in, my shoulder pressed so hard against the rough metal bars that it hurts like hell. If I can't reach it now, I've already decided to bust open the wall and rip apart the mesh cage to get at it.

My anxiety is rising and my stomach's in knots because I think I already know what it is, but I keep stretching until my fingers catch the smooth black leather surface, the finely stitched corner, and I pull it back. It opens, and I recognize the ID inside.

It's the absolutely worst thing I could've imagined.

I'm dizzy, struggling to push my way out of this deep, dark hole. It's all I can do to yell. "Charlie! He's got her. Harriet's got Gekas. That asshole's got Gekas!"

chapter 112

Jack races down the highway, car-top down. The air is brisk around him, but the sun is warm against his smiling face.

He's never felt such freedom.

Since releasing himself of the lunar pull, of the wait for the ritual to begin, he's come into his full power; he is free now to choose who and when. Before, he believed the moon had given him strength, had dictated his fate; now he knows it was a burden holding him back, the ritual nothing more than a self-imposed stricture. He'd been capable of so much more.

He feels a ferocity of passion, not just now, in this moment, but for the time to come. He can envision a future of her and him, of killing, that he once could never have imagined.

But he must do things right if he is to achieve his goals.

The boys will be coming soon. They triggered the motion alarm at the house; he's seen them on the security camera. They've seen his work and they'll put the pieces together quickly. They may already be on their way.

If he does things right, the trap will be sprung. He will kill the impostor and the boys, and put an end to the harm they've caused. And once it is finished, she'll finally be whole and strong again.

And then he can kill.

Again and again and again.

part 4

I push myself back through the partition and twist around to get out of the crawl space. I'm still yelling at Charlie when I see his head pop through the hole.

"He's taken Gekas." I say, throwing her police ID toward him.

I push past him and land on the floor, soaked in sweat and covered in filth. I drag myself to the window and take in fresh breaths of spring air.

"What was in there?"

"A cage, way at the back." I gesture to the other side of the room. "There's likely a false wall or something."

Charlie's on his feet and across the room, searching along the drywall. "I don't see anything—" He gives a swift kick with his shoe and cracks the wall, and it doesn't even faze me. He drops down and tears it away.

"What the hell, dude?" he yells as the mesh enclosure is revealed.

When I can breathe again, I crawl over to him. "He must've covered the whole thing up—" I start to say.

"But why? Because of *us*?" Charlie interrupts. "Who's he trying to hide it from?"

I look at Charlie. "Maybe he's never coming back. Maybe he's moved on."

"But why?" Charlie asks again.

His question irritates me and I yell, "I don't know!"

I have to take another breath, and Charlie stares again at the cage and the hole he's made in the wall.

"Okay, let's think this through," he says. He leans in and studies the wall more carefully, giving it a sniff. "The paint is fresh. Probably just dried the other day. That's why he's kept the windows open."

I work to get into his headspace. "So he's trying to cover his tracks. Maybe he really isn't planning on coming back."

"He seems to have known that we went into his condo—"

"How? Because of Mike? You said—"

"I know what I said," Charlie growls. "We're not responsible for his actions. But if he knows we went into the condo, he must've figured we'd show up here too."

"And why haven't we heard about Gekas on the news?" I ask, and Charlie grabs his phone and scrolls through various social media feeds.

"Nothing. No one's mentioned a damn thing."

"So either she's not really missing or no one knows yet," I say, and pull out my phone. I scroll through contacts and bring up Gekas's office number. I call it.

It rings until her voicemail picks up.

I don't leave a message.

"Try her cell," Charlie says.

I dial it and immediately hear, *The caller is temporarily unavailable…* I hang up.

"She could be travelling—"

"Or out of the service area."

Now Charlie's dialing a number.

"Who are you calling?" I ask.

"Her boyfriend."

"Spencer? How do you have his number?" I've got a dozen questions and concerns about what Charlie's doing.

But his rationale is simple. "He's dating Gekas. You can be damn sure I'm going to check on him," he says.

Huh. I've never known him to feel protective about many people, especially a cop—*especially* Gekas. I want to say something, but this is not the time.

"What are you planning to say?" I ask.

"Nothing," he says, flipping on the speaker phone and handing the phone to me.

Dammit, Charlie!

The other end of the line clicks. "Hello?"

My brain scurries to figure out what to say. "Hello, is this Spencer?"

"Speaking. Who is this?"

I expect shit's going to hit the fan as soon as I say my name, but I do it anyway. "Anthony Shepherd."

There's a long pause. "Anthony Shepherd? Ah, yes." Another pause. "Why are you calling, Anthony?"

Definitely not what I was anticipating. As long as I keep things natural, this might go okay. "Uh. Just wondering if you've talked to Detective—to, uh, Maggie lately?"

"She told me she'd be out of town for a little while."

"Oh."

Charlie grabs the phone out of my hand, covering the mouthpiece. "Don't sound so desperate," he hisses.

"Hello? Anthony?" Spencer says.

"Sorry about that. The phone slipped out of my hand." I say, though I'm not sure he believes me. "Do you know when she'll be back?"

"Not exactly. Anything I can pass on to her for you?"

"I, uh, have some information—"

Charlie punches me in the arm and I wince, struggling to hold back the pain.

"I see. Anything I can help with?"

"No, no," I answer, feeling cornered.

I try to run the different scenarios in my head. If I tell him what we think is happening, it could create unnecessary worry. It's all speculation at this point, and I can't even imagine all the trouble we'll be in if we're wrong. But if Gekas *is* in trouble, we need people looking for her—

Finally I say, "Nothing's wrong. I just wasn't able to reach her. I was hoping she might be with you."

He's not convinced. "Anthony, I don't really know you, but whatever you're up to, I'm sure Maggie would likely tell you to stop and let her do her job."

I'm pretty sure she would too—if I didn't think she was already in trouble. "Okay. Thanks anyway," I say, before hanging up.

Charlie stares at me, anxious to know what was said.

I stare back at him. "We need to find Gekas."

chapter 114

Charlie heads for the stairs, but I don't move.

"Come on, Shepherd. We've got to go."

"Wait."

"What? Why? Harriet might not be here, but pretty soon that neighbour's going to realize we're breaking and entering."

I ignore Charlie, though. Until we know where to find Gekas and Harriet, we really have no direction.

"Is there any way to track Gekas's phone?" I ask.

"Nothing I can do now. I tried getting into her phone a long time ago, but she was too crafty for me." His hint of admiration makes me smile.

"If we tell the cops, can they do anything?"

He considers. "They might be able to see where her phone last contacted cell towers. They've probably also LoJacked her car, so they could track her with that."

"And we could warn them with an anonymous call?" I'm still worrying about the consequences if we're wrong. Not only will we be in a heap of shit, but Charlie would probably get booted to some juvenile facility. But neither do I want Gekas's life in only our hands. The more people looking for her, the better.

"I know a good payphone. No cameras around or anything," Charlie says.

"Okay. Anything else we can do?"

Charlie runs a hand through his mop of hair. "Let's flip this. What do we know about Harriet?"

"Besides that he's a psycho stalker, kidnapper, and possibly ruthless killer?"

"Yeah, besides that."

I scan the room, looking at the bookshelves. "He teaches—" I catch myself "—*taught* biology..."

"After we're done with him, he's not going to be doing much of anything anymore," Charlie murmurs.

I try to ignore that and keep listing what we know. "He seems to like the sciences. He's divorced."

"His wife is from Winnipeg," Charlie adds.

"And he's from...," I trail off, heading for the desk.

"What?" Charlie demands.

"Statten said he's from a farm north of the city," I say, pulling open drawers only to find them empty. I race down to the second floor and into the room with the moving boxes.

Charlie appears at the door behind me.

"If you were hiding or on the run," I ask him, "where would it be your first instinct to go?"

"Shit," he says, realizing, crossing to a second box and tearing off the lid. "Home."

"Look for anything. Pictures, ID," I say.

"You find me a relative's name—parent or grandparent—

and I can track down an address for you," Charlie says, grinning. "I can get access to every land title, every owner. Even if he tried to change the name on it, I can tell you any property owner all the way back to 1884, and whether they still owe money on it."

I shake my head. "Seriously, how did you survive without the internet last summer?" Despite the seriousness of the moment, Charlie's dependence on all things technological amuses me.

He ignores my question, though, and pulls out a thick folder full of bills. He's flipping through it when he exclaims, "Man, *that* explains how he paid for the condo."

He shows me a stack of credit card bills. Every one of them is maxed out and months behind. Mixed in with them are notices from collection agencies.

"He must've applied for every loan he could find and just kept borrowing. Aw, hell..."

"What?

He hands over a bank document.

"What's this? A loan agreement?" I ask.

"Look at the name of the bank officer."

I flip through the pages and scan to the bottom. "Aw, hell...," I say too.

The bank signatory is Paul Gulley.

"Victim number one?" I ask.

Charlie nods.

"So, the first guy is the bank officer that gives Harriet a—" I turn to the front of the document, "wow, a fifty-grand loan, which Harriet then doesn't repay."

"Then he kills a student he got into an altercation with—"

"But he taught Rudy years ago—"

"Maybe he held a grudge. Doesn't matter. Harriet's connected to both of them."

"What about the third victim?" I ask.

"Who knows? Maybe he went on a date with Harriet's ex. Whatever, we've got a pattern forming: revenge."

"Which maybe explains the others, but what about Mike?"

"Maybe they had a run-in. Maybe Mike rubbed him the wrong way—"

"Or maybe he went after Mike to threaten *us*."

Charlie quickly dismisses this. "Doesn't matter. He chose to do it."

"And now he's got Gekas, the lead detective on his case."

"No better motive than that."

I continue to dig into the boxful of loose items, finding old computer equipment—a keyboard, a mouse, and a rat's nest of cables. Beneath it are several old wristwatches and an old wallet. I open it to find an expired driver's license, along with a social insurance card, and an old credit card.

"I think I have something," I say, handing over the ID.

"Elias Harriet. Born 1931."

"Harriet's father, maybe?"

"Sounds about right." He pops open his phone and starts tapping and scrolling through pages.

If Harriet has Gekas, I don't know how long he'll keep her alive. He kept his other victims for only days, a week at most, before killing them. And we don't know how long she's been missing.

Whatever Charlie discovers about Harriet's father in the next few minutes we'll need to act on immediately. There can't be any second-guessing. We might choose wrong—wrong place, wrong direction—but I'm certain that doing nothing would be the worst thing we could do.

"Got it. It's—dammit!—his farm is almost an hour and a half out of the city," Charlie says.

"If we're wrong, we risk Gekas's life, and get in a whole ton of shit—"

"And if we're right, we save Gekas, and stop the bad guy—"

"And *still* get in a whole ton of shit," I finish.

"Either way, there's no going back." He shrugs. "Your call, boss."

I don't even need to think about it. "Let's go get Dad's car."

chapter 115

We hurry downstairs, but instead of going through the back, we step out the front door to avoid Harriet's neighbour. We don't need him slowing us down. Once we're on the street, we race straight for home.

I'm hoping Mom and Dad haven't come home yet. Not only will they be pissed that we aren't obeying orders, but they'll shut down our plans completely. No taking the car, no driving out of town, no trying to find Gekas. Sure, we'll be in deep shit for everything we've done so far—Charlie will be sent away and I'll never see the light of day again—but I just hope that if they're home, we'll be able to convince them to go after Gekas. Right now, every second counts, and we still may not have enough time.

We arrive at the house, and thankfully my parents are nowhere around. I rush in and grab Dad's car keys.

"You know there's no way we're going to get away with this, Shepherd," Charlie says, echoing my thoughts as we climb into the car. "Your parents are going to come back while we're out. We're going to bury ourselves with this."

"Since when did you become the voice of reason?"

"Since you started crossing the line," is his immediate response.

I hit the garage door button and start the car. "It's the right thing to do, and you know it."

He nods. "I do. I'm just not used to you being the one to tell me."

I slide the car into reverse and we pull onto the street.

chapter 116

Charlie guides me to a phone booth on Albert Street across from a Dairy Queen. It's an old-style one, closed in on all sides, with a door that folds open. I'm a little surprised to learn that one still exists.

"Trust me," he says, indicating the area. "Not a single camera around."

"How do you know these things?"

"A kid got cold-cocked here by a couple of thugs last spring and they took his wallet. I tried to help him out."

I feel bad. I always expect Charlie's knowledge to come from some illicit thing like a drug deal. "Did you ever figure it out?"

"Nope. Couldn't find an image of them or of the attack."

I can hear the disappointment in his tone. He'd really wanted to help.

"Anyway, go make your call. I'm going to grab us a couple of coffees and food for the road," he says, pointing at the 24-hour doughnut shop across the street.

I step inside, closing the door behind me. I don't need change, since all emergency calls are free, so I dial, and the operator picks up quickly. I give minimal information, telling the woman on the other end that it's important she contact the proper people and locate Gekas. The operator wants me to stay on the line and answer more questions, to know why I think the detective is in trouble, but all I want is to end the call and go.

When I see Charlie walking back, I stumble out a thank you, and hang up.

"All good?" Charlie asks, handing me a coffee. "Done our due diligence?"

"Good enough."

"Then let's roll."

We follow Albert Street north out of the city until it merges with Highway 6. As we leave the city limits, I feel the uncertainty of this decision weigh on me. What was it Charlie had said: No way out of this? No way to go back? As the downtown office buildings shrink in the rearview mirror, I feel quite certain he's right.

Fear rises in my gut, but I push it away.

Charlie's quiet in the passenger seat, sipping his coffee, checking his phone. He cracks open the box of doughnuts and takes an apple fritter before offering them to me.

I grab a maple.

He takes a big bite and savours the flavour. "I'm not really a fan of chain bakeries, but after being stuck in the house for as long as we have, I'm willing to take anything."

He falls silent again.

I can't stop thinking about the cage in Harriet's house.

"Harriet's a small guy," I say.

"Uh huh," Charlie answers.

I think back to Harriet's class. He always wore a suit jacket, button-down shirt, no tie. "I never thought of him as particularly strong."

"Okay." Charlie twists in his seat toward me. "So, what's on your mind?"

"Mike's a big guy—"

"Which is why he shot him in the back of the head."

The thought makes me cringe. I hate talking about my friend this way. But I need to keep working it through.

"So then what? We don't really know where he was killed—" I say.

"Correct. All we know is that it was sometime after his meeting with Autumn—which may very well have been the reason he died."

I stare down the long, straight highway, considering this.

Charlie continues, "Since we know where he ended up, you're wondering how Harriet got him there if he's too small to carry him?"

I nod.

"Could explain why Harriet finishes his victims the way he does." He takes another sip of coffee. "All of them had to be above 160 pounds. That's a lot for anyone to deal with. Maybe he needed to dismember them to move them."

Mike's one of those victims, and I struggle to keep from imagining his chopped-up body. I force the thought out of my head. I can't get emotional. I need to keep my wits and help Charlie. Gekas is our priority now.

I clear my throat. "It's messy work. Has to be lots of blood."

"Plus the privacy you'd need to do it," Charlie adds.

"Plus once in the bag, you're still dealing with the same amount of weight—"

"Well, minus about seven percent from blood loss."

I stare at him, disgusted that he knows this sort of gruesome detail.

He shrugs off my look. "So, say a 160-pound dude, that's—" he runs the math in his head, "only over ten pounds' blood loss. Not a lot of difference."

"So, he has to haul the bag the body's in to wherever he's going to dump it."

"Or use a wheelbarrow. Or take them a piece or two at a time."

All these thoughts are revolting, and I don't want to think of them in connection to Mike, so I focus on the practicality of whether Harriet could even pull it off. "And that takes him more time, with more chance of being discovered..."

"What are you getting at, Shepherd?"

"Something's not quite adding up. It still feels like we're missing something."

"We usually are," he says, matter-of-fact.

He's right. We're usually running full steam ahead with half the information, trying to dig up our answers as we go. If Gekas's life weren't at risk, I would definitely try to find out more before heading into danger.

"We're doing the right thing, aren't we?" I ask.

Charlie picks up another doughnut. "I don't know, Shepherd. But I trust your gut, and if you say this is what we've got to do, then I'm willing to follow."

I'm astonished by the compliment, and he notices.

"Aww, Shepherd, don't get all blubbery just because I said something nice."

I smile and shake my head, secretly thankful his smart-assery saves me from having to come up with a response.

chapter 118

As we dip into the river valley, Charlie grumbles, "Shit, service is getting spotty."

"How will you ever survive without the internet?" I say sarcastically.

"You can be a smartass, but I need it to direct us to the house," he says sharply.

When we come up the other side, the signal returns. Barely.

Charlie opens the glove compartment and pulls out a road map. "Good thing your dad's old-school."

He digs through the centre console and grabs a pen. Studying his phone, he starts sketching out the path to the farmhouse while giving me directions. "Turn right here and drive down this road for about ten miles."

We hit gravel, and I have to slow down a bit. It's fresh and loose and Dad's car swings and whips until I steer into the smooth-packed tracks.

"Pretty sure your dad wouldn't be happy with you totalling

his ride," Charlie says as he takes a quick snapshot of the map.

"Especially since we've broken parole and I took it without permission."

"Yeah, that too."

We drive through another valley with a creek running through it, and Charlie lifts his phone, looking for a signal. Finally he sighs and gives up. "I think that's it. All we've got now is a paper map and our wits."

I smile. "Well then, we're screwed."

Charlie grins, and turns to stare out at the curves and undulations of the countryside. "Everything around here must run into that big valley we just went through."

I look over at him.

"You know, you should study geology or geography after you graduate. Could be a career in it for you."

"Ha. Yeah, right."

"Well, you seem *reasonably* smart—" I say.

"Thank you, oh wise one."

"Seriously, though. You're good at this stuff. You must have the grades—"

"Shepherd, I'd need to graduate first, then I'd need to care about university—"

"Why wouldn't you?" I ask, incredulous.

He sighs, staring out the window. He never answers.

I push. "Charlie, why not?"

He ignores the question. "Turn right at the next road."

"Charlie—?"

"Next right, Shepherd."

He's not going to say any more and I accept that this conversation is done.

At the crossroads, I slow and take the turn, heading back toward the large river valley.

chapter 119

The wide gravel road narrows and, after the last intersection, the road turns to dirt. Charlie tells me to keep driving until we're almost on the edge of the valley.

"Slow down," Charlie mutters. "This is it."

On our left is a small wooded area. I wouldn't even think there was a farmyard in there if it weren't for the windmill poking above the tree-tops.

"Keep going. There's a road into that field on the other side of the yard," he instructs.

Makes sense. The less chance Harriet is aware of our arrival, the better.

If he's here.

I peer down the driveway as we pass it, but it's long and bends, so I'm not able to catch a glimpse of the house. I drive on and pull into the second approach. The tires sink immediately. If I don't back out now, I'm going to get stuck for sure. I put the car in reverse and pull us back out onto the main road.

"Looks a little soft. Might wreck your kicks," Charlie says.

Ruining my shoes is the least of my concerns. I grab my phone and climb out of the car. Instead of using the remote and letting it beep, I handlock the doors.

"Thought we should stay quiet," I say.

"Good idea," Charlie says, pulling the lockpick out of his backpack before tossing the bag into the backseat with a clunk. "Probably best to travel light, too."

He takes the lead, walking along the shoulder of the road. It's mucky and soft, but the deep grass holds the earth together, making for fairly easy going. As we enter the driveway, we trek along the treeline so we can scout the place out. The poplar trees lining the road are thick and wild. Fallen logs and solid underbrush make it seem menacing. Although walking through it looks impossible, a wild animal or Harriet himself could easily be lurking somewhere in its depths, waiting to pounce.

"I thought we were done with spooky woods after last summer," Charlie says.

"You and me both."

He grins. "At least you came out of it better than me."

I know he doesn't blame me for what happened, but I feel responsible.

"I really wish I knew what we're walking into," I say.

He looks at his phone. "And I really wish there was some damn cell service when we're tracking a killer."

We round the bend of the driveway and the trees open to reveal the farmyard. It's overgrown and wild; small saplings have begun to reclaim the clearing. A half-collapsed barn with white peeling paint lies in the rubble of its foundations on our left, and on the right, the windmill reaches up to the sky. One of its blades has fallen off, leaving it lopsided and useless. In the centre of the clearing is a large brick farmhouse. Caraganas sprout high along its sides. The place would look abandoned with its wild, weathered look and its boarded-up windows, if it weren't for the freshly crushed swath of grass that tracks a path toward the house.

"Somebody's been here," Charlie says.

"Fairly regularly by the looks of it."

We stay close to the trees, studying the yard.

"No good way to approach the place," Charlie says. "If someone's in there, they'll spot us."

I consider the caraganas. "Let's sneak in from the side. Maybe the bush will give us some coverage."

We track along the perimeter of the yard and flank the house.

Charlie finds an old, fallen tree, and kicks off a branch, removing its extra limbs, gripping it tightly in his fist like a club. "Just in case," he says.

As we move quietly toward the house, I realize it's less weathered and forgotten-looking than I'd first thought. Some of the windows are boarded up, but a few of them on the main floor still have glass, though they're dirty and covered by newspaper on the inside. I'm surprised to see solar panels on the roof. And there's a small shack behind the house with wires running to it, most likely housing a gas generator like I've seen at cabins at our lake.

"How much you want to bet this place is off the grid?"

Charlie nods. "And do you smell that?"

"Yup, he's been burning stuff here too."

"No vehicles around here, but—"

"We might not be alone."

We arrive at a porch that runs around the front of the house. Although the railing is dilapidated and the flooring is broken and rotten, the front door looks solid.

Charlie hands me his stick. "I'll check it. You stay here. Watch my back."

He climbs the steps, stepping on the side of each tread to avoid making too much noise. The porch is a minefield of loose boards, and he's cautious as he crosses to the door. He turns the handle and gives it a shove, but it remains firmly shut.

He moves back down to me. "Jammed tight," he whispers.

Let's go around, I signal, and we move farther along the right side of the house.

We duck to avoid being seen through any of the windows. Even though they're covered with newspaper and overgrown caraganas, someone might still be able to see us from the inside. The basement windows are also boarded up, but some small animal about the size of a fox has made a trail through the thick, low brambles and found a way inside through a broken slat along the back of the house.

"Something stinks around here, and not in an ice-cream-gone-bad sort of way," Charlie says quietly.

I agree. The stench is deep and nasty, soaked into the soil and soul of the place.

We edge around to the back until we find a second door on the far side. A padlock holds it shut. It has a small, grimy window, and I peek through a thin sliver where the newspaper doesn't quite cover.

"Could be the kitchen. I think I see a sink."

Charlie works on the lock, unclasps it, and pushes.

The heavy door sticks on the frame and the two of us work together to force it open as quietly as possible.

chapter 120

The smell is worse inside.

We creep cautiously through a small mudroom into a large kitchen. An old gas stove sits beside a counter that leads to a sink on the left. There is a row of cupboards next to a small pantry and a pale green and chrome fridge on the right. Everything has a layer of dust on it, but Charlie runs his hand along the bottom of the sink basin.

"It's been used recently," he whispers.

On the floor is a square outline in the wood with a metal ring.

"Either leads to the basement or a cold cellar," Charlie says.

"Should we look?" I ask, keeping my voice low to match his.

He shakes his head, but kneels down anyway and grabs hold of the clasp. "Get that club ready. One... Two..." On "three," he yanks it open and the stench of sweet rot rises up, followed by a flurry of fruit flies.

Holding a deep breath, I grab my phone and shine a light

down. At first, it looks like just dirt, but then I see crumbled wood and broken glass jars.

"Cold cellar," Charlie says. "What a mess. The whole thing has collapsed. The shelves must have rotted out and everything just fell." He shuts it quickly.

"It'd be nice if that's all the smell was," I say.

The stench is more pungent and meaty than can be accounted for by fermented fruit.

"Yes, it would be," he says as we weigh the options of where to go from here.

Ahead is a dimly lit dining room with an opening to the living room in one wall, and on our left is a doorway leading from the kitchen to a dark hallway.

I have the sinking feeling that we're eventually going to have to go into that darkness. Charlie must think so too, because before we leave the kitchen, he searches the drawers for a knife. He finds nothing.

I lead us into the dining room first, though, the big stick ready to swing. The table and chairs are draped with a white cloth; a tall cabinet, also covered, rests against the far wall. Dust rises into the air as I pull back the sheet on the table and look beneath. It's a solid piece of furniture, handcrafted out of two-by-fours. Well-worn, comfortable-looking chairs surround it.

"Quality craftsmanship," Charlie whispers.

Only he would comment on such a thing when our lives might be in jeopardy.

We continue into the living room, where the years have been less than kind. Maybe it was once nicely decorated, but this side of the house is away from the sun, shrouding the room in cold, menacing shadow. The floral wallpaper is faded and stained, and here and there someone has been blasting it apart with a shotgun. A rocking chair squats in the corner beside an ancient upright piano, its guts ripped out, keys and wires hanging down to where the keybed used to be. On our left is a set of double French doors, and on the right, a fireplace. Though it's no longer roaring, the ashes are still warm—probably the source of the smoke we smelled earlier.

Charlie peers into a sort of sunroom off the living room at the front of the house. A single glance is enough to see that it's completely empty, its windows covered with newspapers. He doubles back and follows me through the glass doors.

We find ourselves standing in a small room, a sort of foyer. Our eyes adjust to the gloom and we can make out a staircase going up to the second floor, dividing this part of the house front from back. On the left is another opening to the dark hallway we saw earlier. I stick my head around the corner and see the kitchen entry, as well another door at the back of the stairwell.

I suppress a shudder, imagining what's behind it, then go back to where Charlie's waiting.

The front porch is on our right, and it's clear now that, even if he'd tried, Charlie would never have gotten in. Most of the space has been filled with furniture, pushed so tight against the door it blocks the exit.

"I don't feel very welcome," Charlie says in hushed tones as he steps up to a closed door beside the staircase. He listens for a moment then moves away. "I don't want to go in there."

"Why?" I ask.

"It doesn't sound...right."

"What if it's Gekas? At least check," I whisper.

He shakes his head at my insistence but lightly raps a knuckle on the wood.

Something bangs against the door with a scurry of claws, then rushes up into the walls.

Charlie leaps back.

"I *told* you I didn't want to try," he says, shooting me a look that's easy to interpret, even in the shadows.

So we have two choices: take the stairs to the second floor, or follow the hallway back into the murk and see what's behind the door at the end. Again, it seems like a simple choice—the afternoon sunlight streaking between the boarded windows casts at least a few shards of warm light. However, as I climb the first few steps, I hear the drone of flies, and that sickly smell of rot makes me queasy.

Charlie looks down the hall to the kitchen, then back at me. "I can't believe I'm about to say this, but what do you say we get the hell out of here and call for backup?"

"What about Gekas? We're already here—and she might not be able to wait."

He shakes his head and says something that throws me off guard. "I think we're in over our heads. This whole place feels wrong. Most of the time we have some sort of odds in our favour, but we're playing on his turf here; he's got the advantage, and I don't like it."

I'm not used to cautious Charlie. His confidence has helped me deal with most of what we've been through.

If he's nervous, *I'm* nervous.

But if Gekas is here and we abandon her, I don't know that I could live with myself. Especially after Mike.

"Seriously, Shepherd. Let's pull back and wait for the cavalry to arrive."

"You're serious?"

He gives a short, sharp nod. "Let the cops deal with this. What with that smell and the cage back in the city, there's enough weirdness going on that they have enough cause to conduct a search."

There's something about the way he says this that bugs me—like maybe the cops are already on their way.

But he's right and I know he's right, and I'm about to agree when we hear the *tap tap tap* of metal against metal somewhere beneath us.

"Shit," Charlie says.

"Do you think it's Gekas?" I whisper.

He looks at me, cold. "Maybe. Does it matter?"

He's got a point. Either it's someone who needs our help or something we don't want to mess with; either way it could be dangerous.

Tap tap tap.

"Definitely sounds intentional," I say.

"So if we go find a cell signal—" Charlie's doing the math in his head "—over ten miles back, that's about twenty minutes' drive time, plus another ten to hike back to the car first."

I follow it through. "Thirty to call for help and get someone to take us seriously, another hour or so for someone to get out here."

Tap tap tap.

"I still say we go and get help," he says. "We can even come back and keep an eye on the place afterwards, if you want.

But I think it's time we split. This could be a trap; something literally doesn't smell right."

I trust Charlie's instincts. "Fine. Let's move."

Tap tap tap.

We ignore the sound and leave the foyer, crossing through to the kitchen and back into the mudroom.

My hand is on the doorknob when Charlie hisses, "Stop!"

I glare at him. "What?"

He points through the crack in the newspaper, and I see what he sees: a silver convertible, with no one inside.

chapter 122

We haven't heard any doors bang shut, so Charlie and I scuttle back to the stairs before the driver comes in.

"What do you want to do?" I ask, tightening my grip on the club. "Catch him off guard? Try and overpower him?"

"The guy uses a gun. No thanks."

I consider our options. The upstairs windows are boarded up. We might be able to crack off some boards and climb out, but we'd have to do it both without him hearing us and without breaking our legs when we jump down. Then I remember the rotten wood of the basement window outside, and the narrow path made by the fox. If we're lucky, maybe it goes all the way through—

"There could be a way out downstairs," I hiss.

We race down the dark hall to the door at its end and descend into the blackness beyond. The stench of decay is now overwhelming, and I immediately realize that we've made a terrible mistake—but there's no time to second guess ourselves.

Charlie pulls out his phone and turns the flashlight on. He swings it around to reveal we're in a long hallway with several padlocked doors on the right and one that's open a crack on the far left.

"Shepherd, which way out?" Charlie asks, and I try to orient myself in the house, doing my best to figure out where the broken wood might be.

"Down the hall," I say, hoping I'm right.

We hustle to the end of the hall and slip through the open door, shutting it as quietly as we can.

chapter 123

Charlie swoops his light around.

It's small, with an opening to another room on the left. The space is filled with junk. Stacks upon stacks of newspapers, books, and boxes line the walls. A couch and two armchairs have been pushed to one side; beside them is a large pile of paint cans and thinner.

Charlie flips open a crate full of files. "Someone's a hoarder. Looks like old journals, birthday cards, anniversary cards—" he says.

"*Shh...*," I hiss.

I climb on the couch and check the window, but it's boarded up tight. This isn't the one I'm looking for.

"Keep going," I say, urging him on.

We rush into the next room, and the beam of Charlie's phone jitters across the walls. On the left, several lengths of pipe run horizontally at different heights along one side serving as a sort of open-air closet for suits, dresses, pants— even someone's wedding dress. On the right are shelves filled with blankets, towels, and sheets, and open cupboards full of children's toys: cars, wooden blocks, construction sets, a row of books.

Charlie pushes into the musty clothing. "Think we can hide?" he whispers.

"No. We've *really* got to get the hell out of here."

No sign of a window, but there's a doorway to yet another room. The closer I get to it, the more the hairs on my neck rise. It's boarded up from the inside, except for the lowest slat, which hangs loose.

"We're like rats in a maze, heading toward the trap," Charlie says, and it feels like he might be right.

An astoundingly rancid smell hangs in the air. I force my-self closer still and gag.

"Holy moly, that's nasty!" Charlie exclaims. "We can't go in there."

"We have to," I insist, swallowing hard. "I'm pretty sure that's where the window is."

Charlie takes a deep breath and tries to look through the open hole. "I can't see anything."

I give the bottom board a swift, hard kick, and it goes spin-ning into the darkness of the next room. I try knocking the one above it off but only end up hurting my toe.

Charlie looks beneath the boards again. He's choking on the atrocious stench, but doesn't give up. He yanks his shirt up over his mouth and holds it in place with one hand. He studies the boards.

"Whoever put this wood in place meant for it to stay. There's about half a dozen screws on each side. He looks inside with his light. "I can't see a window, but there's a lot in here."

"Like what?"

"A cot, an old clawfoot tub. There's another door. Could be a closet, maybe another room—" Charlie pulls back, coughing, then spits on the dusty cement floor. "It's disgusting in there. Smells like shit and dead people. You sure this is the way?"

I trace my finger in the dust of the floor illuminated by his flashlight and recount our movements. "We came around the porch, along the right side of the house, and through the back. The hallway by the kitchen took us to the stairwell and down, so that puts us somewhere in the middle of the house. We went along the hall, turned left and then double-backed through these rooms. There can't be that much left of the house. This has to be it. The window *has* to be in there."

Charlie shakes his head, resigned to our fate. "Okay, fine, let's do this."

He takes another big breath and lunges forward. He shoves his arms in first, twisting his head sideways and pushing with his feet to get a little way into the room. To get completely through requires a lot of wriggling and grunting and struggle, and I hold onto the big stick, watching for anyone coming through from that first storage room while he works his way inside. I'm so intent on protecting our asses, I don't even notice when his feet disappear beneath the boards.

"Okay, I'm in," he says in tight, compressed breaths.

"I'm right behind you."

"Let me look around before you..." His voice falls away.

"Charlie?" I whisper.

Nothing.

I drop down and look through the gap at the bottom.

He's standing in the corner, staring into the tub. "Charlie?"

His voice rises in panic, and he's no longer conserving his breath. "Get out of here, Shepherd. Run, hide. Do whatever it takes."

"What? Why?"

"He's been killing for years."

"What do you mean?"

"Bodies, Shepherd. This place is full of bodies."

chapter 124

I don't want to leave my friend.

"Can you see the way out?"

"I don't..." Charlie no longer seems capable of thinking rationally.

I've never heard him sound like this, and it's freaking me out. "Charlie, you need to look for the window."

He drops back to the ground to look at me. "No, Shepherd, you need to go."

We're at an impasse. I want to go further—the window's *got* to be there—but he's flat-out refusing. I'm ready to drag him out of there—he's so panicked, it won't be hard—but I don't know that there's any other way to escape, except back the way we came, and if Harriet's got a gun...

"Charlie," I make my tone firm. "I'm coming in."

He appears at the opening. "No!"

"We have to—"

I can see his eyes dart back and forth, his mind racing,

trying to reason his way back to rationality. "Okay, I'll look. Let me look. But if anyone comes—"

"I'll hide," I say, nodding.

He's nodding too, as if parroting my action is all he can handle. Then he's up and gone.

I stay low, looking back to make sure no one's coming, but constantly glance under the boards, watching his light sweep around the room.

"There's no way out, Shepherd. Whatever you saw outside—this is a dead end."

That's when I see...*something* behind him: first just a grotesque silhouette, then lit for a brief flash in the light of Charlie's phone.

A leg—or what was once a leg—dangling over the edge of the bathtub. It's formless. Some of the skin is gone, some of the muscle. Hints of bone. It's red and black and white and yellow. Then I see a torso lying in another corner. There's an arm beside it, not attached to anything, and I have to close my eyes, but my brain holds onto the images and won't let go.

I realize my mistake. I never should've pushed Charlie to keep looking, I should've gotten him out of there right away so we could fight this evil together.

But it's too late now, because someone flips a breaker and the lights go on.

chapter 125

Footsteps thump down the stairs.

"Charlie, get out of there!" I hiss.

"Shepherd, go!" he grunts back.

"Not without you!"

Someone's at the door at the end of the hall.

The threat seems to focus Charlie's thinking. "Hide. Get out. Find help. Don't try to take this guy alone."

I don't have any time to argue. If he's got a gun, that's it.

"Take your stick," I say, pushing it through the hole in one quick shove, hoping it'll help if he gets a chance to use it.

I crawl to the back corner with the rack of hanging clothes, edging my way as silently as I can behind the wedding dress and musty long coats. Hopefully, Harriet won't look too carefully.

I can't see anything but listen intently to his footsteps cross the first room and pause somewhere close to me—probably in the doorway. I try to slow my breathing so he won't notice it, but I'm sure he'd hear the pounding of my heart if he paid attention, it's so loud.

Harriet isn't moving, probably trying to assess the situation before proceeding. Then he slowly enters the room, shoes scraping against the cement, small pebbles of dirt cracking under his soles.

He stops again.

It feels like he's standing there for an eternity, and I'm sweating and scared. I'm doing my best to keep my breaths steady but shallow when I realize he's left the room and is in the hallway, going back up the steps.

I climb out from behind the clothing. "Come on," I tell Charlie, urgent but quiet. "Let's get you out of there."

"And go where? He's still in the house," Charlie murmurs from the other side of the boards.

"What do you think he's doing?" I whisper. "Did you see him?"

"No, I hid," Charlie says. "But I think he was listening, trying to decide if someone's in here."

With the lights on, I can see we've left scuff marks in the dust where Charlie crawled under the boards. Harriet can't have missed it, but I keep this to myself. Telling Charlie isn't going to help.

Floorboards creak in the hallway upstairs. Harriet's on his way back down.

"I'm going to work on getting you out," I whisper at him before hurrying into the first room and ducking behind the couch. I keep as tight and low as I can, but it seems impossible to hide completely, as tall as I am.

Harriet moves past me and I don't dare look. There's a

tumble of boards striking cement, the metallic *clank* of a coffee can full of nails, and I suddenly realize he's fixing the broken board, sealing Charlie in!

Dammit!

If I'd kept the stick, I'd consider rushing him, but even then there'd be no guarantee I'd be able to overpower him.

And if he has a gun, I'd be even worse off.

The best option is to get away, and either get help or come back with something that will do a better job of kicking Harriet's ass.

When he starts hammering, I sneak out into the hallway. I go up the stairs, my movements quick and stealthy, trying to time my steps with every strike of a nail. There's only a dozen steps, so I get to the top fast.

Shit! He's locked the door at the top of the stairs!

I don't waste time and rush back down the steps, my brain all the while trying to untangle what that locked door means.

Harriet doesn't know who all is in the house. He suspects someone's in the back room that he's nailing shut, but if Charlie's hidden well enough, he can't be certain. But he must also suspect that there could be others here too, so he's being cautious.

Which means I have to remain extra alert.

Back in the hallway, there are three other doors to choose from, all padlocked—except the one closest to the stairs, whose lock hangs open. I pull it off its hasp and slip inside, shutting the door behind me.

The further I am from Harriet, the better.

chapter 126

It's dark in here. I try the switch—the bulb must be broken, so I pull out my phone and turn on the light. I regret it instantly. In an alcove in the corner of the room is a heavy wooden workbench, tools organized neatly on shelves above. The wood is stained a dark reddish-brown, and I have to quickly look away when I see what's caught between the jagged teeth of a saw. I back away, knowing what he does here, hands shaking uncontrollably.

Shit! I'm still holding the padlock!

I need to get control of myself. I need to focus. I need to solve the problem.

The rest of the room is filled with shovels, gardening tools, and sledgehammers. There are jerry cans of gas in the back corner and a closet beside the alcove.

Hurrying, I tuck the lock into the shadows behind the tools where it won't easily be found—it's the best I can do. Even if he notices it's missing from the door, I can't give Harriet the chance to shut me in too.

I think I now understand the basement's layout and open the closet, shining my light inside.

A large chunk of plaster has been smashed away, leaving lathe and boards exposed. I could probably crawl through to the room beyond. But propped in a corner is a burlap sack tied with a purple ribbon. It sits in a pool of dried blood. Something—it's way too small to be someone—is inside. I don't need to—don't want to—look, but it's like some sick test subject of what he's been leaving for Gekas to find.

Oh God. Gekas.

I've been so scared, so worried about Charlie, the thought of her possibly trapped somewhere in the depths of this hell-hole had escaped my mind. I have to help Charlie but I also have to find Gekas.

That tapping we heard earlier—she *must* be down here somewhere. We've been through one half of the basement, and if Charlie had found Gekas in that...that place, he would have said something. So the tapping *has* to have come from somewhere on this side. I need to check the other two rooms—the ones with padlocks.

I hear movement in the hall and pray that Harriet doesn't notice the missing lock as he goes past. He must be done sealing Charlie in, and for a moment I'm hopeful that my friend will be safer locked in there than in the hands of this psycho.

Harriet must be preoccupied because he climbs the stairs; I listen hard for the sound of the basement door. It opens and closes and there's the distant *click click* of the lock.

For the time being, we're alone.

I get down on my hands and knees, and shine my light

through the hole in the closet wall. I can see broken black and white tiles and realize it's an old bathroom. There's a sink with a grimy mirror beside the door, and a nasty looking toilet on the opposite side, its tank lid shattered on the floor next to it. I've already decided not to look in either of them. The room once held a bathtub, but it's been pulled out: pipes stick out of the walls. It must be the one in the room where Charlie's hiding. I can't imagine what he's going through in that nightmare of a place.

Focus. Keep looking.

Finally, I spot something. The plaster has chipped away where the tub's plumbing disappears into the wall, and I think I see a small opening. If someone's in the last room on this side, I might be able to at least talk to them.

I pull myself halfway into the bathroom, and the hem of my shirt catches on an old, rusty nail, but I don't care and let it rip. I just need to get through. I drag myself across the floor, chunks of plaster scraping the tile beneath me. I have to lift myself higher so that I can move more quietly.

Next to the pipes now, I squat low and lean over, trying to peer through the small chink in the wall.

It's pitch black. I can't see a thing.

"Hello?" I whisper tentatively.

"Who's there?" croaks a voice in the darkness.

"Shh...," I caution. "He'll hear you."

"Who are you?"

"Detective Gekas—?"

"Who...?"

I'm confused. "Who are *you*?"

"Tom Harriet."

chapter 127

I fall silent and drop back from the hole. I'm *sure* I heard Harriet going up the stairs—I'm positive. My head spins, trying to piece things together.

"Hello? Are you there?" the voice calls out. "Who are you?"

Is he messing with me? Is this a trick?

I don't say anything.

"Hello?" Harriet asks.

What's going on? It's his house; he's got all the keys. So what's with the mind games?

"Why don't you come get me?" I say, trying to keep my voice as even as possible.

A low, pitiful sob emits from the hole, and I want him to shut up. Maybe he's trying to confuse me—or Charlie and I have misread everything. And if he's *not* the guy we thought he was, then he's going to draw attention to whoever's upstairs.

"Quiet!" I hiss at the hole in the wall.

"We're going to die."

"No, we're not. But you need to shut up."

"We're going to—"

"Stop."

Harriet quits wailing, but I can still hear him sniffling.

I don't trust him, but I need information—whether he's telling the truth or not. If he's lying, he might reveal himself. If not, then I need to find out what's really going on.

"How long have you been here?"

"I—I don't know."

"If you had to guess?"

It seems his mind is a shattered, jumbled pinwheel of thoughts. "There was— He put me in a cage in my— And then—"

I consider the situation. The basement is pitch black; he has no sense of day or night. He'd sleep when he was exhausted, wake, and sleep again. Even a few days would probably disorient a person. Add to that the isolation and lack of sensory input. On any average day, I need distraction, whether from an electronic device or the world around me. Down here, he's had nothing. He's been stuck alone in his head with only his thoughts for company, his dire situation playing over and over in a loop. It would drive anyone insane.

"Who put you in here?" I ask.

I hear a cackle, but it seems to draw clarity rather than crack his sanity further. "My brother."

Brother?

Charlie and I never knew Harriet had a sibling.

He repeats, "Who are you, again? Maybe you told me— My memory— I don't... I can't..." He's quiet again.

I'm starting to believe he is who he says he is—I can't figure out what he'd be scheming at otherwise—but if I'm wrong, he'll recognize me, and I need to protect myself.

So I think fast. "Tony Wolfe," I say.

He doesn't pause or even question it. He only asks, "Tony, can you get me out of here?"

"I'm going to do my best."

chapter 128

I need answers and I need them now. The sooner I know what I'm dealing with, the sooner I can get us all out of here.

"Mr. Harriet, who's your brother?" I ask.

Again, that clear, cynical laugh. "Ha. 'Mister!' I haven't been called that in—"

"Who's your brother?" I interrupt.

"Jack—Jack Harriet."

I don't recognize the name at all. "Why's he doing this to you?"

"I think, Tony—I can call you Tony, right?"

"Yes." I wait for him to continue, but he doesn't, so I repeat the question. "Why is he—?"

"I don't know, Tony. He's— If I had to guess...I'd say he's jealous."

"Jealous?"

"Parents, Tony. Our parents."

Every time he repeats my name, he seems to find focus. I

think my name has become a lifeline out of the darkness toward sanity.

"Didn't they love him?"

"Of course they did. What parent wouldn't?"

Charlie could probably name a few.

"The trouble, Tony, is that he wanted all of it."

"He didn't want your parents to love you?"

Harriet hesitates.

I can hear him—I'm guessing he's leaning against the wall, breathing right into the hole.

"Mr. Harriet?"

"He doesn't think they're my parents."

"What do you mean?"

"I was adopted, Tony."

Is Harriet's brother so messed up that he thinks this makes a difference?

"The sad thing, Tony, is that after...everything, I was just happy to see him again."

I'm guessing he's talking about what happened with Autumn, about his divorce.

"We thought he was dead," he adds.

Harriet no longer needs prompting. He chatters continuously. After being alone so long, this opportunity to speak must feel good, like a logjam bursting open to let the river of his thoughts flow out.

"After high school, he went away to university, and we heard less and less from him. Then one day, the phone calls stopped. My parents went looking for him, but the school said he'd quit and the dorm said he'd moved out.

"My parents kept searching—they tried not to lose hope—

but as each year passed, they grew more heartbroken. It finished Dad. He went out to the barn and— And, well, Mom didn't last much longer without him."

Harriet's quiet, and I worry I'll have to prompt him again, but he takes another shaky breath and continues, keeping his voice low. "I was *so* angry at him. Our parents loved us both, tried to give to us equally. But he couldn't get past his own selfishness. And now—"

Here Harriet stops, unable to continue, because we hear his brother, Jack, coming down the stairs.

chapter 129

Jack is in the hallway, outside the door to Harriet's cell. Quietly, I grab a sharp sliver of the shattered toilet bowl lid, and tuck myself into a corner of the room.

"What's going on down here?" Jack says. His voice is deep, sonorous. It sounds familiar but the tone is icy, threatening. I can't think where I've heard it.

"Nothing," Harriet says, and relief floods me. I'd worried he'd been so far gone, he'd tell his brother I was here.

"Bullshit. Who're you talking to?"

"An angel, come to save me."

Jack's shoes scrape back and forth against the cement of the hall floor. Like me, he's probably wondering whether his brother's crazy

"Yeah? What's this angel's name?"

"It's— He's—" Harriet's memory fails him. Then he improvises. "It's the boy in the other room."

Crap.

Jack laughs, and it's cold and mean. "Oh, he's no angel."

I exhale a shaky sigh. Jack thinks he meant Charlie. Hopefully my luck will continue to hold.

"Keep quiet down here," he says, going back toward the stairs. But there are no footsteps going up.

I realize far too late that he's stepped into the workroom I've just come from.

Did I leave any sign of my presence? Any traces?

The missing lock!

I listen to him cross to the closet and scramble to remember: was it open or closed when I came into the room? And will he notice if it's different?

He walks back out of the room, and now I'm on high alert. A moment later, I hear him on the other side of the bathroom door. The length of time it takes to open the padlock is all that separates us.

I drop down and shimmy back through the hole into the workroom closet.

I hear a key scrape in the bathroom's padlock and the small *shhhck* as it pops open. I pull myself all the way back into the closet just as the door swings wide, light from the hall spilling through the hole in the closet.

I stand in the workroom breathlessly, trying to anticipate his next move. The bathroom door slams shut again and I don't delay. I climb back into the closet and push myself into the corner beside the bloody bag.

This is the worst frickin' game of hide-and-seek ever.

He returns to the workroom, ready to catch Harriet's angel. The closet door is ajar and I can see a narrow slice of the room. If I tried to peer around the door, we'd be face to face.

I don't move a muscle, hoping against hope that he doesn't search the closet.

Fortunately, he doesn't spend too long examining the room, and he steps out. Unfortunately, as soon as the door to the workroom closes, I hear the rattle and *shwick* of another padlock being fastened to the door.

I wait to hear his footsteps go up the stairs before I risk moving—but I only hear a *tap tap tap* at the door.

"Is that you, Anthony?" *Why* does Jack's voice sound so familiar? "Are you Tom's angel?"

I don't answer, hoping he'll wonder if anyone's actually here.

That hope is immediately shattered.

"No need to be shy, Anthony. I know you're in there." Then he shouts down the hall to all of us, "Don't go far, any of you. I'll be back for you all really soon."

chapter 130

Once I know Jack has gone back upstairs for sure this time, I crawl back into the bathroom to double-check the door. Yup, still locked, but a guy can hope. I need to figure a way out before he gets back.

"Hello? Who's there?" Harriet calls out again.

I crawl back to the hole.

"Tony."

"Oh, I thought—I thought I had imagined you."

"Nope, I'm real."

He's quiet for a moment. "How—how can I be sure?"

This guy is going to need a lot of therapy.

If we get out of here.

"You'll just have to trust me. Do you know what your brother has planned for us?"

"My brother—?" I certainly hope he hasn't forgotten who's locked us in here. "He says I must be punished for my sins."

"Sins? What sins?"

"I suffer from temptation. I desire. Covet."

I wonder if this has something to do with Autumn. "But did you actually *do* anything?"

"I don't— I'm not sure anymore."

Harriet's pretty fragile, but I hope he'll be able to help me figure this out.

"What do you remember?" I ask.

"There was a student..." There's another long pause, and if I could see him, I'm sure it would be obvious that he's doing his best to fit the fractured pieces together.

"Were you close?"

"I—we—talked."

"But did you like her?"

"She...was trouble."

At least he'd figured *that* out. "And that stopped you?"

"I—I spoke to her. At school— And I would see her at her job—" Then clarity comes, all at once. "They said I was texting her, Tony. Sending her pictures. Asking *her* for pictures."

"And did you?"

"No, she's a *student*..." The disconnect returns. "But she had proof. I don't remember. But I must have. And then... oh God, Tony. Carol—she left..."

As he remembers and relives every troubling moment, his voice rises in pitch. Better ease off, slow him down before he gets his brother down here again. Jack might not have been ready to deal with us a minute ago, but I'm sure not going to push our luck.

"Mr. Harriet, can I tell you something?"

"Yes?"

"I thought you were a good teacher."

He's hyperventilating, breath whistling through the hole, but he's listening. "I—I was?"

"You were. You taught me Grade 11 biology."

"I did?"

I know what the next question will be.

"What was your name again?"

I no longer need to lie. "Anthony Shepherd."

"Anthony? I—I remember—"

"I'm going to look for a way out, okay?" I say. "I'll be back."

"Promise?"

"Yes. I promise."

chapter 131

I crawl back to the workroom and consider the situation. I check my phone—it's got battery, but still no signal.

I study the workbench, thinking maybe one of these tools might help bust me out, but I'm not getting through any of these doors without a lot of noise, and none of them will be particularly helpful if I come face to face with him. You don't bring a hacksaw to a gunfight.

I need a different plan.

Across from the workbench are shelves filled with old paint cans, power cords, leftover insulation, even an old fish tank—all of which are covered in a thick layer of dust, and none of which will help. Above are the exposed beams and floor joists of the main floor, and the subfloor itself.

Basically, I'm in a box.

However, I now notice that where the wall behind the shelving meets the ceiling, there's a gap. When I stick my hand up to it, I feel a cool draft. I close my eyes, visualizing the house and how it's put together, where all the rooms are above me. The kitchen should be directly overhead—almost. This room feels like it's half the size it should be.

I push the aquarium aside and rap my fingers against the drywall until I find a thick-sounding solid section. I clear away more of the shelves, exposing a piece of wall that's all water-stained and mouldy from years of moisture.

I know exactly what's behind it: the kitchen's cold cellar—and its collapsed walls.

I push my hand against the soft plaster and it crumbles with ease. I pull and yank, and the smell of rot hits my nostrils. I nearly gag and have to take a step back to catch my breath. Still, it's got to be better than what Charlie's smelling right now, and the thought makes me move faster, pulling my shirt off and wrapping it around my face to reduce the impact of the stench.

I dig, and dirt and crumbling brick spills through the hole. It doesn't take long for me to work my way into the slick, slimy peat of vegetable matter. I have to actually climb onto the shelf to dig deeper into the hole, being careful not tip the whole structure over. As I stretch halfway through, long, orangey-pink earthworms spill down over my arms, and oval sow bugs skitter their many, many legs over my face.

I don't care. I get enough traction to push against the wood studs in the wall, forcing my way up through the muck until I break through the surface in the cold cellar in an explosion of flies and sludge. The deep muck stinks and my eyes water, but I drag myself through the rest of the way.

I want to get out of this cellar. I feel disgusting—and smell worse—and I'm pretty sure there are bugs crawling into every one of my crevices. I listen for Jack but can't hear any-thing over the buzz of flies.

I risk it, and push the trapdoor to the root cellar open a crack. My field of vision is limited: I can only see the back door and the entrance to the hallway. I don't know where Jack is or what he's doing. He could be right behind me for all I know. I hope like hell he isn't.

I smell smoke.

Jack must have lit the fireplace, but that doesn't matter to me at the moment. The smart thing to do would be to climb out of here and get as far away from this house as possible—

There's a scream from downstairs—Harriet—followed by the growl of Jack's voice saying, "Come on."

They struggle at the bottom of the basement steps.

Then a gun goes off.

Even though I've half-expected it all along, his gun is now a reality I have to deal with.

In the ringing silence that follows, I think Harriet's dead. Then I hear the heavy scuffle of two pairs of feet coming up the stairs.

There's the sickening thud of a body hitting a wall, and through the crack, I see Harriet's head hit the hall floor so hard it bounces. He's gaunt and pale and looking my way. He blinks and scrambles to regain his feet. I can't believe he's still alive. I hope he has the sense to keep his mouth shut—any indication from him that I'm here and I'm a dead man, no question.

I let the trapdoor sink back down, staying quiet. The strug-gle continues above me, hollow clomps echoing through the boards. They stumble through the hallway, and then up the second flight of stairs.

What's Jack doing with him?

As soon as it's quiet, I don't waste any more time. I quickly climb out of the cellar, the noxious odour making me dizzy, and gasp for air, only to be assaulted by the taste of smoke at the back of my throat.

The air is hazy. I'm coughing and retching and have to fight to clear my head. Is the chimney blocked? We've got to get out of here.

I need to get to Charlie.

chapter 132

I look around corners and get back down to the basement. Although I'm almost certain Jack is upstairs with Harriet, I'm really hoping I'm not walking into a trap. It would *really* suck if he were waiting for me, gun pointed dead centre.

The padlocks are still in place on both tool room and bathroom, but the door to Harriet's cell is wide open. Inside is fuel for the wickedest nightmare.

The room reeks of human filth and is nearly engulfed in darkness. The hallway light casts a thin sliver across the floor and wall, illuminating the folds of a grimy blanket.

Harriet's been living like a beaten animal. I have no idea how he's lasted so long.

I don't waste time, though—there's none to spare—and I rush through the storage rooms on the other side of the hall to the boarded-up doorway and my friend.

I kneel down to a crack between the wood. "Charlie?"

There's movement and his eye appears. "Shepherd," he says solemnly from behind the wood slats.

"You okay in there?"

"I am now that you're back," he says, renewed hope in his voice.

"I'm going to get you out."

"About damn time."

There's no way I can pull off the board Jack's just hammered into place, but I'm hoping I can break the others.

"Step back," I call out, and throw a desperate shoulder check into the wood. It hurts like hell but nothing seems to move.

"Again," Charlie says.

I put a little more force into it this time and definitely hear the wood crack. I take two steps back and literally run at the doorway, and a couple of the two-by-sixes bust off.

Charlie's face appears in the hole. "Took you long enough," he says.

I'm so grateful to see he's okay that my comeback couldn't be more lame. "Sorry, princess. I was a bit busy."

"That all you got?" he asks, rolling his eyes.

Gah. This guy.

"Can you just help me here?" I ask, ramming against the rest of the boards.

"Gladly."

It takes us no time to knock out enough pieces so that Charlie's able to climb through. He reaches back to grab the big stick. As he does, I fill him in.

"Haven't you been a busy boy," he says with a smartass grin.

Now that I've got him beside me again, my own humour returns. "Well, *someone* has to cover your ass!"

The smile fades. "Seriously, Shepherd, thanks for coming back for me."

"No problem, brother."

He looks shocked at the word. "Brother, huh? You know, I like the sound of that!"

And I think he honestly does.

chapter 133

We race to the top of stairs. Smoke now hangs low in the room, making our eyes tear up, and we drop to our hands and knees. I pull my shirt up over my face again and wait while Charlie adjusts his.

"What the hell's Jack doing?" I ask.

"Besides trying to murder all of us and frame Harriet for it?" Charlie asks.

That aspect hadn't occurred to me. Jack might be mad at his brother, but what did we ever do to him?

"Why's he pissed at us, do you think?"

That's when we hear Jack clomping down the stairs from the second floor, and Charlie makes a suggestion. "Why don't we ask?"

"Because he's got a gun," I say.

"Yeah, but there's two of us," Charlie replies, hefting the club.

We hide in the hallway as Jack moves into the living room.

Charlie signals for me to wait as he cuts through the kitchen into the dining room.

I sneak to the living room doorway.

Jack's at the fireplace, back turned.

He's a tall guy, well-built, and again I get the feeling that I've met him before. At the moment he's wearing what looks like a breathing apparatus from a dive suit, so I can't be sure. The gun is tucked into the back of his pants and he's leaning over the fireplace, digging at it with a poker, trying to dislodge a burning log.

He pulls it loose and pushes it into the corner beside the rocking chair. It won't take long for it to catch fire and turn the place into an inferno.

We need to act fast.

As if reading my mind, Charlie races from the dining room, but Jack sees him coming and reaches for his gun. He's not fast enough, though, and Charlie's already swinging the club, hard. It connects with the mask on Jack's face and the plexiglass cracks. It's got to hurt, and the gun skitters across the floor, but Jack takes the hit and turns on Charlie.

Shit!

I dive for the gun.

Jack rushes Charlie and tackles him, shoving him hard against the wall. Charlie's head makes a resounding *thunk*, splitting the old plaster into a web of shards. He drops like a rock and Jack's on top of him, bludgeoning him with his fists. They're one big tangle and I don't dare shoot without risk of hitting Charlie, so I fire a warning shot into the floor instead. My ears ring and the gun kicks in my hand—I feel it through my whole arm.

Jack freezes, mask askew, and lifts his hands in surrender. He twists toward me, furious, and I find myself staring at Gekas's boyfriend, Spencer.

chapter 134

The rocking chair has caught fire and the flames promptly spread up the wall. We need to get out of here quickly.

"Why couldn't you boys have just stayed in your rooms?" Spencer shouts.

"Get off him," I growl, and he pulls himself off Charlie, rising slowly.

"I knew you were persistent, but I didn't expect you to be *this* much trouble."

I ignore him and focus on my friend. "Charlie? You okay?"

He's moving but slowly, trying to clear his vision.

"What are you going to do, Anthony?" Spencer asks, edging this way, though his hands remain raised in surrender. "Are you going to shoot me? Eye for an eye for Mike?"

"Shut up!" I yell.

The fire climbs the wall; flames lick at the ceiling.

"Charlie, you need to get up now," I say, not taking my eyes off Spencer.

"That was a nice touch, calling me about Maggie," he says,

and the fact that his tone is so...so *normal* creeps me right out. "Very caring," he adds with a sneer as he inches closer.

I have a clear shot. My finger is on the trigger. One squeeze would bring him down. But fear grips me.

There are only two moments: this moment and the moment after I pull the trigger. Am I ready to take a life?

Spencer sees the hesitation and rushes at me, but my game instincts kick in and I deke to the right. He stumbles and falls into the hallway.

"Charlie!" I yell, turning to my friend for a split-second.

Spencer recovers more quickly than I thought possible, and he sucker punches me in the kidney. I buckle to the floor.

He's on me at once, going for the gun, but I tighten my grip. He fights to loosen my hold, but I've got the advantage of both arm length and strength, and he can't get it away from me. But neither can I do much except hold on, he's gripping the barrel so tightly.

He starts twisting it in my hand, and I think he's trying to wrench it from my grasp, but then I realize he's trying to turn it on me instead.

I counter, trying to aim it anywhere else.

He forces a finger between mine and the trigger guard—

Bang!

It's a deafening sound and the pistol nearly shakes free of my sweaty palm. I'm breathless but feel no searing pain. I'm sure it hasn't hit me, but I'm not positive about him—

Bang!

The gun fires again, and other than the ringing in my ears, neither of us seems affected. As long as I keep out of range,

I have no problem emptying the chamber this way. It'll be one less thing to worry about.

Spencer tries to force me onto my back. He's built solid like Charlie, but I spread myself out, making it harder for him to flip me over. He slams a knee into the side where he punched me, over and over, and I crumple up tight.

It's enough.

Now he's on top, still grabbing at the pistol, bringing it up between our chests, using all his weight and strength against me. But I've got the floor to push against—as long as he doesn't pin my arms, I might still hold him off. I struggle hard to get the gun out of the tight space between our bodies, certain he'll headbutt me if I don't do something to stop him. My strength is wearing thin...I won't be able to keep this standoff going much longer—

That's when I see Charlie rise up behind Spencer, tree branch in hand, and he has time to aim carefully and take a full swing.

The club catches Spencer in the ribs, but he doesn't loosen his grip. Still, he's weakened enough that I can pull the gun away completely.

Charlie yanks him off me. "I knew those golf lessons would come in handy," Charlie says as he helps pull me up.

We turn on Spencer together, Charlie holding the stick, me holding the gun. I feel pretty good about our odds.

But he's not scared. At all. His hands are out, half in defense, half in preparation to attack, always advancing, looking for an opportunity to strike.

"You're just a couple of dumb kids who've let your friends

get stabbed and murdered, and ruined the lives of those around you with your stupid actions."

"So why come after us, then?" I spit at him. "Why kill Mike—?"

"Dammit!" Charlie exclaims, realizing. "He did it for love."

I look from Charlie to Spencer, trying to follow. "Wait. You blame *us* for Gekas?"

"She was strong and capable before the two of you came into her life. You nearly got her killed!"

I shake my head. "But why Harriet, then?" I ask.

It's only a flash across his face, but it tells me enough.

"Shit, Charlie, this has nothing to do with *love*," I say. "This is all about revenge!"

Spencer lunges, and Charlie swings the stick, pushing him back into the thickening swirl of smoke.

"We need to get out of here," I say, tugging Charlie by the shoulder, keeping the gun trained on Spencer.

"What are we going to do with him?"

A voice behind me speaks. "Let me take care of him."

I turn to see Gekas amid the flames and smoke in the dining room, service revolver drawn.

chapter 135

We only have a minute or two before this whole place goes up.

"We have to get out," I yell.

"You two go," she says calmly, though I can see the raging tempest building inside. "I think he and I are going to stay here a moment."

"Maggie—" Spencer says, but she cuts him off.

"You don't get to use my name anymore."

"But this is all for you!"

"No," she shakes her head slowly. "None of this is on me. You chose—"

"For *you*. To make you strong again."

"This has nothing to do with me!"

The heat of the fire is unbearable, the flames have spread to the far side of the dining room. Soon there won't be a way out.

"Detective, we have to go, *now*!"

"No!" Her storm breaks and tears stream down her face. "Why should *he* get to live?"

I've never seen Gekas so exposed, so raw. It frightens me.

"Did he give anyone else a chance? The people he killed? The families he hurt? How about what he was going to do to you two?"

She's ready to kill him, to let him die here, and she doesn't want us to see it.

But I can't give her that permission.

I step up to her, and reach out a hand, setting it gently on her forearm. "No, Detective. We both know this isn't the way."

I can feel her whole body shake under my touch. I know how close she is to pulling the trigger.

"Detective? We've stopped him. He can't hurt anyone anymore."

She tenses and looks at me, and I can see all the pain and sorrow in her eyes—then she finally breathes and lowers her gun.

chapter 136

We have little time left.

"There's someone still upstairs. Charlie, you good?" I ask.

After the pounding Spencer gave him, he's still shaking out some of the cobwebs. But he's on his feet and running on adrenaline. "Good enough," he says.

Gekas wants to argue, but I'm not having it. I rush for the stairs and Charlie's close behind.

I take a quick breath as I reach the top, and hope it lasts long enough for me to find Harriet. The smoke hangs low and stings my eyes.

I'm going by instinct, and head to the end of the hall, checking the door first—it's cool enough, I think—before Charlie drives his heel into the wood by the knob, shattering it.

We're hit by a roomful of smoke that immediately worms its way into my nostrils. Only by squinting can I make out the blurry vision of a body on the floor. Lungs bursting, we rush over to him. I barely register the sledgehammer and the busted rubble of a chimney beside him.

I get between Harriet's legs as Charlie grabs him by the shoulders. Together, we hoist his limp body and move out the door. The hallway is already thick and sooty, and we can no longer see at all, stumbling down the hall, and bouncing off walls.

I'm dizzy and my lungs can no longer wait. I exhale in an explosion and my body fights for more oxygen. I'm running on empty as we reach the top of the stairs, and I inhale against my will, smoke searing my throat and lungs.

By the time we're back on the main floor, the living room is an inferno; the heat singes our hair and clothes, but I barely notice. I stumble and drop Harriet's legs, but Charlie keeps dragging him down the hallway.

"Shepherd, come on!" Charlie calls out, and I pick myself up and follow them into the kitchen. Charlie throws his body against the back door, and the three of us tumble into the cool spring air.

chapter 137

I grab Harriet's legs again and we stagger out past Spencer's car, getting as far as we can from the burning building before collapsing into a heap.

My eyes and throat feel like they're on fire and I'm retching out black, tarry spit, but my brain is crying out to help Harriet. I roll him over, struggling to see if he's alive—struggling to see anything in the bright sunlight—but everything's a messy blur, and I can't breathe without hacking up a lung.

It isn't until I feel Gekas's hand on my shoulder that I know she's beside me, helping.

"Where's Spencer?" I stammer.

"In my car, not going anywhere."

I give her an uncertain look.

"Don't worry. He's alive." She puts a bottle of water in my hand. "Drink."

I take a swig, and it tastes sooty and brackish and I cough it up. I have to rinse and spit before I can finally take a long swallow, and the cool water feels good in my throat. I pour some on my face, washing my eyes until the stinging fades a bit.

Gekas works on Harriet, cutting away his shirt and attaching an AED she must have brought from her car. She yells, "Clear," and while the machine analyzes Harriet's state, she radios dispatch from a walkie-talkie and updates them on the situation.

Charlie's beside me, cleaning his eyes with another bottle of water, and it's only now that I can fully see how much of a beating Spencer gave him. His face is swollen and bloody, and I'm impressed he was even able to rally enough to stand, let alone help get Harriet out of there.

The machine says, "Shock advised," in a cold electronic voice, and Harriet jolts as Gekas pushes the button. He's still not breathing, so she starts chest compressions.

Watching Gekas at work is impressive. Whatever she felt earlier in the house, it's gone. She's in the moment, handling the situation, and I have nothing but respect for her.

She checks Harriet's heart rhythm then moves onto CPR. She delivers two quick breaths and his chest rises, then she starts compressions again.

All at once, Harriet coughs violently, his whole body fighting to breathe on its own, and he's suddenly aggressive, arms swing wildly.

Gekas holds him back, protecting herself and him, all the while speaking calmly. "EMS is on the way. You're going to be okay."

As soon as he settles, she drops, the energy drained from her.

"I think this is yours," I say, pulling her badge out of my front pocket and tossing it to her.

"I figured that son of a bitch had it." She glares toward her car where Spencer waits in the backseat. "Used it as bait, hoping you two would be foolish enough to come looking for me."

Her words hurt, but she's likely just dumping on us to cover the real pain. "Detective, are you okay?" I ask.

"No. Not yet," she says, her voice cracking. "But maybe one day."

chapter 138

It doesn't take long for police and emergency personnel to arrive. Police cars and firetrucks pull up the driveway, and an air ambulance touches down in a corner of the yard. It's already too late to save most of the house. I'm not surprised to see my parents arrive in a police car while Charlie and I are being treated for our wounds and smoke inhalation.

I can see they're pissed—why wouldn't they be—but surprisingly Gekas cuts them off on their way to us.

Charlie gestures to where they're talking and grins. "You're never going to see the light of day again, Shepherd."

"Probably not."

Neither of us is ready to face the fact that he's going to be booted from our home as well. We look at the huddle of cops around Gekas's car.

"So he did all this because he hated his brother," Charlie says to me, and it's like he can't quite believe it.

"When we were inside, Harriet told me his brother accused him of desire, temptation—"

"You didn't see that room in the basement," Charlie puts in. "He'd been killing for a while. I think he was just looking for a direction."

"So he projected all his weaknesses and insecurities onto his brother? Onto Gekas?"

Charlie nods. "Everyone who crossed his path was a potential victim."

"Even Mike?"

"Like I said before, Shepherd, it's not your fault. You can't be responsible for the actions of someone like Spencer."

I look over at Gekas and my folks. "How did she find us? How did she know where we were?"

Charlie shows me his phone. On it is a single message to my dad: a picture of the road map that he took when the service was spotty.

"You sent it to them?"

"Normally, I don't worry about myself, but your parents would never forgive me if I let something happen to you," he says with a wink.

I still can't get used to this new version of Charlie. What a difference two years, a couple of near-death experiences, and too much time spent with my parents can do to a guy.

"Why didn't you just tell me you were worried?" I ask.

"Hey," he shrugs. "Just because I'm worried about a situation doesn't mean I don't think we should do the right thing. No such thing as an innocent bystander, Shepherd."

"You really believe that, don't you?" I say.

"Always."

I never doubted otherwise.

chapter 139

The ride home is long and quiet. Not even Charlie is willing to speak, and I'm glad my smoke-damaged throat buys me a bit of time to think. When we pull up to the house, we all climb out of the car and walk in. No one suggests it, but we all go into the kitchen. Charlie puts the kettle on, Dad pulls out cups, and Mom grabs the collection of tea bags.

My throat is tight, but I can't wait. "I'm not going to say sorry—"

"Anthony—" Mom warns.

"No," I say, unable to believe it comes out of my mouth. "You can punish me all you want, but I want to have my say."

Mom looks pissed, but Dad lays his hand on hers. She doesn't say another word, but she takes hold of his fingers in a white-knuckled fist.

All eyes are on me. Better make this quick.

"This is my fault. This has nothing to do with Charlie. He did the right thing. He let you know where we were. He was the voice of reason. Don't punish him for my mistakes. I made every choice. I take responsibility for it all."

I pause, thinking through my next words. "I thought we were helping Gekas, but I was wrong. And my actions might have killed Mike."

Charlie starts to argue, but I ignore him, the pain of my words bubbling in my throat and stinging my eyes like no smoke ever could.

"But I don't take back what I did. That man was a monster and he wouldn't have stopped until he was caught. And Charlie and I did that."

I take a big breath. "So much of what we thought and did was wrong. I put my life and other people's lives at risk. But we also found Spencer, and stopped him and saved Mr. Harriet, and what we did was *right*. I know it. I feel it in my gut."

I look my parents in the eye. "I'm *always* going to do what I believe is right. Nothing you're going to do will stop me from doing that. That's why I'm going to apply to be a police officer when I'm finished school so at least I can do the right thing the right way."

Judging by the looks on everyone's faces, it seems I'm the only one who hadn't figured out that this was the path I was taking until now.

chapter 140

Even though I meant every word, none of it gets us completely off the hook. I guess angry parents will always beat great speeches.

But Mom and Dad surprise us.

"As long as you live in our house, you need to follow our rules," Mom starts out. "However, we also can't keep treating you like teenagers. You'll soon be eighteen and on your own. You'll have to make your own choices. So, tell us, what do *you* think a just punishment would be?"

I don't say anything, unsure how best to proceed, but Charlie sits up straighter. "I say ground us until the end of the school year."

"Charlie!" I yell. He's totally buried us before we've even had a chance to negotiate.

"What?" he shoots me a look. "We disobeyed their rules. We snuck out of the house, took the car without their permission, and went into a serial killer's house."

"We didn't know he'd be there!"

"Oh, we knew," he says smugly.

"So what's that mean? Straight home after school?" Dad asks.

"Definitely no weekends out—"

"*Charlie!*"

He ignores me. "Give us extracurricular chores, walking the dog, doing homework, and working at our jobs. Deal?"

Mom and Dad stare at us.

There's not much I can say at this point, so I toss up my hands. "Fine." I look over at him. "You actually wanted this, didn't you?"

He raises an eyebrow. "It's good to have some discipline."

Mom and Dad aren't done with us, though.

One day, when we come home from school, we find a bunch of wireless security cameras installed around the place to keep track of any movement in the house—which I'm sure includes Charlie and me. And we all start going to weekly family therapy, despite the fact that our shrink tells us repeatedly that we would have been fine with once-a-month visits.

My parents also make Charlie and me take a course with Victim Services at the police station—something I think Gekas recommended. These are group sessions that are a combination of sitting around in a circle and discussing our situations, as well as one-on-one and classroom talks. I hate sharing the events that led us into Harriet's farmhouse—it sounds like I was pretending to play hero—but Charlie always seems energized after his private sessions.

Despite all this, I regret nothing. I know that I'd go out to the farmhouse again, and sit in those therapy sessions again, listening to the stories of other victims.

I know there are a lot more people out there waiting to be helped.

chapter 141

One day, Mom takes me to the graveyard.

I visit Sheri's grave first and leave flowers. It's been so long since she's been gone that her absence has become part of my norm.

But when I visit Mike, the dirt is still fresh and piled high.

I'm past feeling numb and crying, but some days I catch myself thinking of calling him for a game of basketball or for a ride to school, until I realize it can never happen.

He's dead and there's a hole in my life.

I miss my friend.

chapter 142

We don't see Gekas for a long while after, so when she shows up on our doorstep on a Saturday morning almost a month after our encounter at the house, I'm a little surprised.

"Hello, Detective Gekas."

"Please, Anthony. Just call me Maggie."

"You and I both know I'll never be able to call you that."

"Fair enough," she smiles. "I just wanted to drop off—"

"Maggie?" Mom calls from the living room before appearing at the door beside me. "I thought I heard you! What are doing out here?" She pushes past me to pull Gekas into a hug. "It's so good to see you! You're staying for breakfast." Mom's insistent and Gekas doesn't even get a chance to argue before she's pulled inside. "Ben's just finishing up the cooking."

"*Ackee* and saltfish with fried dumplings, and cinnamon banana pancakes," Dad hollers out from the kitchen as Gekas is ushered down the hallway.

Mom calls to Charlie, "Please pour Maggie some coffee."

"For sure, Mrs. S.! Hope you don't mind flavour, Mags," He gets a glare from the adults in the room. "Okay, okay! Gekas, it is!" Then, without a pause, he looks at her conspiratorially and adds, "You wouldn't believe the swill they drank around here before I came along."

"Hey, careful there, Charlie-boy. That was *my* swill," Dad cautions.

As soon as he's done filling Gekas's cup, Charlie rushes back to the stove. "Gah! Mr. S., you're burning my pancakes!"

Gekas smiles at the orchestrated chaos of our household.

The food is served, and my family and Gekas sit at the table together. Ollie comes from his spot in the living room to set himself on Gekas's feet, and it's clear she's one of us.

"You're almost finished with your time off," Mom says like she knows, even though this is the first I've heard of it.

"Yes," Gekas nods. "Back to work Monday."

"Aren't you going to miss it?" Dad asks.

She shakes her head. "Group counselling and therapy work? No thank you!"

I laugh at our similarities. "Did your parents install a half-dozen nanny cams too?"

She smiles. "No, but considering the trouble the two of you get into, I'd've installed two dozen."

Dad raises his cup to her.

She turns to me. "Actually, you're the reason I'm here."

"Not my cooking?" Dad teases.

"Or my coffee?" Charlie adds.

She laughs. "Well, not before, but after tasting all this, you may need to keep an extra plate ready for me!" She pulls out two envelopes from the inside pocket of her leather jacket and lays them on the table. One is thin and the other is thick, bursting at the seams.

"Who are the envelopes for? Are they full pardons for our sins?" Charlie asks, grinning.

Gekas laughs again. "With *your* history? I'd have to get the prime minister on the line to get your record wiped clean."

Charlie pulls away her plate and she shoots him a look. He puts his arms up in surrender.

She hands the thick envelope to him. "I went through the files we have," she glances quickly at the rest of us then meets Charlie's eyes. "I gathered some information you might find meaningful."

"Thank you," he says, but he doesn't open it, opting instead to slip it under his butt and pick up another forkful of pancake.

Gekas looks at me. "Your mom and dad told me about your career plans. I've checked into it and you're way past the registration due date."

"But I thought I could apply for training any time?"

"Not if you're going for a university degree in police studies," Mom says.

"Wait? What?"

Dad steps in. "You're not going straight into training. You're going into justice and specializing in police studies—"

"But that's a four-year program!" I sputter.

"Yes, but it will build your skills in critical thinking—" says Mom.

"And theory—" Dad adds.

"And ethics," Gekas finishes.

"Why do I feel like the three of you have been conspiring against me?"

Now they're all grinning at me, and Gekas pushes the thin envelope forward. "Your parents have shown me your marks. You're a little low on some of them."

I'd tell her it's been a tough semester, but everyone at this table already knows it.

"However, I did a little work behind your back—you should be used to that sort of thing by now," Gekas says with a wink. "I spoke to the dean, and after submitting recommendation letters from me and my boss, you've got a spot for the fall."

I open the envelope and find an acceptance letter to the local university. I'm at a loss for words, but manage to croak out a thank you.

"Aww, Shepherd, don't start with the tears," Charlie says, looking at Mom and Dad. "I don't know how you raised him, but he's a sensitive waif."

I suck in a breath, always thankful for his ability to get me out of a tight spot, whether it's physically or emotionally—though I'm not about to show it. "I'm just crying because I won't be moving out on my own, far away from all of you."

"Pfft." Charlie's dismissive. "You'd miss us!"

And we all laugh because it's true.

chapter 143

After that meal and a good visit, I feel bad about what I'm about to do.

"Detective Gekas?" I call out, catching her at her car before she leaves.

She waits, one hand on the door latch, and her head drops. She straightens, then turns to me. "Anthony."

I walk down the steps toward her. "I was wondering if you could tell me..." I don't know how to finish the sentence.

"You want to know why it all happened," she says, voice cracking. There's still heartbreak in her soul that a month of counselling won't ever erase.

I nod. "Who was it Charlie and I were chasing?"

She shakes her head. She's still not happy about the two of us taking the law into our own hands.

She comes to sit on the step.

I feel like I'm looming over her, so I drop down beside her.

"Spencer seems like a ghost to me now. Full of lies and deception. Floating through life, stealing the identities of the people he'd killed...," she trails off, not looking at me, staring at the quiet street.

"But I thought he was the love of my life," she says finally, point blank, making her voice solid. "We met about two years ago, not long before I crossed paths with you. I went south for a holiday and met him on an island in a bar. We hit it off right away."

Gekas repositions herself on the cold, hard steps.

"It was nice that he was from the States. I was always working, so we could schedule visits and not play the usual couples' games. I never worried about other women; I trusted him. My *instinct* was to trust him. He was convincing. I never thought—" She closes her eyes, and her body deflates a bit.

I couldn't imagine believing that the love of your life was a decent, faithful man—only to discover he is a serial killer.

"What I didn't know was that he was actually from here." She sits up, rigid, and I can almost see her step into full cop mode. "After his parents adopted his brother, he became jealous, and eventually left. After that, all we have are pieces of his life, hints of where he went and what he did, though we're pretty certain he started killing at about the time he met me."

"You never suspected him?"

"No. Well, not until you boys went to the condo."

I glance at her. She'd told us the condo was a bust.

"He's the one who told me that it's easier to fake an ID than it is a passport," she says. "But that wasn't what made me start questioning him." Before I can ask, she goes on. "One of the shirts," she says. "A handmade brand from Italy."

This time her voice doesn't crack, but it's as cold and hard as the steps. "Something about that detail stuck with me for days. I couldn't shake it. Until I figured it out. It was the same as his."

"Did he leave it for you?"

She shakes her head. "I don't know if it was intentional. But it was enough for me to start looking more carefully into his history. Of course, he had no connections to his family. But he also had no friends, no other life. It was just him and the law firm."

"He *was* a ghost."

She nods. "And he's been killing for a long time, crossing provincial borders and state lines. The investigation has escalated to a federal, inter-agency level."

"So that's what you were doing when you weren't answering your phone?"

She nods again.

I ask the question I can't let go of. "Why Mike?"

She contemplates her answer. "When he came back here with me, he turned his hatred on his brother. At first, it was about destroying Harriet's life."

"Was Spencer responsible for ruining his marriage?"

"Well, Harriet was hardly perfect. And Autumn was a temptation."

"But did he cheat on his wife?" I really don't want to know about Harriet's sex life but I do want to understand what happened.

"No. He wised up before he did something too stupid. But Spencer caught scent of it and used it against him. He was responsible for laying out all the digital breadcrumbs to point the finger at his brother."

I think about all the naughty texts and pictures that were sent between Autumn and Spencer. Gekas can't be happy.

"He kept at it. Stole his identity, put him into financial ruin with debt, sabotaged every relationship he had."

"And then kidnapped him."

"Yes." She's staring at the ground.

The papers had been following her investigation at Harriet's house in the city and the basement of the farmhouse. I know what she's seen.

"After his wife left, Spencer arrived at his door." Her eyes are fiery, she's wrestling with a stewing anger, and she closes them to continue. "Harriet was thrilled to see his brother. At first. Then Spencer drugged him and chained him up in the attic."

She laughs and it isn't until she wipes away a tear that I realize she's crying. "Harriet almost got away once—and that's when Spencer took him out of the city, made it harder for him to escape."

"That means he's been held hostage for—"

"Months. Harriet had lost everyone, so no one knew he was missing."

The utter terror and hopelessness he must have suffered!

But she still hasn't answered my question.

"But why Mike?" I ask again, and she looks at me, frustrated.

"Last summer," she says finally.

I stare at her, trying to figure out what she's getting at.

She sighs. "After the attack at the lake, I wasn't myself. Like I said, lots of physical therapy, then they stuck me at a desk. But I wasn't rushing back. I was—"

She doesn't finish the sentence, but I know exactly what

she was. She was scared of the consequences of going back into the field and chasing bad guys. Just like Charlie was. Just like Ollie. And why *shouldn't* she be nervous?

"He thought he could fix me by doing what he was good at. It was—his gift to me."

"He even wrapped them with a bow…" I trail off.

She nods.

"But if you *had* figured it out—?"

"We think he planned to frame Harriet for the murders." She pauses. "Personally, I think he was willing to be caught. He thought of it all as an act of love. But I don't think he knows love. I think it was just his way of trying to *control* love."

"And Mike was just someone else who got in his way—because of Autumn?"

She nods, but I can tell she's avoiding something.

I have to say it. "He blames us for what happened to you, doesn't he? If it weren't for us, you wouldn't have been wounded. He held a grudge, and when we found his condo, he turned all his hate and anger on Mike—"

"Don't blame yourself, Anthony."

"I don't."

She studies me, seeing that I mean it. "The farmhouse was his end-game," she says. "The plan was to kill you and Charlie, blame it on Harriet, and burn the evidence to the ground."

"He just didn't expect Charlie to show up with his big stick," I say, trying to lighten the mood.

Gekas doesn't crack a smile, though; she only searches my eyes. "I've talked with Charles. This was all you, Anthony. *You* went after this case, despite the fact that I said no."

I try to disagree, but she interrupts. "Quit arguing. If it weren't for you, we'd never have found him. Your persistence tracked him down. And you saved your friend and Harriet and yourself from that slaughterhouse by being smart and resourceful. We stopped him, and you and Charlie survived because of your determination, quick wit, and inner strength."

She stands, stuffs her hands in her pockets, takes a deep breath, then smiles down at me. "I'm glad you've chosen law enforcement. Knowing that you'll be out there, fighting the good fight, and helping others. I'll be proud to work beside you."

With that, she turns and heads to her car, not turning back.

And I can't help but smile.

chapter 144

Graduation arrives. Since I'm still grounded, I don't get to participate in most of the pre-grad activities. But Mom and Dad let us out early on good behaviour, and we get to attend the last big bash. I don't expect Charlie cares much for this sort of thing, but I think he's happy just to get outside the house.

Despite Mom's persistent pestering, I choose to attend the ceremony on my own, without a date. Although I was asked by a few girls in my class and heard rumours of a few others too shy to approach me, I felt it was only right. But I've promised myself that once this year is done, it's time to move on. As Charlie has reminded me countless times, Sheri wouldn't want me to mourn her forever.

Although Charlie doesn't have enough classes to graduate this year, Elaina takes him along as her date. Nothing surprising about that since she's been bringing take-out or appetizers over to our place on a regular basis, and watching movies with Charlie and my family. The two of them have grown quite close, and it's still weird to see Charlie acting so normal and un-Charlie-like.

Mom and Dad rent a limo so that Charlie and Elaina, Laura, Maxine, Gretchen, and their dates, and me, the third-wheel, have a ride to the ceremony. At first I protest—it seems a little too much hype—but once we're on our way, it feels good to be surrounded by all these people.

We pull up to the Centre of the Arts, where the ceremony is being held, and pile out. Everyone looks fantastic, and we take plenty of selfies together before heading in. We're sorting out where we have to be and Charlie's telling Elaina where he'll meet her after the ceremony since he's got to go sit in the audience with my parents, when his phone rings.

He checks the number but doesn't answer. He pulls me aside. "Hey, Shepherd, do you mind helping Elaina inside? I just need to take this."

"Everything all right?" I ask as the phone rings again.

"Yup, totally fine. I've just been trying to track down my mom and I think this might be her." He grins. "Wouldn't surprise me. Her timing has always sucked."

His *mom's* calling?!

"You sure everything's cool?" I double-check.

"Yeah, yeah, go on in before they decide to renege on your diploma."

He pushes me along, and I look back and see him take the call, stepping back outside.

I catch up to Elaina. She asks where Charlie is and I tell her. She gives me a funny look, and it's exactly the way I feel, but people are herding us into a big room so we don't get to discuss it further.

There are long aisles cordoned off, and I feel like a cow being led to graduation slaughter. At one point they hustle us into caps and gowns, and at another, they hand us a program for the evening and a little graduation pin with the school's emblem. Another stop, and this time they tell us they don't want our phones going off during the ceremony, and make us put them into envelopes with our names written on them and hand them over.

We shuffle further along and people are telling us a lot about what to do once the ceremony begins and where to go, but there's so much information all at once, I barely register any of it.

Once we're organized, they lead us out onto the stage alphabetically by last name. The lights are bright and I can barely see the crowd, but I follow my line and take a seat between a girl from my homeroom and a guy from my basketball team way at the back of the risers. The background music fades, the school band starts up, and Mrs. Johnson walks out on stage.

It takes over an hour, and I'm already exhausted before my name is called. But I feel only gratitude when I walk across the stage and Mrs. Johnson hands me my diploma. Afterward, they have a special dedication to Mike, and she presents an honorary degree to his parents.

Mike's mom looks my way to whisper *thank you* to me, and all I can do is nod, choking back the emotion.

When they finally announce that we are officially this year's graduating class, we all throw our caps in the air. Mike would've loved that. Ceremony complete, they usher us off the stage and back into the big room to return our gowns.

The cap—if we can find it again—is ours to keep. There's a lot of celebration and happy tears, and I get lots of hugs and a couple of kisses and I can't say I mind.

All the grad chaperones look totally done with us, like they want us out of here yesterday, and push us to finish hugging and changing clothes and primping so that we can go to the grad dinner downstairs and they can go home. We line up one last time to grab the envelopes with our phones in them.

I get my envelope and tear it open.

Right away I see the text, already forty minutes old, already too late for me to do anything about.

It's from Charlie and it's only one word:

help

acknowledgments

This book has been one of our biggest challenges and it took many people to help us get it across the finish line. We have a lot of questions during the writing process, and our thanks go to Angie's students, David's former students, Madame Dryburgh's class, Jeff Gegner, Kevin Johnson, Mike Park, and Constable Blair Randall of the Regina Police Service for helping to answer some of them. Nial McFadyen gets a big shout out from us for being our *numero uno* patron. We are indebted to Creative Saskatchewan for their generous assistance in the production of our books, and to Donovan Bergman and the print team at Friesens. We'd also like to recognize our early reader, Kate Gane; our proofreader, Brian Mlazgar; our photographer, Jeff Sawatzky; and our translators, Anna Maria Kontsiotis and Ulyses Rocha, for helping us with final touches; and give a huge special thanks to Heather Nickel, who works with us to bring our books to life.

Angie would like to thank Kevin Leflar for his support, Katerina Voyatzis for letting her play with the elevator, her coffee girl Maria Plastaras, and the Creator for this beautiful, crazy adventure. David would like to thank his wife and kids for their love and support, and the staff and former manager at Starbucks for putting up with him every early morning this past summer. Finally, a big thank you to our friends, family, and YOU (yes, you!), our reader, who picked up our book and bought our book, and maybe shared our book. We're forever grateful for your kindness and support on our journey.

about the authors

DAVID GANE is a writer, teacher, and stay-at-home dad. He writes film scripts and fiction, and has also composed poetry, plays, and academic film reviews. He occasionally teaches screenwriting at the University of Regina.

ANGIE COUNIOS teaches by day, and writes film scripts and fiction the rest of the time. When she's not teaching or writing, she's packing a bag for another adventure, completing a goal list, playing with her camera or practising yoga.

Find them at
www.couniosandgane.com